MW01252334

THE PRETTY PLACE

LAURA LESLIE

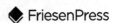

FriesenPress

Suite 300 - 990 Fort St
Victoria, BC, V8V 3K2
Canada

www.friesenpress.com

Copyright © 2020 by Laura Leslie
First Edition — 2020

Edited by Caroline Kaiser
Book cover design done by Laura Leslie

All rights reserved.

No part of this publication may be reproduced in any form, or by any means, electronic or mechanical, including photocopying, recording, or any information browsing, storage, or retrieval system, without permission in writing from FriesenPress.

ISBN
978-1-5255-9028-3 (Hardcover)
978-1-5255-9027-6 (Paperback)
978-1-5255-9029-0 (eBook)

1. FICTION, COMING OF AGE

Distributed to the trade by The Ingram Book Company

PROLOGUE

I hadn't known what I was capable of when I took my first heedless steps toward the Pretty Place. Steps that unknowingly set into motion a ticking metronome of tragedy that would swing back and forth, keeping perfect time throughout the imperfect sorrows of the rest of my life.

It was nearing the end of spring then, and I could still smell the earthy scent of the ground thawing and coming alive after an achingly long Ontario winter. Normally, I wouldn't have ventured into the backwoods alone, but the concealing branches of one particular forest beckoned, pulling me from the trail I had travelled so many times before.

Silence enveloped me as I entered the forest, a quiet so heavy it weighed on my eardrums like the underwater pressure of a dive that's almost taken you down too deep. It wasn't a sunny day, but delicate rays of light still broke through the canopy, creating little spotlights on my surroundings. The trees were glistening, flaunting their fresh green leaves, their roots tucked neatly away. Emboldened with a bravery I didn't recognize, I journeyed to the depths of the forest where a creek flowed slowly from the west, glittering with gold as it trickled down to the reservoir at the heart of it all. Everything was serenely ordered there—as if it existed only to please me.

There were no signs of recent life, save for the footprints that trailed behind me, the same footprints I'd need to find my way out. The only proof that anyone had ever been there was a Coca-Cola bottle, so old the sun had robbed the label of its colour. Peering out from under a rock, the green-tinted glass offered its broken remnants to the light, reflecting on the water, contributing beauty in its own little way.

I wanted to bring it home with me, a souvenir to prove what I had found that day, my very own piece of the magic. Carelessly, I grabbed it from its resting place, the glass cutting deep into my palm at the base of my thumb. Blood dripped from my wound like the creek flowing to the pool—from its vein into its heart. I felt no pain as I washed my hand in the water, becoming blood brothers with my newest companion. I remember feeling as if every step I'd taken for months, maybe years, had all been leading me there, to that place, to that moment.

I was just a silly little kid when I decided to call it the Pretty Place, a simple name derived from its most obvious quality. To me, it was a place where solidarity felt like inclusion, and invisibility felt like truly being seen. It became like a dear friend whose every dark secret I wanted to loyally harbour. Though, in the end, it harboured mine. Had I never returned, I may have doubted its existence. Looking down at my palm now, I see that the thin, faded scar remains, an ever-present reminder that beauty once existed in my life, even if at its purest, it was fleeting.

PART ONE

1

CHAPTER 1

Wednesday, June 16th, 1999—36 days until my birthday

Mom's upset again. She's been upset a lot lately. I can feel an ominous tension in the house. The halls are darker than normal, as if even the blinds know to let less sunlight in. Could the furniture be sensing a bad night brewing? The chairs are pulled in tightly, sulking around the kitchen table.

When I got in, Mom was sitting in the family room with piles of presumably clean clothes mounding around her. It was a scene I was used to on her days off, though typically, the mounds were accompanied by baskets and neatly folded piles—the markings of laundry day. Today she just sat there, curtains drawn, silent, still. Possibly enjoying the warmth of a freshly dried pile. Possibly sleeping with her eyes open.

Normally, she greeted me with the standard inquiries. *How was your day, Ivy? What did you do? Where did you go? Have you eaten?* I waited for the interrogation to begin, watching her have a staring contest with the antique radio on the wall unit in front of her. The TV was on, but she stared at the radio.

"Mom! Snap out of it," I said as I walked into the laundry

room to feed Chelsea, our overweight and underintelligent Old English sheepdog.

"Hi, honey," she whispered, barely audible from the next room. Quiet, but I could still detect a hint of breathy despair, a disappointment that made me wish I'd picked a more thoughtful greeting. She didn't like being alone very much, and of course, Isaac wasn't around either; it felt as though he hadn't been since he hit puberty.

I'd been gone since sun-up. My best friend, Robyn, and I had taken our first day of summer vacation, scheduling a full-day hike into the valuable hours before dinnertime. It was the most grown-up adventure we could think of to commence our adolescence. Junior high was finally over, and we would be entering high school in September. It was a big day for me, but somehow I was still the only one who managed to honour our family-dinner curfew.

I wondered how late Dad would be. With the way Mom had been acting, he should've been home on time, though lately, he never was. Mom got like this sometimes, quiet and slow, and it worried me. It worried me even more that I was the only one who seemed to notice. If I looked to Dad for support, he'd explain again why it was so hard for him to work the typical nine-to-five. Working in finance required a lot of late nights, early mornings, business meetings, etc., etc. Those were the details I understood about his job—and that he wore a suit and carried his beloved, off-limits briefcase.

I grabbed my book from the deck and headed to the bay window in the front of the house, which overlooked Lake Scugog. If Mom wasn't making dinner, then I wasn't needed to help—a small bonus of her current preoccupation with inanimate objects.

I wasn't surprised to see that my reading nook hadn't been affected by the tension I was feeling in the house. Nothing could put a damper on that perfect time at dusk when the sun was just warm enough to offer comfort but not quite hot enough to burn. Even my freshly burned summer skin welcomed the invisible blanket it cloaked me in. I'd only spent one day in the sun, but I'd already begun to turn a swarthy shade of brown no one ever expected (even though it happened every year). With my white-blonde hair, light eyes, and freckles, I think people found my olive skin a bit . . . surprising. Unusual even, though not in a good way.

I flipped through the old book, searching earnestly for the folded corner that marked where I'd left off. The mystery novel wore its age unabashedly all over its creased pages and torn-off cover. Every time I thought I'd found my place, I'd read a line, only to realize the fold belonged to a predecessor of mine—someone who'd solved the case years ago. *This is why I should use bookmarks,* I thought as the garage door screeched open. I didn't have to look out the window to know that next, I'd hear the familiar crackling pop of Dad's car moving slowly up our long gravel driveway. Chelsea, summoned by those wonted sounds, readied herself at the laundry room door, her tail wagging so intensely, her whole lower body gyrated with excitement.

Dad walked in looking uneasy—as he did most nights, which made me feel uneasy, as I did most nights. "An hour-and-a-half commute will do that to ya," he often reminded us. Without acknowledging his four-legged admirer, he quickly fulfilled his home-from-work routine, gently placing his briefcase on the piano bench and his shoes in the front foyer closet.

And so the night began. I sat patiently, waiting for him to find me in my usual spot, dismissing my increased heart rate. Like the harmless drive-by of a patrolling cop car, Dad had an uncanny ability to make me feel as though I'd done something wrong, even when I hadn't. Exactly thirty-three seconds later, he found and greeted me with a warm hello.

"Where's Isaac?" he grunted.

I shrugged. Isaac had become an enigmatic stranger to me in the last year. It was as if turning eighteen had made him blind, deaf, and mute, stumbling around the house at all hours of the night, not caring or being totally aware of what day it was or what planet he was on.

"What's your mother doing in there? Is she all right?" Dad asked, untucking his striped shirt and loosening his tie.

I shrugged again.

"Ivy, don't shrug at me. We're humans, and we communicate verbally, remember?"

He shook his head so vigorously, I had no choice but to be impressed. Not a single brown hair on his rigidly styled head had moved out of place—that dippity-do gel meant business, and so did he. I wanted to reply in my best robot voice, asking him to enlighten me about this strange *human race* he spoke of. It was my preferred response—fighting fire with fire—when it came to his patronizing questions. But I didn't want to start the night off with a conversation about my attitude. Instead, I got up and moved our predinner pleasantries to the kitchen, obliging him with verbal communication in my best *human* voice.

"I don't really know, Dad. She's taking an extra-long time on the laundry today. That's about all I've gathered from the disaster in the family room." I answered what I knew his next question would be before he had to ask. "And sorry—no, dinner isn't ready either. Maybe we should just order pizza."

He peered through the window that extended from the kitchen to the family room. We'd cut a chunk out of the adjoining wall a few years earlier; Mom had been right to say it opened up the space and made both rooms feel larger. He could see the top of her curly blonde head tilted down as she stared at the radio while the TV looped an infomercial on mute. His pale-blue eyes darted back to mine; they were ice-cold but still beautiful. Even when he was angry, they reminded me of the colour of the sky on a crisp spring day before any clouds came to remind you that rain was always possible (even imminent).

He waited for an explanation; I lifted my hands up in defeat. Again I didn't have the answers. I had no idea what Mom found so fascinating about the radio. I mean, I enjoyed that radio too; music was my first love, so any conduit to it was an object I was fond of. But not, like, *that* fond. Dad broke his gaze abruptly, as if to show me the appropriate amount of time to stare in one direction.

"Pretty sure there's a pizza in the freezer," I said, hoping he wasn't too annoyed to appease me.

Frozen pizza was our family go-to, especially when Mom was feeling "tired." Living as far as we did from town made it hard to get deliveries. In the winter, it was next to impossible—par for the course when you live on the Island (Scugog Island, to be more exact). Although I'd recently learned in school that "No man is an island," islands were in fact islands, and it was hard to deliver pizza to them. Some winters, the one causeway that connected us to the mainland (Didn't that mean we lived on a peninsula?) would freeze over or be so covered in snow, there'd be no battling it. Much as there'd be no battling Dad if he had other things in mind for dinner. Reluctantly, he grabbed the pizza and slid it onto the tea-stained counter before turning the oven on to four hundred degrees. Could there be anything simpler than frozen pizza? *I should have handled dinner,* I thought. A pang of guilt settled over me like the blanket of sun in the bay window, only there was nothing comforting about it.

I heard Isaac's music loud and clear before I saw him. A predictable scenario. His CD Walkman was blasting Pearl Jam, so I'd have bet money he was wearing his favourite Pearl Jam tee. Matching his shirt to that day's musical choice was about as much coordination as his outfits ever saw. Jean shorts riding low beneath his butt, he meandered around with his own soundtrack, obviously not interested in sneaking up on anyone. You could say that about his questionable hygiene too, which gave a whole new meaning to "Smell ya later." He never used to be like this. He'd become a foreign object in a home I knew like the back of my hand.

When Isaac and I were younger (and still best friends), we'd turn off all the lights and run around the main floor with our arms wrapped around ourselves, not allowed to reach out and feel for the walls, competing to see who knew the house best. I guess you could call it a game we played with each other, but really it was a game of chicken you'd play with yourself. The faster you ran, the more courageous you'd feel—until an out-of-place footstool threw you headfirst into the sliding glass door in the family room. I hadn't been able to live that down, probably because Dad hadn't gotten around to fixing the glass. A thin piece of plastic and some over-ambitious tape held the large shards together still, a hilarious reminder that despite being frequently referred to as a *precocious* child, I was actually (a bit of) an idiot.

Isaac was (a lot of) an idiot, but since he was older, I felt as though he got away with (a lot) more. He got special treatment all because he had the audacity to be born first. He was living proof that *older* didn't necessarily mean *wiser*, and I was particularly sensitive to the double standard Dad applied. By the time the pizza had cooked, Dad had wrongfully taken Isaac's side twice while we bickered about trivial things like whose dishes were still in the sink and whose turn it was to pick up Chelsea's poop. Dad had lovingly created a chore calendar for us on graph paper using his metal ruler and skills from his formative years as a bridge architect (his vocation prior to banking, which was only slightly cooler). The calendar was stuck prominently to the freezer door and showed a glaring lack of check marks in the "done" boxes for the last three days.

"Summer vacation doesn't mean a vacation from your chores, you know," Dad said as he searched the silverware drawer for the pizza cutter.

"It's in the dishwasher," I whispered, remembering I'd forgotten to turn it on.

"And you could have helped your mother with whatever she's doing in there if you saw she was . . . struggling."

"Isaac has been home too," I quickly pointed out. "Just because he's a half-wit loser doesn't mean he's exempt from family duties, does it?"

They stared blankly in my direction. Expressionless, but I could tell

I'd crossed an invisible insult line and took it upon myself to gracefully exit stage left. The crowd wouldn't be so tough in the family room.

I called to my canine companion for emotional support as I sat down beside Mom in the hilly town of Laundryville. Chelsea sauntered in, stumbling across the clothing without a care in the world and, as usual, with what appeared to be a distinct lack of a thought in her head. She obediently sat next to me, leaning up against the wood-burning stove, something she'd done in winter, singeing her grey and white fur orange-brown.

"What's going on, Mom? Why are you just sitting here? Are you okay?"

Her tired green eyes continued to stare vacantly at the radio, her breaths so shallow I had to touch her to make sure she was still warm. Chelsea lay down between us, slowly resting her head on Mom's knee, licking gently at her elegant navy-blue sundress. It was as if the dog sensed her distress and was offering comfort in the only way she could—non-verbally.

"Yes, yes, I'm fine, honey," she said as she moved her leg just enough to let Chelsea know she didn't need her consolation (or her slobber). "Get her off the clean clothes, please."

Some people just aren't worthy of these fine creatures, I thought as I looked around at the jumbled disarray of everyone's clothing. I had trouble identifying what was clean and what was dirty, but I ordered Chelsea to "get" anyway. She stared at me as contentedly as Mom stared at the radio, and with about as much understanding of what I expected her to do. Chelsea wasn't the smartest pup around, but with her big, fluffy coat and bright eyes, she was definitely the cutest. A similar comparison would never be made with me in mind, but I wasn't sure if that made me proud or disappointed.

"I've got it from here," I said to Mom as I grabbed one of Dad's checkered work shirts and laid it out flat in front of me. "Dinner's ready!"

As though I'd broken the spell, she rose to her feet, stood tall atop Laundryville, and then made her way to its bordering

9

municipality—Dinnertown. Despite her well-known allegiance to Dad and me, Chelsea trotted closely behind her; if someone was moving toward food, she followed like a lost puppy. Half the time, I think she actually *was* lost.

As I tried to sort out the mess in front of me, it became clear Mom had strayed from her usual laundry-doing methodology in more ways than one. Under her fine tutelage, I'd learned the intricacies of load separation based on colour, though today she'd abandoned her own best practices. Instead, she'd assembled the loads based on item type. All of the shirts and all of the pants were living harmoniously—segregated from one another. Even if one shirt was white and the next was red, they were all just shirts in the wash (pink shirts, ultimately). It was a bit unorthodox, but I liked it.

I set to work:

1. Straighten collar.

2. Criss-cross sleeves.

3. Fold in half.

4. Half again.

5. Stack.

6. Repeat.

I'd been trained well (despite inconsistencies in the curriculum), and it wasn't long before the tattered burgundy rug peeked out from underneath the chaos. Soon I had successfully cleaned up Laundryville. *They should really make me mayor!*

I looked through the hole in the wall into the kitchen. What wonderful utility the window served—spying on each other from one room to the other. At the table, Mom was fidgeting, picking away at her uneaten pizza. She insisted on using a fork and knife to eat everything, even finger food. Dad and Isaac were done with their meagre meals, but the trite dinnertime chatter remained. It was refreshing to hear Mom questioning Isaac for once. She peppered him with questions as if she were seasoning a cheap steak.

"Where did you go today? Who were you with? Did you see Jessie again?"

Jessie was Isaac's flavour of the week—or if she was lucky, maybe she'd be a whole-summer fling. Dad appeared indifferent, and after Mom's lengthy interaction with the antique radio, her standards of conversation weren't high. I'm sure even Isaac's one-word replies felt riveting.

I decided to make my grand re-entrance with a peace offering. If Mom wasn't going to eat, I'd make her a tea. Tea was better than nothing.

CHAPTER 2

2012—It's been thirteen years

Suzie says it's important I think about *that* time in my life. To recall details with more accuracy and less "psychological projection." If I'm so fixated on it, I need to understand why. Apparently, journalling is an effective way to analyze issues and concerns, both past and present. She's lucky I was such a fastidious child, keeping detailed notes of every occurrence as if I planned to write a bestselling memoir one day. Oh, the disappointment I'd see on young Ivy's face if I told her the state her life would be in—certainly not memoir worthy—as she rounded her twenty-eighth year. Basically, I am paying a therapist to tell me I should write in a diary, something I've been doing on and off since I was six. She's encouraged me to let my old journals "guide" me as I write a new one—as if the incoherent drivel I wrote as a child will be some kind of spirit guide on my complicated journey through egocentric validation.

It's true that a lot of my adolescence has escaped me, but I like it that way. I *made* it that way. It's why I had to travel all the way to Mom's house out in the boonies to get the few diaries that survived—the diaries she insisted on keeping. When I read them now, disparate memories materialize, forming together like a shitty book report written by a student who's only read the Coles Notes. The details are dodgy, but the overarching conclusion is resounding: there are two kinds of people in this world, those who look back in anger, and those who don't.

I have to sing (or in this case, write) at least three lines of "Don't Look Back in Anger" by Oasis or I won't be able to complete this juvenile soul-searching exercise. All because I accidentally thought a thought that came close to a lyric I know. I've been doing it since childhood; at first it was an endearing quirk, now it's more of an annoying burden. What kind of life is it to sit in fear on a first date, praying he won't unwittingly say something that makes me break into song? I've gotten a bit better in recent years with the help of some cognitive behavioural therapy (I snap a hair tie around my wrist when things are getting bad), and I don't have to sing the lyrics out loud anymore. Now I can sing them in my head while I talk on autopilot or pretend to listen. Before, I'd get antsy if I didn't recite the full song or at the very least a whole verse, but now I can move on after a few bars.

The upside of this specific symptom of obsessive-compulsive disorder (OCD) is that I'm occasionally reminded of songs I've forgotten—unless the lyrics are already tattooed somewhere on my body, that is. This song, however, I didn't forget (it isn't tattooed on me either, thank God). I loved it when I was younger, playing it relentlessly on repeat. Now I resent it. *Don't look back in anger?* Easy for *you* to say. I'm not the type to pick up my rose-coloured spectacles every time I take a stroll down memory lane. I'm more of a . . . *blinders* person. If the blinders are off, the anger train goes full steam ahead, so it's really a matter of picking my poison. I'd say all the good memories came *flooding back* to me (upon reading my journals), but if I said that, it would only be because I'm trying to fit another stupid cliché into this therapy-ordered nonsense.

Okay, okay, you caught me—I'm being defensive again. I'd be lying if I said nothing at all came of my self-indulgent historical research.

14

I've been reminded of some rather interesting details—for better or for worse (there's another one—God, I'm good). It's fascinating what details you can forget about yourself if they don't fit perfectly into the narrative of who you think you've become. Somehow (or maybe it was on purpose) I forgot I'd been held back a year, which meant I would have been the ripe age of fifteen when I entered high school. I remember people, like my Mom's church friends, saying I was *beyond my years*. Did I ever tell them why?

When I was eleven, I fell ill after an avoidable accident took place involving me, a raccoon, a half-frozen Lake Scugog, and my unwavering desire to be a child heroine. The infection that followed kept me out of school for almost three months. It was an unmanageable absence, even in middle school, especially because I wasn't an A+ student to begin with.

Apparently, I relished the decision to be held back a year, the way any naive child would, I suppose: excitedly counting my extra days of summer, laughing at how easy retaking tests would be, and bragging to Isaac about all the new friends I'd collect in my new (second) grade five class.

I quickly learned that reality paled in comparison to what I imagined, and the raccoon I'd tried to save from its cold, watery casket wasn't worth the divide I felt in myself and my schooling from that time onward. A stranger among my peers, I didn't collect friends; instead, I collected books. Sitting in the library proved a welcome distraction from the day-to-day hardships of feeling too old or too young, ostracized by both groups. Reading was the only thing I was good at, so I adjusted to the sobering cruelty of my academic purgatory by spending every free moment devouring novels hidden between the shelves of the mystery-fiction section. I was determined to be ahead of my whole school in reading if I was going to be behind my age group in everything else. A small victory, since that alienation led me to a somewhat fulfilling career in publishing.

"Books! Yes!" Henry agreed—perfect for a girl who looked like me.

A jest wrapped painfully in truth, as all jokes are. I was big for my age, even before I was held back a grade. Often the tallest girl in my class (an award I could have done without winning), I wore Isaac's hand-me-downs and pretended it was an androgynous statement rather than a necessity. I must have been into self-deprecating comedy at an early age because I took rigorous note of my shortcomings:

1. My crooked teeth had once been compared to that of a beaver, Canada's honoured national symbol.

2. My frizzy, often unkempt curls had been compared to a lion's unruly mane.

3. My prepubescent acne was akin to a Dalmatian's spots.

4. My robust figure could be categorized as belonging to the marine-mammal family (with the other walruses).

Blessed with a healthy dose of character-building misfortune at an early age (and an undeniable affinity for animal comparisons), I think it's safe to say that times were tough for my not-so-burgeoning self-esteem. In my head, I had a heinous picture of what I'd look like when I grew up. I assumed every one of my physical flaws would steadily worsen, and every small blessing would naturally lessen. No one told me I'd outgrow my awkwardness and grow into my looks. Mom said I was beautiful no matter what, but I knew the essentiality of white lies even as a child. That's who I see when I look in a mirror now—a younger version of my mother. Loose honey curls, pillowy lips, a sharp nose, sage-green eyes, and faded freckles—I see the woman I stared at with disdain as a child, bitter because I thought I'd never grow up to look like her. More so than growing into *my* looks, I think I grew into hers.

I remember having two sets of friends when I was a kid: my Catholic-school friends (or lack thereof) by day, and my street friends by night. Robyn was my best friend, and I still occasionally talk to her on Facebook—nothing major, just the odd check-in. Congratulations are usually in order for her most recent pregnancy, while condolences are usually in order for the demise of my latest relationship, etc., etc. During those elementary school years, every evening when I got off the bus after my forty-five-minute ride, I'd transform into anyone I wanted to be, anyone I told my street friends I was. I wrote about the way I'd change every June as though the tough skin I wore during the school year would slowly begin to fall off and be replaced by my care-free summer skin, as in that Death Cab for Cutie song, "Summer Skin."

Although roughened by the intense heat of the sun, my summer skin was my softer skin, and because I was only ever around real friends then, it was my thinner skin too. What I'd give to find that skin again, so innocent and pure (and most importantly, wrinkle-free). I have different versions of myself I share with people now, but no matter how hard I've searched, I've never found the skin I wore at the beginning of *that* summer. It was the shell of a happy but ignorant girl who thought the biggest hardship she'd ever have had something to do with a dead cow.

CHAPTER 3

─────

Sunday, June 20th, 1999—32 days until my birthday

Today was church day. Despite being raised Catholic, we're
Pentecostal. This past year, when I had a choice to be confirmed into
the Catholic religion, I decided to emancipate myself—the same way
Mom did a few years ago when she stopped going to Mass and started
attending Living Light on the Island.

I usually attended Sunday morning service with Mom. Like Isaac,
once I turned sixteen, I'd be afforded the right to choose if I wanted
to keep God in my life. Until then, Mom preferred I kept her and
God company. The day Isaac turned sixteen, he claimed his only religion was rock 'n' roll, and he never set foot inside a church again. In a
strange way, it felt as though his defiance almost pleased Dad, though
he and Mom usually tried to maintain a united moral front.

Since Mom's staring contest with the radio, her mood seemed to
have lightened. Dinners were less round and saucy, and she'd successfully resumed mayorship of Laundryville.

"I like it when it's just the two of us," she said as she sped down
Pine Point Road in our grey Chrysler Caravan.

Mom's flagrant disregard for the loosely enforced speed limits freaked me out a bit. It didn't help that the roads on the Island seldom had dividing lines and were even less likely to be paved. She reached over and gently took my hand. Even in sunny, twenty-six-degree weather, her hand was as cold as the early spring waters of Lake Scugog.

"I like it too," I said, trying to warm her hand between both of mine.

Her mouth rippled the way it always did right before she was about to cry. She withdrew her hand and rubbed the knuckle of her index finger around the outline of her lips, tracing it slowly as if she was putting on invisible lipliner. It was a nervous tic I'd caught myself doing more than once, despite my reluctance to inherit any quirky habits from either parent. She looked distant, consumed in thought, as if her mind were somewhere outside the car and she'd only sent her body to drive us to church.

"What's wrong, Mom? Do you want me to drive?" I asked, sincere in my offer.

I didn't have my learner's permit yet, but sometimes she'd let me drive around in parking lots after the stores had closed. It was a strictly forbidden (and, as such, coveted) activity that started as a "one-time" gift on my thirteenth birthday. Henry, the safety freak of the family, would file for divorce if he ever found out; the unnecessary risk and insolent law-breaking would horrify him. To Mom, driving in an empty parking lot was pretty harmless, but nothing was harmless to Henry, who proudly headed up his office's health and safety committee. He'd read every hypothetical emergency situation in the book (literally—he brought home a huge first-aid manual to study after he was elected), and as a result, he preferred us to experience fun only in written form. *Why go skydiving when you could read someone's detailed account of it from the safety of the ground?* We weren't even allowed to have scented candles. Fundamentally, Mom letting me drive without a licence was our biggest secret. It's strange how secrets (good or bad, big or small) have a way of bringing people closer to each other. Mutually assured destruction was a powerful thing.

"No, no, I'm just tired, and you know how I get when I'm tired," she said, placing both hands on the wheel at ten and two (just as she'd taught me).

"Why are you so tired lately? Just go to bed earlier!"

The solution was so simple. Who needed a life coach when they could have me? Free of charge.

"It's not that easy, hon. When I worry, I can't sleep, and when I can't sleep, I worry."

I struggled to relate. I may have taken for granted the absence of worry in my own life, but I still thought an earlier bedtime was a reasonable suggestion.

"Well, what do you really have to worry about, anyway?" I asked, sounding more flippant than I'd meant to.

She pulled onto Island Road, the busiest road on the Island, and *undeniably* the most creatively named. Treacherous in the winter and scenic in the summer, it led us along wily curves to the causeway that carried us off the Island and into town. We giggled as she careened from side to side, turning the van's wheels to the beat of the gospel music that blasted from the radio. Driving like a maniac while keeping in time to the music was something she'd done when I was younger as a way to cheer me up. But I wasn't going to let her tomfoolery distract me from doing the same for her; I turned down the radio and prodded further.

"If it's about Isaac or me, I promise we're fine. He should shower more, but other than that, you've raised two well-adjusted and, may I add, rather attractive kids."

She didn't attempt to humour me. Not even a half-hearted smirk.

"No, Ivory," she replied, using the nickname only she and my Aunt Sam used. "It's bigger than that—*way* bigger. But I think it's safer that I don't share the details." She rubbed her finger around her mouth again, warding off a tear-induced tremble. "I just want you to promise me one thing, okay?"

It wasn't unlike me to assume her entire world revolved around Isaac and me. The potential for her worry to extend beyond us hadn't

21

even occurred to me. As my hand hovered over the passenger-side dashboard, she reached over and lightly smacked it away. I'd been destructively picking away at the foamy white interior (a nasty habit I hadn't inherited from anyone). I exhaled slowly, letting out a breath I'd been holding since we were on Pine Point.

"Of course, Mom."

"Just be careful, okay? Always leave the house in pairs, and don't answer the phone if you don't know the number or if it's my work calling—*especially* if it's my work calling." She let out a long sigh—a heavy release she must've been holding it in for a while too. "Don't talk to strangers either. I know it sounds silly, but it's about time we get more serious about our family's safety."

"Are you for real? You're not considering making a bomb shelter again, are you?"

She rolled her eyes. Still not humouring me.

"Grandpa just about fainted when I told him we didn't lock the doors—that no one on our street did. Next year will be the year 2000! Who knows what kind of crazies that'll bring out? We should start preparing now!"

I'd heard her far-fetched Y2K theories before, but this sounded different. Her fear was rooted in something more imminent, something she cloaked in the deranged guise of millennium preparedness.

"Sure, no problemo. You know what? I'll just never leave the house. And we can start saving canned food now if you want," I quipped, hoping to add some comic relief to an unexpectedly serious (and seemingly irrational) conversation.

"Okay, Ivy—never mind, then."

***

After church, Robyn and I decided to go to Sunrise Beach, not to catch frogs as we used to (when she was still interested in having fun), but to suntan. It seemed a bit boring, but nevertheless, it was *adult*.

Dad asked if we wanted some lunch before we left. He was going to make a sandwich and sit by "the clean, warm, well-kept body of water I've paid dearly for out back." The detailed description was his passive way of mentioning that we didn't have to go all the way to Sunrise Beach—we had everything we needed right in our own backyard. I found his transparent plea endearing.

"No thanks, Dad! But thanks for asking!" I made sure to sound sincere. Isaac had gone all teenager-tude on him, but I wanted to suppress the sass as much as I could and stay Daddy's little girl for a least the summer. Things were just easier that way.

"Wear your shoes, for shit's sakes!" he yelled as I grabbed my bike, readying myself for takeoff. Leaving the house shoeless gave me a weird sense of freedom. It made me feel as though I hadn't been confined by the evolutionary development of soft soles. By the end of each summer, I'd be able to run up and down our gravel driveway without a single wince of pain. Anyone could dare me—I'd prove it.

Dad stood in the backyard, dutifully watching from around the corner of the house as we rode away. He stationed himself there so he could wave goodbye (the car-less equivalent of the *beep* we'd sound whenever we pulled out of Grandpa Perruzza's driveway). Soon a tall, dignified wooden fence would go up between the front and backyards so you wouldn't be able to see one from the other. Until we could afford it, there would just be the embarrassingly floppy plastic fence that was neither keeping anything in nor keeping anything out— not even a stiff breeze, which posed a problem for our four-legged, runaway family member, Chelsea. We had to chain her to the side of the house near the back door. I hated tying her up, but last summer, she'd escaped and wreaked havoc on the Langley house. The Langleys were waterside neighbours we didn't know very well. She'd plowed through their screen door like a menace, making herself at home on their expensive furniture. To say they were perturbed would be an understatement. Isaac took responsibility, even though we were both supposed to have been watching her (a small benefit of being the

23

younger sibling), and he had to pay for the damage with the money he'd made at Blue Feather Farm, a local farm-turned-retailer. His offer to take the fall was a gracious one, though he spent the rest of the summer whining about the money and how it had been meant for a new amp—not an overpriced throw pillow.

"How's Patty-Poo doing?" Robyn asked as we rode side by side toward Sunrise Beach. Patty-Poo was her annoying, yet somehow charming, nickname for Mom, whose real name was Patricia.

"She's fine, I think. We talked in the car this morning. She's just bugging out about something, said I had to promise I'd be *safe*." I laughed, raising my eyebrows so high I thought they'd hit my hairline. "Then she asked me to only leave the house if I was with someone— so it looks like you're stuck with me for the summer."

She rang her bike bell wildly in celebration, standing on the pedals as she rode, clearly not getting the memo about discretion. "Oh man, I hope it's something juicy. We could use a little excitement around here."

I sang aloud a verse from "Round Here," my favourite Counting Crows song, about how sad mundanity can make you. Robyn waited patiently before she went on; she knew the drill.

"What do you think it's about?"

"I honestly have no idea. She works with a motley crew of creeps at Sternwood Construction," I whispered, looking around with shifty eyes, pretending to be scared. "But she's going to work tomorrow, so it must be fine. She's just been watching too much *Law & Order*."

She laughed with me; I could always count on Robyn to humour me, unlike Mom.

"And how's Isaac doing?"

I could always count on her to ask about Isaac too. We swerved onto the dirt pathway that led us down to the beach. It was lined with wise-looking willow trees, and I tried to let the placid scenery calm my budding irritation.

Robyn and I talked about everything. She knew every detail of my life since I'd moved to the Island when I was five and she was four. She'd probably be considered the sixth member of our family (I counted the dog, of course) if it weren't painfully obvious she was in love with Isaac. I was used to my friends falling for my brother, or at least joking about it to piss me off, but with Robyn, it stung. I thought our friendship came with an unwritten rulebook (when I say unwritten, I really meant written, because I wrote it out in my journal three years ago and made her sign it at the bottom, like a contract):

- *Never steal your best friend's things*
- *Never talk about your best friend when she's not around*
- *Always lie for your best friend to her parents*
- *Always tell your best friend everything first*
- *Never fall for your best friend's brother*

BF: *Robyn* Witness: IVY

Pretty simple, really—Isaac was off limits, not to mention mean and foul smelling. Ever since Robyn had "become a woman," her interests had strayed slightly from mine. And that was okay. It just wasn't okay that I was subjected to transparent interrogations about Isaac's band, his girlfriend, or his, quote unquote, "favourite cologne."

I dropped my bike to the ground and pulled off my beaded cover-up; Mom and Dad had gotten us both one the last time they went to Jamaica. Robyn wasn't wearing hers; she wasn't even wearing a shirt over her red bikini top. Her long black hair wasn't pulled back in a ponytail as it normally was either, and when I stared closely, it almost looked as though she was wearing lipstick. I guess we had a different dress code now that we were about to go to high school.

"He's fine." I hoped the hardness in my voice was as transparent as her inquiry.

My response set the tone for the trip: it would be a quiet afternoon spent intentionally burning in the sun. Not a single frog would be caught, not a single word would be said. Very *adult*.

CHAPTER 4

Tuesday, June 22nd, 1999—30 days until my birthday

Robyn and I caught wind (which usually smelled of manure from the surrounding farms) of the fact that the summer's first game of manhunt was happening. Manhunt is a "game" that really isn't a game at all. It's something a handful of us kids on the street say we're playing when we need a valid excuse to leave the house dressed entirely in black in order to terrorize the neighbourhood after sunset.

On the Island, only one road travels along Lake Scugog. You have the waterside houses, and then you have the less affluent houses, like mine, directly across from them. Behind the waterless properties are acres upon acres of fields and forests, filled with what we liked to call "uncharted territory" (basically just useless land no longer good enough for farming). Our nights often led us through the vast acreage, sometimes as a shortcut, sometimes just to explore. It could be a bit creepy in the darkness, but most of us found it more fun than disconcerting. It was the kind of eerie pastime you'd only appreciate if you enjoyed horror flicks—which I did.

If we were feeling brave, we'd explore deep into the forests, finding abandoned barns and forgotten stables. We'd taken to naming our discoveries things like Devil's Den or Bloody's Barn—as if the decrepit structures weren't spooky enough. We often believed we'd never seen them before (and might never again), but in the light of day, it was anyone's guess.

Most manhunt nights started off with nicky nicky nine doors—a game we took to impressively deviant heights. After picking a victim, we'd station ourselves separately around their house, knocking on all the doors and a select few windows. We'd repeat the prank every three minutes or so, stealing something from their porch each time so they'd know they weren't just hearing things. The homeowner would emerge, usually frightened and always confused, unsure of which entrance to check first. By the time they made it to a door, we'd already be hidden safely in our preordained meeting spot (truly menacing). After recently reading about the details of the Manson murders in 1969, I was beginning to think our tactics were a bit cruel, but I wasn't one to object—I was the oldest in the group, so it would be too predictable.

Robyn and I met with the other kids at the foot of my driveway at 8:30 p.m. sharp.

"It's not dark enough," said Nick, a small, homely boy who lived four doors down.

It wasn't often I agreed with him, but I knew sunset was at least thirty minutes away.

"He's right," I said to the rest of the group. Robyn, Crystal, and Sarah (and sometimes Nick) were the kids whose names most often littered the pages of my journal and the friends who saw me as the person I wanted to be outside the walls of the school library.

Crystal and Sarah were sisters, both with mouse-brown hair and prominent noses. Some people assumed they were twins, even though Sarah was two years Crystal's senior. Thankfully, we were starting to outgrow the stage in our lives where people guessed your age based purely on your height. Crystal and Sarah's house, extravagant both inside and out, was on the rich side of the street. If not for them, Robyn and I wouldn't have known the joys of speeding across the water on an inflatable death trap, tethered to a boat by a thin rope liable to snap or fling you off at any moment (otherwise known as tubing). Their family didn't have to choose between a lot of toys or a nice, big house—they were lucky enough to have both. With them, we'd go boating in the summer and snowmobiling in the winter. We had an above-ground pool, and of course they had an in-ground pool with a diving board and a slide. We had a second-hand Super Nintendo, and they had a brand-new Nintendo 64. They had a dock with unlimited access to the lake, while we had a wobbly fence that once let a cow into our backyard.

"Let's walk to Pine Point and back around," Sarah said. "By then it'll be dark, and we can hit the houses on the Darley Road side."

The walk up Pine Point was a traditional prerequisite to our manhunt games each summer. We'd discuss our final report-card grades while Nick bragged about how late his curfew was. Realistically, he didn't have one at all because his parents never cared enough to enforce it. His dad was usually at the bar, but if he was home, he'd have just arrived, belligerent and violent, from the bar. His mom, on the other hand, never went anywhere; she was always home drunk—drunk enough to put up with Nick's dad, which meant too drunk to notice Nick had left.

We walked until we reached the Candy Lady's house, which marked the top of the tallest hill our tired legs would have to trek up. It was too late to knock on her door, but if it hadn't been, we'd have gone right up the driveway to the front porch for our allotted piece of candy. Visiting the Candy Lady was a long-standing tradition, dating back long before our Pine Point walks. It was the Candy Lady's mother who'd earned the title by opening her home to the neighbour-hood children, repaying a knock at the door with candy in hand—like Halloween but all year round. It was one of the few small things that made the Island kind of special. Out here, we took what we could get.

"She's fostering two Native kids from the reserve by the casino now, eh?" Crystal said.

"No way. Really?" Nick asked, wide-eyed. I wondered if he ever had daydreams of being in foster care—in a more stable home with caring parents.

"Yeah." Crystal nodded, proud of her intel. "I saw them a few days ago. Must be around our age, but it's hard to tell. Think we should try and be their friends?"

I shrugged. Making new friends had become less and less important to me with every candle added to my birthday cake.

"Jeez, it's already nine," Robyn gasped, looking down at her green, glowing digital watch, a graduation present from her parents. "Let's just go do a farm frenzy instead!"

Farm frenzy was another game that wasn't really a game at all, where we'd sneak into farms and mess with the animals. Harmless stuff—no biggie. Sometimes we'd play tag with the goats or move the rooster closer to the farmhouse. We hadn't been caught yet because we'd gotten really good at staying out of sight and stifling our laughter. The closest we'd come was last summer, when we narrowly escaped a round of BB shots followed by the exposing flash of a hand-held floodlight. A peculiar order to present the defence in, though common sense wasn't always abundant in the secluded, rural towns of Durham Region.

We neared Old Man Spooner's farm—he owned all the acreage that sprawled up behind the houses on our street. Despite possessing so much real estate, he and his son lived humbly, side by side in old farmhouses that were both in desperate need of updating. Mr. Spooner was an affable, quiet man whose tanned, leathery skin told you everything you needed to know about his work ethic. However, his son, Junior, was constantly the subject of whispered pettiness in the community. His distinct *lack* of work ethic usually resulted in an unsightly yard—much to his neighbours' dismay.

We chose to start the night at the unkempt farm because it was easy to hide in the tall grass. We dipped to the right side of the dirt road, crouching low in the dug-out ditch. Though our steps were hurried, we'd learned exactly how to wade through the deep, smelly swamp water without making a sound any louder than a bullfrog's splash.

CHAPTER 5

Wednesday, June 23rd, 1999—29 days until my birthday

Crystal thought it would be funny to actually try to tip a cow—we'd never had the guts to do it before. Despite what some may think, cows are actually malevolent creatures, angry and short-tempered. They look even bigger close up, not exactly approachable (especially the bulls).

"Are we going to jail?" Crystal asked once we'd all arrived at Mount Everest.

Mount Everest was our landmark meeting place on the long, torrid days we devoted to staying out of sight of our parents. The pile of boulders had been stacked dangerously high, dug out of the surrounding farmland years ago to prepare the plots for cultivation. The rocks were the only reminder that the barren land around us had once been filled with crops.

"No, we're not going to jail, Crystal. It's just a cow," I tried to reassure her.

We hadn't meant to do it; it was hard to believe we actually had. At first we thought we'd just shocked the cow, but after a while, we realized we had shocked it to death. Cows were expensive, and its death would be costly to Junior. Mom and Dad bought a full cow from the Spooners every year. It was delivered in hundreds of neatly wrapped brown paper packages, tied with white string and labelled precisely—right to the point. Heart. Brain. Flank. Tongue. Most years we'd have to split the order with one or two families on the street, depending on what we could afford.

"Well, should we tell someone?" Nick asked. He looked particularly feeble in his faded Blue Jays T-shirt that was covered with holes and stains.

Too late now, I thought. "Well, hind legs are twenty-twenty . . . or whatever," I said, hoping to provoke a laugh.

"No!" Robyn barked. "Are you insane, Nick? Cattle die all the time. As long as Junior didn't see any of us running away, we're safe. Let's just leave it and stick to nicky nicky nine doors from now on. Farm frenzying is over!"

I knew it was disappointing for her, since it was her favourite game. But farm frenzying had become risky, and Robyn was the most risk-averse teen I'd ever met. Dad predicted she'd end up working in banking—"Investments," he claimed with so much confidence, it made nine-year-old Robyn cry.

"I agree, no one says a word," said Sarah, unpacking the snacks she brought from her purple *Beverly Hills, 90210* lunch bag. We could always count on her to feed us in a time of crisis.

I looked around at everyone's faces, scrunched with worry but less panicked than they had been last night when it happened, when we'd realized the cow was dead—dead as a doornail. At that moment the silence was amplified, and I could hear the blood running through my veins, settling in my throbbing earlobes. I was sweating all over, but at the same time, it felt as though every hair on my body was covered in a thin layer of ice that would pierce my skin if anyone touched me. We stood there staring at the cow for at least ten minutes, frozen in disbelief, waiting for time to reverse itself or for the future to meet us there. Robyn finally yelled, "*Run!*" and we followed like lemmings behind her—more afraid of being left alone in the dark than being caught. The getaway run wasn't like the thrilling and hilarious sprints we were used to. Normally, we'd struggle to control our laughter, but as we fled I struggled to put one foot in front of the other. Witnessing death for the first time had rendered me useless.

I'd seen dead things before many times while exploring the back fields. I knew the smell of rotting animal flesh and could pick it out on the breeze before anyone else even noticed it. At first I found it repulsive, unlike anything I'd ever smelled in my life. Over time I'd grown to like it. Maybe not the smell itself, but knowing what it meant: I got to examine something dead close up. Sometimes we'd find unlucky baby deer or sickly coyotes overlooked by predators not enticed by an easy meal (especially if it meant the meat wasn't fresh). Last summer we found a dismembered leg of a goat, and while were crouched down inspecting the maggot-infested tibia, Chelsea, thinking it was a stick, grabbed it and bolted. The memory used to make me laugh, reminding me how dark my sense of humour was, but today it just felt sinister. I know now there's a big difference between seeing a dead *thing* and seeing a thing *die* right in front of you. Cows, next to horses, were the biggest, sturdiest animals I'd ever interacted with. Their strength and stature explained why my remorse was coupled with surprise. *How had we pushed it to such an inconceivable death?* We didn't even "tip" it per se; its centre of gravity had other things in mind. The startled, slow-moving cow stumbled around for a minute and then fell to the ground like a baby taking its first steps.

"Let's get out of here," I said. "We all agree—no one mentions it, and we'll be fine."

"We have to go into town," Crystal said.

"We only came out to talk about . . . it, but we gotta head home now," Sarah finished.

Nick took it as his cue to head home too. The five of us hung out together a lot, but Nick would never hang out with Robyn and me alone. We were the fearsome twosome, and he knew three was a crowd.

***

"Let's get as far from Junior's place as possible," I said, marching with purpose northeast toward the sun. Robyn followed behind me along one of the many paths we'd come to know in the back fields, one we hadn't made ourselves. There were foot trails and driven pathways all around us, some well defined, others overgrown and ambiguous. The haphazard thoroughfares provided a semblance of order in the areas that most often felt the footsteps of local transit, but they weren't labelled or maintained, leaving their legitimacy in question.

"What are you thinking about?" Robyn asked, breaking the silence I'd made while thinking.

"Nothing really—just Patty-Poo. Still kinda worried about her."

I knew Mom was feeling more than uneasy about work. As Sternwood Construction's secretary and part-time accountant, she found that her job was normally low pressure and low stress (something Dad said she should appreciate more), but this seemed no longer true. Last night I'd heard Mom and Dad talking about her work troubles while they were in the living room having their after-dinner tea. They spoke in hushed tones, but Isaac (a master eavesdropper) turned off the faucet and stopped doing dishes long enough for us to get the gist. Now it was all I could think about.

"Do you want to talk about it?" Robyn asked.

"No."

"That's okay. Let's just have some fun! We'll stay out all day—that way we'll have an alibi!"

"Sure, okay."

I'd read enough murder mysteries to know that wasn't how alibis worked, but I didn't feel like correcting her. I'd be happy to stay out all day—whether it supported our innocence or not.

I swung my old canvas backpack around and put it on backwards, covering what would have been my breasts—if God didn't have such a cruel sense of humour. I took out the little portable radio I'd gotten for Christmas from Aunt Sam and turned it up to full volume.

Aunt Sam was Mom's younger sister. She was wild and free and unapologetically herself. She lived an hour away in Toronto (instead of the boonies) and was a punk-rock city girl who loved music as much as I did. We'd always been close—she kind of just *got* me. Not to mention she was only fifteen years older than Isaac (making her my coolest relative by far). She told me once that I was an old soul, and she was young at heart, which meant we met somewhere in the middle. Whenever she came over, she brought me a new burnt CD with different versions of my favourite rock songs and newer radio tunes she doesn't think are garbage. I looked forward to Aunt Sam's visits and her gifts; they never let me down, and the boom box was no exception. Without needing to adjust the antenna, we could hear Fleetwood Mac's Stevie Nicks coming in loud and clear, singing "Dreams."

"Can you put on something written in *this* decade, please?" she begged.

I shook my head. "Nope!"

Classic rock music wasn't something I'd ever compromise on. I'd rather wander around in silence than subject Mother Nature to the banal melodies of another boy band. Especially because of where we were. By the time "Dreams" was done playing, we'd made our way onto sacred ground, standing ten feet from my favourite spot on the Island—the Pretty Place.

The Pretty Place was a special spot to both of us, but we tried not to come too often. I wanted to preserve its rarity; it felt fragile, dissipating with every stolen visit. I almost believed we'd one day find an overgrown field in its place with no indication it had ever really existed, as if it were only visible to those who appreciated it (just as children see magic only because they believe). A silly thought, but it was so beautiful there, it had the power to make you accept the inexplicable.

"Let's go to the Pretty Place, Robyn. It feels like we should!"

"Nah . . . you sure? Don't you think we'll, like, bring bad juju into it because of the cow or whatever?"

I stepped back, dramatically darting my eyes around in every direction, practically punching myself in the mouth to do the universal *shh* sign.

"No one's around," she said, shrugging off her carelessness.

"Still!" I said, gawking. "And no, if anything, it'll wash all that off of us."

"Okay, okay, let's go!"

She threw her crimped hair up in a scrunchy and used the inside collar of her neon-orange T-shirt to wipe the sweat from her upper lip. Her shirt, like her general appearance, demanded attention. *Really inconspicuous*—but at least she wouldn't get shot.

We veered off the path, meticulously weaving through the poison ivy that marked the opening where our furtive trail began. We hadn't cleared a path on purpose. From the outside, the woodland looked ordinary, and we knew better than to draw attention to it. When we were younger, we'd painted rocks and left them at the base of a few trees, creating a secret trail that led us to the core of the forest. Years later the rocks still wore their full paint. Effectively carrying out their God-given vocation, they were working rocks. We knew there were smarter ways of marking the route (this was only slightly more practical than a proverbial trail of bread crumbs), but it added to the mystery of it all.

Following the rocks in as deep as she could, Robyn fell back and let me lead the rest of the way. I'd been there more times than she had, but I saw it with fresh eyes even still. Inside, the trees appeared old and wise but young and spry too—familiar yet exotic. At the very centre of the forest was a shallow, shimmering reservoir surrounded by dainty white flowers. Beside it was a willow tree with a rope swing and a makeshift ladder nailed precariously to its side. Across from the water were the ruins of an ancient yellow Volkswagen Beetle. Windowless and invaded with overgrown brush, it was pierced through the sunroof by a pine tree, making it look more like a lawn ornament than an abandoned, old vehicle.

We could play cards in the tree fort we built last summer, and if the willow branches were strong enough, we'd tie them together and make swings to sit and have our lunches on. There'd be no bad juju in the Pretty Place, only beauty and good times—our very own Garden of Eden, only without all the forbidden fruit crap.

CHAPTER 6

Friday, June 25th, 1999—27 days until my birthday

We were relieved no one had heard anything from even the most gossipy neighbours. I thought we'd gotten away with it (the cow—dead—doornail), but damn, were we ever wrong.

Friday night was family night, something that increasingly posed a problem for Isaac as his teen-boy charm intensified. By the time he was sixteen, he'd already started dating at least two girls at a time, making family night a distant third on his priority list. Mom, however, was unwavering about its importance—if our weekday dinners as a family were going to become few and far between, then Friday night game night was non-optional.

Monday, Wednesday, and Friday, Mom worked her shift at Sternwood. On those summer days, Isaac and I were totally free of supervision and mostly free of prudence too. Today we broke into Mom and Dad's room (locked because of us), popped the screen off the bathroom window, climbed onto the roof, and jumped two storeys down onto the trampoline.

"Let's dry off," I said, heaving myself up the rickety pool ladder. We'd decided to end our parent-free day with a swim because it was less likely (though not impossible) I'd break a bone (or rather, another bone) in a small body of water. Isaac, who'd recently become aware of his blossoming male physique, continued swimming laps as if he were training for the 2000 Summer Olympics. After all, swimming was (and I quote) "the best full-body workout you can do!" He loved to exercise as much as I loved to avoid it. It was as though his athletic build made him immune to the perils of calf cramps, side cramps, foot cramps, and every other cramp I got whenever I tried to be physically active. I wish I could say his enthusiasm was infectious, but it wasn't. If anything, it made me more disdainfully aware of my place in the world (this being in the front bay window reading a book). Why exercise when you could read about exercising from the comfort of your large, cramp-free ass, right?

I grabbed my towel off the back deck as Chelsea's rattling chain announced someone was home. I struggled to free her while she flailed around like a fish out of water. Seeing her so excited about their arrival made me feel guilty about how little I cared. Both the van and the Supra were already inside the garage when I opened the door, an unusual sight, since typically, Mom and Dad didn't arrive home at the same time. Mom's garage door was still open, and I could hear a heated conversation going on in front of Dad's. Dripping wet and shivering, I tiptoed up to the door, stationing myself in prime eavesdropping position. I held my breath and closed my eyes—I was old enough to know it didn't actually make me invisible but young enough to think I should still try.

"Why would you even say that, Patty?" Dad asked. His words were curt and as cold as the concrete beneath my bare feet.

"I don't know. I just have a feeling! I prepped their books for audit this year, you know? Is it so far-fetched to think they're mixed up in something illegal? Organized crime, even? Open your eyes!" she shot back (I wasn't the only Marshall who preferred to fight fire with fire). "I know we don't live in Toronto anymore, but that doesn't mean there aren't still criminals all around us."

"Well, that's just great," he said. "Things aren't exactly going well at work for me either—the timing couldn't be more perfect."

(Sarcasm runs in the family too.)

"I'm not saying I'm quitting. I'm just letting you know I could get caught up in all this. But don't worry—I know the paycheque is what's most important!"

(In fact, it dripped from every word.)

"I'm not saying that. I'm just saying, let's wait it out and see if it really does affect you. Keep your head down, and don't ask questions. No one's going to notice a part-time secretary unless you start causing a fuss."

I didn't have to see them to know Mom would be rolling her eyes and Dad would be crossing his arms—the ticked-off tango.

"Sure, okay," said Mom. "I wish I could offer you the same advice for your work issues, but we both know you've dug yourself a bigger hole."

With that, the dance was over.

Mom stormed into the garage and headed for the back door while Dad swung around and stomped up the porch steps and through the front door. I felt a cool whoosh of air on my face as she rushed past me, leaving the familiar scent of vanilla musk lingering in her furious path. I kept my eyes shut until she slammed the door, relieved she hadn't noticed my wet footprints during her dramatic exit.

Their conversation made me feel uneasy, nauseous even. They didn't seem to be on the same *team* anymore. The dynamic in our home had definitely changed, but it had been a subtle, slow burn since the Christmas before last. Mom had refused to go see Grandpa Marshall for dinner as planned, and Dad held a grudge about it, not speaking to her until the following year. It may have only been six days, but it felt more like six months. I wasn't sure if that was the turning point or if there was more to it, but things had been undeniably different between them ever since. No more gentle forehead kisses when Dad got home from work. No more holding hands, stolen smiles, laughter, or inside jokes. No more date nights or making plans to go to bed at the same time. And sadly, no more Salisbury steak (because it was Dad's favourite), so ultimately, Isaac and I fell victim to their fallout too. With Mom's new work-related stresses, who knows how much more their marriage could take (or how much more *we* could take)? What if she banned chocolate chip cookies next? Dad said hers were the best he'd ever had.

Inside the house, they effortlessly gave the impression that nothing was amiss—right up until Mom said she wasn't feeling well and bowed out of family game night. Isaac looked at Dad with pleading eyes, plainly hoping for a reprieve.

"Okay, okay," Dad said, waving his white flag of defeat. "Game night is cancelled!"

"Yes!" shouted Isaac. He didn't try to hide his excitement as he thrust his fist into the air.

One by one they dispersed. Dad followed Mom up to their bedroom to either continue their earlier discussion or so they could completely ignore one another (which was more impactful in close quarters). Isaac asked me to let them know he'd gone over to Brett's for impromptu band practice. He was the lead singer and guitarist for the Post Thrills—an *almost* tolerable, *almost* rock band that may or may not have missed the whole mainstream grunge fad. Isaac didn't care what genre they fit into; he played for *himself*, he said, not his (non-existent) audience.

It's just you and me, kid, I thought, looking over at Chelsea, who sat obediently in the doorframe at the entrance of the kitchen. It was her designated spot while we had dinner; she would watch from a comfortable distance. The segregation was a little too totalitarian for my liking; if it were up to me, Chelsea would sit with us at the table eating whatever we ate. But Dad had trained her well, and despite everyone's sudden departure, she remained in her spot, waiting patiently for her own dinner. I let her follow me to the laundry room (which doubled as her kitchen and indoor living space), where she devoured her kibble like a pig in forty-five-seconds flat. Dad had done a bang-up job as her trainer, but it was clear he'd yet to teach her the complicated lessons of sophistication and grace. (Oh, and ladies were always supposed to leave food on their plates, right?)

***

"Crap! Crap! Crap!" I yelled as I bolted outside.

I'd almost read four chapters of my book before I realized Chelsea was still roaming freely alone in the backyard. I searched every corner of the yard—in and around all the poplars, behind the shed and the woodpile, and even under the deck, though I knew she couldn't fit through the lattice openings. Frantically calling her name, I paced like an irate parent waiting for their child to come home after curfew. I'd only meant to leave her out for a few minutes to *do her business* after dinner, but my gracious gift of unfettered bliss had resulted in a pup-free backyard. When I'd yelled her name enough times to make my throat hurt, I knew it was time to panic.

When's an appropriate time to tell Dad? I wondered. He'd gotten home early, meaning we ate dinner early, meaning Chelsea had potentially been gone for two whole hours. The startling realization forced all of the air out of my lungs and back through my ears.

"What's going on?" Dad asked, walking up behind me.

I hadn't realized I'd been crying until he came out of nowhere, frightening me back into the real world. His timing was perfect, as though he'd heard my thoughts from inside the house.

"She's gone, Dad."

"Great," he said, joining the search party in nothing but his pyjama pants.

He started by shouting her name the same way I had (with the same degree of success). Then he switched methods, enlisting his signature whistle call that could be heard from miles away. I had never fully understood what he did to achieve the deafening sound (some

43

kind of hand-to-mouth technique), but it rang out with the force of a foghorn in the night with the same ominous warning.

"You check the neighbours'. I'll check the back fields."

"I'm sorry. She must have gotten off the leash," I lied, scurrying away toward my assigned search ground. I thought he'd feel the dishonesty in the air if I stayed too long and let it linger.

I sang the opening verse to "Linger" by the Cranberries, lost in the song, wholeheartedly resenting the appropriateness of the lyrics. I'd only made it to the side fence when I heard it: Chelsea's thunderous galloping from somewhere in the distance. She'd found her way home, her return swift and ordained like the return of the prodigal son.

"Good girl!" I wailed. Like Dad, her timing was perfect.

She shimmied under our fence, unwittingly showing us the spot that had aided her escape.

"You're lucky," Dad said sharply.

We bent down to welcome her with abundant pats and hugs. If I hadn't known any better, I'd have thought there was a smile on Dad's face as Chelsea rolled over and exposed her pink-and-black speckled belly for a tummy rub. Two hours was the longest she'd ever gone unaccounted for, so the instinct to punish her bad behaviour was outweighed by the relief we felt upon her return.

"I'll tell your mother we found her," he said, grunting. "Not like she was too concerned anyway."

CHAPTER 7

Same Day, Friday, June 25th, 1999—The night she got sick

I stayed outside with Chelsea for a while to suffocate her with the tightest hugs I could muster. She reciprocated, licking my face all over. Her kisses smelled different—almost sweet, and the blue fur around her mouth made it look as if she'd eaten a snow cone!

Chelsea went to her outside water bowl, which looked desolate with two dead flies floating around in an inch of lukewarm sludge. I emptied the fly soup and filled it with some fresh water from the hose, waiting a few seconds for the sun-heated water to come out so her homecoming drink would be as nice and cool as she liked it. She drank the entire bowl without coming up for air. I filled it back up. Parched from her misadventure, she drank the entire thing again as though she'd returned from the desert rather than a field on a balmy summer night.

It was dusk, so I wasn't sure if the looming darkness was playing tricks on my eyes or if Chelsea was, in fact, swaying from side to side as she drank the second bowl. The darkness might have accounted for the swaying, but when she flopped over and then stood back up twice, it was clear she'd appear to be losing her footing in *any* light.

Must have been some adventure, I thought as I filled her bowl a third time to see if (by some impossibility) she was still thirsty. She drank a bit and threw up. Drank some more, then more vomit. Sniff, drink, throw up, sniff that, drink and repeat.

The bluish vomit had chunks of half-chewed grass and a pile of leaves mixed in. With a release like that, I assumed she'd be feeling better soon. It was no big deal; she'd just had some field snacks on her night out—nature's blueberry smoothie. Like all dogs, Chelsea had an affinity for grass sandwiches, of lesser concern than her other snack of choice—poopsicles.

At first it seemed the vomiting made her well again. I sat with her while she napped on and off, sitting up and lying down, stumbling around, then walking straight, acting strangely and then totally normal. Chelsea's behaviour reminded me of Nick's the first time I'd seen him drunk. He'd stolen vodka from his mom and drank it straight from the bottle before a night of manhunt. He was only twelve at the time. Nick's body didn't know what to do with the substance he'd consumed, and his limbs were even less certain. He stumbled around like a baffled idiot, and it took all four of us an hour and a half to return him safely to his not-so-safe home, where his not-so-concerned mother told him to "walk it off" and "be a man." Chelsea was acting as though she'd gotten into Dad's whisky too, crossing her legs as if she'd forgotten how to walk, smashing headfirst into anything that proved itself an obstacle. The light on the side of the house was on a motion sensor and was turning on and off like a strobe light at our school dances, making me feel (as most school dances did) as if I was going to have a seizure or, at the very least, join the vomit club. We were both in rough shape, but I didn't know if I should get Dad; after the conversation I'd overheard earlier, it was clear he had enough to deal with. I didn't want to add thirsty, tired, (maybe drunk) dog to the list.

When thirsty, tired, (definitely drunk) Isaac got home, he slid under the side fence instead of going through the garage—his sad attempt to prevent Chelsea's inevitable barking. Instead of the usual canine alarm system, he found us lying on the ground, surrounded by grassy vomit.

"What the actual hell is going on here, Ivy?" he yelled.

His confusion had taken his voice to indiscreet volumes, but he didn't seem to care (neither did Chelsea).

"I dunno. Chelsea is really thirsty . . . and kinda tired, I guess. I dunno—she's fine," I said, half believing it and wholly hoping it was true.

"Um, no, she isn't. Look at her. What the hell is wrong with you? Come here, Chels, come here, girl."

Chelsea didn't move.

"See?" I exclaimed. "She's tired!"

"I'm getting Dad."

If Isaac was willing to interact with our father while under the influence, he must have thought something was terribly wrong—an observation that ultimately forced me out of Denialtown and into the land of Realityville. Something *was* terribly wrong, and it was definitely *all* my fault. I tried to get her to stand, to *walk it off* and *be a man.*

"Do you want to go for a walk, girl?" I asked. This would be the true test of wellness. Often her excitement was so overbearing, we'd have to spell it out—*w-a-l-k*—so she wouldn't know our plans before we got outside. When my question yielded only the tiniest of tail wags, I knew Isaac was right.

***

This time, Dad threw a T-shirt on before he came outside. His face wasn't angry, frustrated, or concerned. His emotion was hard to discern, but I think he was . . . scared. He looked at me and then at Chelsea, scanning the area like a detective looking for clues. Then, as if she were weightless, he picked up our big, furry pup, put her in the back seat of his tiny sports car, and drove away without saying a word. It happened so fast. I'd wanted him to at least try to help her, right there and then. I couldn't understand why he hadn't administered his own first aid when he was the one who'd told me every second mattered in an emergency situation—that there wasn't always time to get to a hospital. His first aid and CPR training was something he'd done "to avoid life-altering regret" after a co-worker had a fatal heart attack right in front of him. He said everyone stood around looking as useless as tits on a bull, and he'd never be caught idle in that situation again, though he'd seemed pretty idle tonight. After every training course, he had come home and taught Isaac and me everything he could remember: *What colour is blood? RED! What does that stand for? Rest, Elevate, and Direct pressure!* And for CPR, I'd remember the breath-to-compression ratio by memorizing, *Five and two will pull them through* or *One and three if they're wee.*

But none of that stupid stuff would've helped me with Chelsea. Did that mean I'd have life-altering regret? Why hadn't he taught us what to do when someone was acting really, really drunk? Maybe then I wouldn't feel like such a tit.

Isaac sat down and put his arm around my shoulders as I sat crouched over, hugging my knees, dripping hot, guilty tears onto the steps. His offer of solace was uncharacteristic and told me he felt at least some remorse for the callous way he'd acted when he got home.

"He's going to take her to the emergency vet. She must have gotten into something in the back field. I'm sure they can pump her stomach. Don't worry," he said.

"I thought she was okay, Isaac, honest," I said as I got up and walked into the backyard. I had to get away from the vomit and the spotlight that periodically lit up Chelsea's things, her chain and her water bowl. It wasn't the light that made me feel ill anymore—it was seeing her things.

Isaac followed and lay with me on the trampoline to look up at the stars, something we'd done a million times before—only this time, it felt different. Huddling close for body heat, not saying a word, I felt more as though we were in a stuffy hospital waiting room than our own backyard. We shared a set of headphones attached to his bright-yellow CD Walkman. Normally, he'd scoff at the idea of sharing his music with me (even if our musical tastes found common ground in the classics), but his uncharacteristic acts of solace continued, and he made another exception. The intro to "The Battle of Evermore" played quietly in our ears, building up slowly with a satisfying crescendo—a small reprieve from the sad silence. *Led Zeppelin IV* was my favourite of their untitled albums, and now it would forever remind me of the night Chelsea got sick.

"It's amazing how they can make such a rad song about something as lame as *The Lord of the Rings*, eh Isaac?" I said in earnest.

I didn't actually think J.R.R. Tolkien was lame, but I couldn't think of anything else worth saying, and I didn't want to be alone with my thoughts. Not even Zeppelin could stop me from analyzing every detail of the night, obsessing over every possible outcome. It made me feel dizzy.

"Sure," he said, turning his head away from mine.

The contrast in our coping mechanisms didn't surprise me—he didn't want to talk, and I didn't want to shut up. I looked around at our backyard, the sanctuary I had passed so much time in. At times the company would be different, but the landmarks were always the same. The vegetable garden I'd planted (with its own fence to keep Chelsea from ravaging the tomatoes). The oval-shaped pool Robyn and I had spent countless hours pretending to do synchronized swim-ming acts in. The alluring birch trees with bark I'd secretly stolen to write silly love notes on. The evergreen trees Dad had planted along the left side of our house to offer some privacy from the neighbours. Our magnificent, towering home—a Viceroy home, I'm told, which meant it was the type of house you'd buy in pieces with a vacant lot and a whole lot of gumption. Whoever originally bought it must have been light on the gumption piece because they'd abandoned it half built and looking emaciated. But Dad hadn't seen a hollow shell of a home with a six-foot-deep hole in the garage and a squirrel living in the towel closet. No, he saw an opportunity to build a dream home in a dream location. It was an escape from the city he'd grown to despise so much. It took years of laborious commitment, but looking around at everything visible under the moth-infested spotlight, I knew he'd feel it was worth it.

All of the things that seemed so integral to making this house a home suddenly felt immaterial compared to the one landmark at the side door that kept coming into focus. There, sturdily placed on its own platform of patio stones, was a doghouse made to look like a tiny replica of our family home. Though Chelsea rarely used it (she was too accustomed to human interaction), its vacancy weighed on my chest like an accidental breath underwater. I had to look away.

The clouds from earlier in the afternoon had cleared. And the night sky was so vibrant, the stars seemed to be floating right above us—as if I could reach out and touch them.

Depeche Mode had it right with "Personal Jesus"—I needed someone to hear my prayers and to care. I wasn't sure if I needed my own Jesus, though—the same Jesus everyone else had was okay. Even though the stars felt close to me, I knew they were light years away. So was heaven. It made me think about how infinite the universe was. It was enormous, and I wasn't exactly sure how that was supposed to make me feel—good or bad, big or small.

CHAPTER 8

Saturday, June 26th, 1999—No days until she dies

This morning Dad came home and found us sleeping on the trampoline. Slowly bouncing us awake, he didn't have to say she was dead—his forlorn face did all the talking.

We walked together to the house, heads down, two-thirds of us successfully holding back tears. I wanted to ask what happened after he got her to the vet, but I wasn't sure I could handle the answers just yet. He'd say something like, "Knowing what happened won't bring her back to life." A predictably stoic response, but painful nonetheless. I reached for his hand; he was holding Chelsea's purple collar, the tag pressed tightly against his palm to prevent a jingling that would now be devastating.

"Do you want it?" he asked, avoiding eye contact.

"Yes, of course," I whispered.

I knew he'd toss it if I said no—being sentimental wasn't high up on Dad's list of emotions, and disposing of a loved one's belongings after they'd died was his dejected form of *cleansing*. I didn't agree with it and would have to claim her things before they found their way into the garbage can. I took the collar and ran up to my room, flinging myself down on my perfectly made bed, the comforter pulled so tightly, it looked like plastic. I tried not to think about what I had done, how simple it would have been to put her on the chain as I'd been told to so many times before. I thought about our last hours together, her throwing up, acting drunk—I wished I'd done everything differently. The feeling I had wasn't just nausea, but something much worse. It was a new feeling, a threat, a looming, a heaviness in my lungs. Subtle but impossible to ignore, taking a little bit of every breath away from me and holding it captive, a constant reminder of what had happened.

Lying still, pinned down by the silence, I decided I needed music. I had to choose wisely because the CD would forever be the soundtrack attached to the day Chelsea died. I found my Sinéad O'Connor album and went to track six: "Nothing Compares 2 U." It was already the song I liked to cry to, but now the sorrow attached to it would be all the more grave.

I cried until I thought my tears were blood because there couldn't possibly be any water left inside of me. Was there actually such a thing as bad juju? Maybe this was karma for what had happened with the cow—maybe Mother Nature takes from you what you take from her. *What a terrifying concept*, I thought as I started to spiral into tears again.

***

"I'm sure I know exactly who did it," Dad said, reaching over the kitchen table to put his burly hand on my shoulder. Looking at my swollen red eyes, he could tell I'd cried all morning.

"I'm sure I know who did it too, Henry," Mom retorted. Her sharp tone implied her *who* was different.

"What do you mean, *who?*" Isaac asked, obviously as confused as I was.

I had hoped they'd discuss the (possibly accusatory) details in my absence, but it was clear Dad hadn't shared his suspicions with anyone yet. I'd already begun the grieving process in my own way—I didn't need anything derailing my progress. Chelsea's name tag hung around my neck on a gold chain I'd received for my First Communion. When I sat down at the kitchen table, the tag caught a stream of sunlight floating in through the solarium window, reflecting fragments of light over everyone's faces. It sparkled so angelically, for a second I believed it: *All dogs really do go to heaven.*

"Bit morbid, don't ya think?" Isaac asked, not one to take days off from bullying, even for bereavement.

"What do you mean, *who?*" I asked, worried the answer was *me.*

Dad sneered at Mom from across the table. She sat hunched over her plate, moving brown beans around like a fussy toddler.

"I told you to be careful, honey, didn't I?" she said, not looking up. "I asked you to promise me to be careful . . . this is how it starts, with a dog, a warning. Then it just gets worse from there."

She wasn't making any sense. Who was warning us? And what were they warning us about? Her gaze was fixed on the food she'd successfully turned to (even more) mush. Dad shook his head slowly, pulling in a long, deep breath; playing with your food at the table was a strict no-no in our house.

"Why do you have to scare them with this shit, Pat?"

"I'm not scared," Isaac and I shouted at once.

"Jinx!" we said in unison, less enthused than usual. "You owe me a Coke!"

The exchange offered twelve seconds of distraction, but Dad wasn't easily amused.

"Stop it! This is serious—not as serious as your mom is saying, but still serious. Chelsea got into something last night, but it wasn't from the back field. The vet said she was poisoned, that she'd gotten into antifreeze."

Antifreeze? How could I have been so naive? Tears welled in the corners of my eyes, every new tear that fell undoing the small amount of progress I'd made.

"Even if there was antifreeze left out, a bottle would be almost impossible for her to get into on her own. The vet said they've seen this before, that it was probably left out . . . intentionally, in a bowl." Mom shuddered as he went on, unprompted by our collective (lack of) responses. "It smells like candy, so animals are attracted to it, but it's really dangerous stuff. Honestly, I'd bet money I know who left it out. That lazy shit would do anything to avoid real work."

"Henry!" Mom exclaimed.

I knew Dad was talking about Junior, and the thought hit me like a dodge ball to the face—if the dodge ball was karma, and my face ... was my face.

CHAPTER 9

2014—It's been fifteen years

Aunt Sam's recent "accident" has me thinking a lot about loss. Not just the loss of life, but the loss you experience when someone chooses to no longer be a part of your life. When I get sad like this, the sadness usually displaces itself into a dull wave of anger directed at Henry. He had nothing to do with Aunt Sam's death, of course, but I feel better about being mad at him for choosing to leave our lives than at her for ending hers.

I remember visiting Aunt Sam in Toronto when I was eighteen and finally allowed to travel to the city alone. I was in awe of everything going on around me, intrigued by the stark differences between city and country life. I found it fascinating to see so many people together in one place, all squished together like herded cattle, yet somehow capable of acting as if everyone around them didn't even exist. No one seemed to care about their fellow commuters—they were just invisible obstacles—and I kind of liked it. I decided to move to Toronto only a year later. I guess I knew there were worse things than being herded around like cattle; you could be living next to *real* cattle—that was definitely worse.

My first subway ride stirred something in me. I remember feeling liberated—truly alive for the first time as the speeding train whooshed by me on the platform. My hair and dress whipped wildly around, dancing in the underground windstorm that was so powerful, I thought I might blow away. I wanted to wait for the next train so I could feel it all over again, but then I noticed a Suicide Helpline poster on the wall next to a pay phone. It stood out—as starkly different as country and city living. It was death posted up boldly among the hustle and bustle of life. It made me think about the reasons I wanted to live, and how they could be the very same reasons someone wanted to die—the gust of wind that put a spring in my step could be the same gust that encouraged a stranger to wait for the next train, only to step out in front of it.

Aunt Sam's suicide has graciously reminded me of my own mortality the same way a newborn baby does. New life and new death—contrary but connected. It makes me obsess about everything I'm missing in my own life. Sleep. I'm missing sleep. I keep looking for it, but I just can't seem to find it anywhere. My ex-therapist encouraged journalling at times like this. She also said I should try to keep things *positive*— that in order to heal (and properly handle any new hardships in my life), I'd eventually have to let go of my anger and bitterness. She was right, but even when I've tasked myself with remembering the good things about Henry and my childhood, my mind wanders to the sad, to the bereaved.

I think I finally understand the metamorphosis I saw in Henry the night Grandma Marshall passed away when I was ten. I saw a version of him I know he didn't realize existed, a version I now see in myself, having lost someone I loved as dearly as he loved his mother. The memory of Grandma Marshall's death has become vivid to me, as if I'm watching a homemade video I found in the attic. It's painful to watch, but this is the closest I've come in years to feeling some form of fondness for Henry.

I remember him getting home, silently pouring himself a drink and heading to the firepit behind the pool. Accompanying him while he had a few drinks out back was our summertime ritual, which Mom quietly protested from the kitchen window. It wasn't uncommon for me to be favoured by one parent while forced to spite the other. I didn't want to displease Mom, but I'd grown to enjoy the smell of fire in my hair and on my pillowcase, permeating everything I touched. I remember being grateful that I got to spend the alone time with Henry and feeling like I knew him better than my brother did because of it. I was his unexpected confidante—I knew him inside and out—though that night, as he sat sipping on rye and tending to the flame, it felt like being in the presence of a stranger.

What I wasn't capable of understanding that sad, late-August night was that he had shed the skin he wore as a provider, a husband, and a father, and settled into the skin of a lost little boy, a part of himself he'd spent many years trying to forget. He wasn't just in the form of a lost boy, but one experiencing devastating loss for the first time. He'd outgrown his boyhood clothes, but in his intense, crippling grief, they had stretched to fit him once again. I listened to him tell stories about his mother, a kind, gentle woman I had only known for the few short years I'd been alive. A woman who had spent so many more years than that protecting him from his own father, a bitter man who'd lived without happiness for the better part of his life. Her battle with lung cancer was the first life battle I'd ever seen anyone fight and lose. Her death felt drawn out but somehow still sudden. She passed in the comfort of her home, in the arms of her eldest and most beloved son. That night, I didn't understand how significant the loss was to him; all I knew was that by the light of the fire flickering across his face, the man sitting in his chair was starting to look a lot like a younger version of my dad. Not the fresh-faced adolescent I'd seen in photos, ready to take on the world, but a scared little kid. What I saw in him that night reminded me then, and now, that despite the invincible, superhero versions we choose to see of our parents, like us, they're merely human.

CHAPTER 10

Sunday, June 27th, 1999—No days until anything

Crystal and Sarah came by the house, but Dad told them I didn't want to see anyone right now. They left homemade cards on the porch with flowers they'd stolen from our neighbours' gardens. It was bad what they did—stealing. But it was done with good intentions. They're Robin Hood flowers, and that makes me smile.

I didn't feel like going to church, so I told Mom I'd rather mourn from the comfort of my own bed. She reminded me that only God could take away the pain I was feeling, but I was fine with wallowing in self-blame instead of off-loading it on to Him or (my own personal) Jesus.

Once I was sure she was gone, I went to find Dad to see how he was doing. Chelsea had been more our dog than Isaac's or Mom's, so I felt more comfortable being miserable in his company. I found him at the back door, hastily putting on his boots. *Boots?* An odd choice for almost-July weather.

"Where are you going?"

"Nowhere—stay here," he snapped, slamming the door behind him.

If he was mourning, he certainly had a funny way of showing it. He may have been going to find every remaining poop in the backyard and throw it in the garbage—despite my sentimentality, I'd probably let him dispose of them without objection. I looked out the laundry room door to see that the platform where Chelsea's doghouse sat was naked. All that was left on the patio stones was a square-shaped dirt outline, as haunting as the chalk that borders a dead body at a crime scene.

What a freak! It had only been two days since she'd died. I ran outside to see what else Dad had managed to erase of her while I was in bed mourning (like a normal person). I tripped over her rawhide bone by the deck and saw her rope toy by the pool, relieved that at least they'd survived the expunging. I'd almost calmed down when I saw it: the doghouse chopped to bits by the firepit. Shingles were scattered on the ground like confetti with bent nails poking out from every piece. I could smell the sticky pieces of tar and freshly splintered wood—scents that I imagined lingered in the aftermath of natural disasters. Our backyard had definitely been the victim of a tornado, only the winds of destruction weren't natural but fed by anger and grief. It was disheartening to see that Dad had treated the doghouse with such crass indifference—not only because it was Chelsea's home, but also because it was a replica of our own home. Seeing the matching roof and identical siding demolished that way made me feel exposed—as if my shelter had been destroyed too.

I searched the rubble for something worthy (worthy of a shrine). A piece of the name sign I'd painted for her house was still partially intact. Dad had chopped it in half right after the *S*, leaving "Chels," her endearing nickname. *Small victory*, I thought. A hidden gem in the unrecognizable pile of remains that would soon fuel the fire Dad would sit beside while he forgot about her.

***

Isaac and I sat at the bottom of the staircase that led up to our bedrooms. The railings were wobbly and unpainted, giving splinters to those who held on too tightly. The steps still wore their original shag carpet, unashamed of the stains they'd endured from countless hours of renovations. Although ugly and unfinished, the staircase was the one place in the house that still bared the soul of its tumultuous past, and for that reason, I'd always felt at ease there.

We sat looking up through the skylight, our elbows resting two steps above our butts and our heads resting a step above that. Upstairs, Mom and Dad yelled at each other from behind their bedroom door (slammed so hard, it had sent a shiver down the stairwell's spine). I'd thought they weren't on the same team before, but this sounded like a championship game with no referees. From our seats, we could make out only a few muffled accusations and the odd berating retort. Without subtitles, it was hard to know for sure, but it may have been the worst argument I'd ever (partially) witnessed between them.

"What do you think is going on?" I asked.

Isaac got up, pulled out the piano bench, sat down, and played the opening bars of "Für Elise," the only piece he remembered from his elementary school piano lessons. He closed his eyes and gently tapped out the whole first theme before answering me.

"*I know* what's going on." He smiled slyly.

"What! How? What is it, then?"

"Dad beat the living shit out Junior Spooner this morning when Mom was at church," he whispered. You could see he was trying not to laugh as he played painfully slowly, desperately in need of a metronome. "And she found out because Sarah's mom told the Candy Lady, and the Candy Lady told Mom while she was getting the newspaper at the end of the driveway."

"Get out of town!"

"Sure, I'd love to." (His tired comeback.)

"Why?" I shouted. "Why would he do that?"

My heart raced, terrified I'd be held responsible for the quarrel in more ways than one.

"Well, you knew he went over there to talk to him, right?"

"Yeah." I nodded, not wanting to appear entirely out of the loop as I motioned to Isaac to move over so we could share the piano bench. As kids, we'd spent hundreds of hours on the bench laughing and carrying on while he played and I sang. Eventually, the piano took a back seat to his guitar, and the bench turned into an overnight home for Dad's precious briefcase. But I still revisited it sometimes, if only to glide my fingertips over where we'd carved our names in the wood underneath.

"Yeah, well, Junior basically flat out admitted it."

"Admitted what?"

"What he did to Chelsea, you idiot."

"What did he do?"

"He poisoned her—like Dad thought."

"What?" I shouted, incredulous. I was going to puke.

"He said that last summer, he caught Kujo tearing apart a goat of his, and last week, one of his cows ended up dead. He said the Geddes' dogs are always terrorizing his animals, and he heard other people complaining about them too—so he did what he had to do."

If that were true, Chelsea had been punished for a crime she hadn't committed. No, she'd been punished for a crime I'd committed—and now she was dead. Cold sweat washed over me, leaving a strange, tingly sensation at the tip of every limb. A circle of darkness closed in around my eyes as if I was looking into a kaleidoscope—only there were no pretty colours at the end, only more darkness.

"Yo, Ivy, are you cool?" Isaac said, grabbing my shoulder before my face slammed into our upright piano.

"Yeah, I'm fine," I lied.

"Well, Junior isn't. He's a lot bigger than Dad, right? But apparently, Dad beat him to within an inch of his life."

Isaac seemed to take great pleasure in that fact, relishing Dad's victory as if it were his own. Although Isaac had an athletic build, he was slender and short for his age, taking after Dad's side of the family (a long line of short men). I wasn't a boy, but from what I'd gathered, being a small boy was the equivalent of being a fat girl—at least God spread the cruelty somewhat equally among siblings.

"I think Mom's scared Junior's going to press charges and we'll have to get a lawyer and shit. Money's already really tight, which I'm sure you know."

I nodded again, making a mental note to ask more questions during family night. I was both relieved and proud—relieved I wouldn't have to add cow killer to my public record (of deadly animal mishaps) and proud we'd avenged Chelsea's murder (kind of).

Dad came down a few minutes later surrounded by a smug cloud of nonchalance. I wanted to give him a taste of his own medicine and tell him that his violent attack on Junior wouldn't bring Chelsea back. But everyone knew revenge didn't have to work like that for it to feel good. I read once that bitterness is what you poison yourself with while expecting the other person to die. If that were true, then revenge was the antidote.

"How cute," Dad said as he walked by us where we sat on the piano bench.

I didn't have to be a psychic to know he'd be heading to the bar in the dining room.

"Which one of you sick bastards took Chelsea's house down?" he asked as he poured himself a drink.

"What? I thought you did that!"

"No, I did," Isaac confessed. "I didn't want to see it there every time I left the house. It's depressing. Not everyone likes being sad like you, Ivy."

I should have known our safety captain wouldn't have left a pile of sharp objects for innocent bystanders to injure themselves on. It was careless and dangerous—it had Isaac's fingerprints all over it.

"You want a drink?" Dad asked, staring at Isaac and not me. He clutched the Crown Royal bottle in his hands so tightly, I thought it might shatter into a million pieces. "Ah, what the hell. Not like I can get in any more trouble than I'm already in."

He filled up a teeny-tiny cup with rye, careful not to waste a drop. Then he poured that little cup into a much bigger cup and handed it to Isaac.

"Fill it to the top with ginger ale, and don't say a word—you either, Ivy."

"I won't, I won't," I said as I got up, ready to leave the party I clearly wasn't invited to.

"I'm gonna go check on Mom, but I won't say anything. Promise."

"Plug the living room phone back in on your way upstairs, would ya," Dad said.

It was an order, not a question. Mom had asked me to unplug the phones the night Chelsea died. She said she could hear a "clicking" sound on the line, and I hadn't questioned her on it. I assumed it had something to do with the phone bill; they argued about that sometimes too. Dad didn't seem to care about the clicking noise or that his order was in direct defiance of hers. I hated being put in this spot, written and then erased from the pages of each of their good books—always in pencil, never in pen.

Upstairs, their bedroom door was left a few inches ajar. I knocked three times before I opened it and slowly walked in.

"Hey, Mom, are you okay?" I asked, sitting down gently beside her on the bed.

She sat cross-legged in a white nightie she'd stretched over her knees. She was reading from the book of Matthew (her version of a rye and ginger ale).

"Sure, hon, I'm fine. Just having a drink," she said. Evidently, the joke was one she'd made many times before.

"At least Chelsea dying wasn't anything to do with your work, right?" I said meekly. It was a poor consolation prize.

"How did you know I thought it had to do with work?"

I had to think fast.

"Well, in the car last Sunday, you told me not to answer any calls from your work, and then on Friday, you said something about it being a warning or something." I was lying for the third time in three days. I didn't want to reveal I'd pieced it together from a number of eavesdropping sessions, though she probably would have just told me had I asked.

"You've always been so perceptive, hon. I don't know why I'd ever try to keep anything from you anyway, my little detective." Her unwarranted accolades made my cheeks hot with shame. Lying to her felt a lot worse when she seemed so vulnerable. "I'm not sure Junior isn't a part of it all, though. He and his dad are both big into real estate investment. And you know I keep the books at work. Well, I help . . . or I used to," she said, "before they asked me to butt out of it because I was seeing some . . . *inconsistencies*, more or less."

The underlying urgency in her voice made it hard to dismiss what she was saying. Before having Isaac and me, Mom had completed her MBA in finance at the top of her class. She did even better than Dad (something she never let him forget). I knew she was an intelligent woman, and if she felt something was going on, it likely was—it was the connection to Chelsea's death I wasn't so sure about.

"But Junior explained what's been happening to his animals. Like, his story checks out, ya know? Everyone knows Kujo's a bad dog. There have been tons of complaints about him from other farmers too."

She took her crocheted bookmark off her nightstand and placed it between the pages of her *Women's Daily Devotional Bible* before clapping it closed.

"Not everything is always as it seems," she said. "If I had a reason to poison a dog, I'd rather blame the town target than tell the truth. Wouldn't you?"

"He didn't have to fess up to it at all, though, right? He could have just denied it."

"Use your head, Ivy. Denying it would have kept him on the suspect list. Admitting it but diverting attention from the real motive is the best way to get away with it, or at least defuse the accuser's anger, though that obviously didn't work."

She had a point.

"Well, crap, that's kind of scary! Is Dad gonna be in trouble for beating him up?"

"That's what I'm most worried about," she said, her lip beginning to tremble. I went in for a hug, knowing tonight would be a night she'd lie awake anxiously without the comfort of Dad sleeping next to her.

"If your dad isn't taking it seriously, I don't know how to protect you guys. And I don't know how we'll pay our mortgage if I quit," she said quietly. "Just be careful, like I said. Always tell us where you're going and when you'll be home. And if I'm ever more than an hour late getting home from work, call the police!"

I let out a breath I'd been holding in since Dad woke us on the trampoline.

"Mom, of course, but it won't be like that. You're blowing it out of proportion. If you're not going to quit, then just keep your head down like Dad said."

I stopped, catching my words before I inadvertently outed myself any more than I already had. She cocked her head to the side, staring at me curiously. If she'd put it together, she didn't have all the pieces.

"I wish it were that easy, but once you know things, and they know you know things—things you probably shouldn't know—it gets more complicated than just quitting." She started to ramble between short, distressed breaths and unfettered tears. "I think that's the message they were trying to get across with Chelsea. I'm so, so sorry, Ivory. I know how much you loved her."

We lay on the bed crying in unspoken reciprocity. We were sharing tears for different versions of the same misfortune, and that was okay because it was still nice to be sad and scared with someone—even if you were sad and scared about different things.

We fell asleep holding hands, tears flowing sideways down our faces into our ears. Later in the night, Dad came upstairs and poked his head inside the door. I pretended to be asleep, an act he'd grown wise to many years ago. Playing along, he turned around and stumbled down the hall to my room. I could hear him take off his belt as he collapsed onto my pink single bed, its wooden headboard creaking with distress under his weight.

CHAPTER 11

Wednesday, June 30th, 1999—
The day we were supposed to bury Chelsea

Dad stopped and picked up Chelsea's ashes on the way home from work. He didn't get home until after 9:00 p.m., which seemed excessively late (even to Mom, who hasn't noticed much lately outside her personal bubble of concern).

Dad saw me glance at the digital clock on the microwave as, carrying a large cardboard box, he walked into the kitchen. I hoped (for Chelsea's sake) the box wasn't filled with soot.

"I'm trying not to worry your mother," he said coldly. "There have been some issues with a couple of us at work. A bad deal. *Real* problems, so yeah, I've been staying late, trying to figure it all out with Doug."

Doug was Dad's best friend and colleague, who'd gotten him the job at his current high-stakes, high-roller, big shot Toronto firm. As a thank you, when they moved into town, Mom got Doug's wife, Nancy, a job with her at Sternwood Construction.

"That's not Chelsea, is it?" I asked, looking at the box. "Couldn't we have gotten her something a little . . . nicer for her eternal slumber?" I tried to diminish my disgust before it found its way to my face.

"Are you not listening to me at all? I'm not getting my mid-year bonus either, so no, we couldn't afford anything nicer. We're lucky to have this."

I'd seen the vet bill on the breakfast bar, poking out from under Mom's address book, asking me to notice it. I couldn't stop myself from reading all the not-so-gory-more-so-clinical details. They'd done two sets of blood tests, pumped Chelsea's stomach, then left her on a fluid-IV for five full hours, an exercise in futility that cost our struggling family a quick $637.98—not including the cremation. It was appalling to think that the garbage in his hands was what he was trying to pass off as her casket, but I knew I should appreciate that he'd paid extra for her ashes at all (even if they came in a Mike's Food Basics box).

"You're right. Sorry, Dad. I'm sorry things aren't going well at work. Is there anything I can do?"

"No, nothing you can do. It'll all come down to semantics, you know?"

I nodded, but I'd have to look the word up later in my pocket dictionary.

"Just keep your mother on track—I'm looking at the big picture here—and if you see anything weird, come to me first, okay?"

"What do you mean, weird?"

"I don't know . . . I just mean if anything your mother's saying seems to be true, tell me first. She thinks I don't believe her, but I'm just trying to defuse any situations as best I can. I have my ear to the ground in this town too. I know what's going on."

I think he intended this information to be comforting—he knew I appreciated it when he treated me like an adult. But sometimes, ignorance really was bliss.

"Okay, whatever you think is best," I said reassuringly. "When should we bury Chelsea?"

"It's late now, hon. Let's do it tomorrow in the backyard."

He put the box on the ground and went upstairs. I was used to being left alone with Chelsea in the kitchen after dinner, but this kind of interaction was new to me. Did she know where she was? And did it bother her that even as a dead dog, she was made to sit on the outskirts of Dinnertown, looking in? I opened the box to look at her ashes. They didn't look anything like I'd expected. They were chunky and white—not at all like the fine grey ashes left over after our bonfires. They were layered in multiple sandwich bags, taking up so much less space than she had when she was alive. I picked up the box and proudly placed her in the middle of the kitchen table. And as a form of protest, I didn't even put her on a placemat.

***

Everyone was mourning the loss of our fifth family member with their own style of sadness. As Isaac said, I preferred to wallow in it, submerging myself in it as if I were holding my head underwater in the bathtub. I found it calming and more manageable when I welcomed the sadness all around me.

Isaac became destructive, Dad became vengeful, and Mom focused on other things. I didn't fault them for their idiosyncrasies. *We are who we are*, I thought, introspective from the paint fumes I'd inhaled. I'd decided to spend the rest of the night maintaining control of my sorrows by using the only outlet I had—painting.

I'd tried different creative outlets in the past; I wrote a few short stories, lyrics, some poems (mostly rhyming couplets), and drew horrible sketches. I even directed a music video using a friend's old camcorder. It wasn't until I painted my first picture that I truly felt an escape from whatever I was dealing with. When I toyed with the possibility of applying to art school, Mrs. Brown graciously suggested I "explore other means of making a living"—so I knew I wasn't very good. But that didn't stop Mom from buying me an easel and letting me take over the dining room for most of the year (outside of Christmas and Easter).

I wanted to paint the Pretty Place because I felt most at peace there, and when I'd taken Chelsea with me, she'd felt at peace there too. I also needed some good juju in my life—if that was even a thing. In theory, my painting should have been as pretty as the place itself, but despite my best efforts, it turned out more abstract than I'd hoped. I had trouble mixing a gold colour that did the water justice, and the creek should have appeared to be moving, but movement was something I hadn't mastered yet. *Maybe it came out abstract as a way to maintain its anonymity*, I thought. Even as art, the Pretty Place was as wise as it was beautiful.

CHAPTER 12

Thursday, July 1st, 1999—Happy Canada Day

By 10:00 a.m. I thought Dad had been in a terrible accident because he'd missed our holiday wake-up call by almost three hours. I was used to him waking us up at the crack of dawn by flinging open our bedroom doors and shouting, "Up and at 'em, Atom Ant!"—a playful phrase he claims is from a show he watched as a kid, but I've seen no evidence to support that. I've only seen evidence to support that his shouting borders on cruel and unusual punishment.

I put my red-and-white jumper on (I'm a sucker for holiday-appropriate attire), organized my drawers, and made my bed three times without feeling rushed—a Canada Day miracle.

Downstairs, I was greeted by the familiar sounds of Counting Crows. I didn't have to listen for more than a millisecond to know what album was playing—*August and Everything After*. It was the album Dad played on repeat when he was depressed, and it somehow managed to be as melancholic as it was inspiriting. I had a full journal devoted to writing out the lyrics in that album, then writing out what they meant to me, then what I thought they meant to Dad. I'd gotten really good at assessing his mood based on the music he was listening to, and today I knew to approach him with trepidation. Dad had clearly fast-tracked himself through the grieving process—moving from anger and revenge to sadness—and the thought of him being sad made my heart hurt more than the lyrics to "Anna Begins."

I had to stop myself from wondering why Chelsea wasn't waiting at the bottom of the stairs, ecstatic to see me, ready for her belly rub. It was an important part of my morning routine I'd taken for granted (which also hurt my heart). Following a predictable morning schedule helped with the "restlessness" I'd feel most days before school. I didn't really understand why Mom called it *restlessness*, but the best way to describe what I felt was to say I was nervous—and I understood that even less. *What could I be nervous about?* As long as I had the time to do the things I liked to do (in the order I liked to do them in), I was usually fine. I tried to maintain a semblance of structure even though it was almost lunchtime, and I moved to step two, pouring myself a glass of milk and a bowl of cereal. The milk made me think about cows, which inadvertently made me think about *the* cow (dead—doornail). I had to mix things up before my day got any more morbid than it already was. Looking out from the solarium, I focused my attention on every living thing around me. Grass in need of a cut, leafy trees, swarming deer flies, and birds chirping incessantly. Could there be anything more (annoyingly) alive than that? Dad was (alive) in the backyard too. He was standing next to a hole in the ground with a shovel in his hand. He must have decided to get a head start on the burial. *Perfect*, I thought—*nothin' like a good hole-digging to help you forget about death for a second.*

He was wearing an undershirt and his old, faded "yard work jeans." Like our staircase, Dad's jeans were marked from countless hours of hard work, but he wore them proudly as if the stains were badges of honour. His hair was slicked back off his face, and his cheeks were smudged with dirt. You could see his skin through his sweat-soaked undershirt, and for the first time, I understood why those thin white tank tops had earned the unfortunate nickname "wife beaters."

There was something intimidating about the whole picture, but he *was* digging a grave, after all, and that wasn't exactly *light and fluffy* behaviour. I watched as he rested his elbow on the garden shovel and his head heavily in his hand; he almost appeared to be taking a break (even though he'd told me breaks were for wussies). I grabbed a bottle of water from the fridge and went out to offer some help and hydration; digging must've been harder than it looked. As I walked toward the birch trees, it dawned on me there was no need to have dug a hole in the first place. Chelsea wasn't a corpse—she was ashes, and we could've kept them inside. I guess we'd all silently agreed we didn't want a Mike's Food Basics box sitting on our fireplace mantel.

"What's up, Dad?" I called while still several yards away. He'd been looking down at the ground since I first saw him through the kitchen window.

"Why did you do this?" he asked as I got closer.

I followed his gaze back to the shallow hole he stood beside and then stopped, frozen in my tracks. *What were the friggin' chances?* Our backyard was as big as a football field, but he'd managed to dig in the one spot I'd already called dibs on.

"Well?" he asked again.

I didn't know how to explain what he was looking at. I could have played dumb and gone with the obvious: "It's a tin box Isaac made in shop class!" But I didn't know how to explain *why* he was seeing what he was either. I didn't know how to tell him I'd been afraid of him and the monster he turned into the weeks following Grandma Marshall's death. I didn't know how to tell him that after he said he was getting rid of her things, I took them out of the garbage can and buried them there in the box. I didn't know how else to keep them safe without . . . keeping them. And most of all, I didn't know how to explain why, of all the perfectly good burial plots in our backyard, he'd picked the exact same grass-less knoll I'd chosen almost five years ago.

"Dad, I'm so sorry. You were just throwing out all of her things— things I knew she gave you to remember her by. It didn't seem right.

What was I supposed to do? I thought you'd thank me one day, that you'd realize you wanted them. I'm so sorry."

He continued to stare blankly at the box, sweat dripping from his temple as he listened to me ramble. Pain was transforming his face; it was the type of sadness that changed your whole demeanour. I could hear my words and my tone, meant to be pleading, but everything I said sounded more like accusations than apologies. With my explanations, I wasn't going to offer any solace—I was just digging the knife in deeper and turning the blade.

"Did your mother put you up to this? Some kind of freaky resurrection ritual or something?"

Whenever Dad decided anger and sadness weren't on the menu anymore, humour was his go-to daily special.

"No," I said, trying not to laugh, "nothing like that."

"Okay, well, as long as you weren't trying to bring her back, lighting candles and dancing around under the full moon, I'm okay with it," he said with a smirk.

I recognized the disingenuous lip curl; I'd felt it on my face before too. It was the kind of forced smile you'd half-heartedly muster when you really wanted to cry, and I didn't know how to wholeheartedly respond to that. I said nothing.

"Put this stuff back in the box and throw it in the shed for me, would ya?" he said, quickly looking away. It was a question, not an order. If I hadn't done it for him, I wasn't sure he could have done it himself.

I gathered Grandma Marshall's belongings and carefully placed them back into the makeshift time capsule Isaac had donated to the cause while Dad sat on the metal two-seater swing by the poplars. I hadn't been able to keep everything he'd thrown out that day, but I'd rescued the things I considered to be the most precious: her handkerchief, her scarf, her gold brooch (A shaped for "Aberdeen"), and her sapphire hairpin. As I walked to the shed, I fingered the items in the box, wrapping the sheer, floral scarf around my wrist and polishing the brooch with the damp handkerchief. I tried to be discreet as I snuck the scarf back out of the box and held it close to my face. I only wanted to breathe it in to see if it still smelled like lavender, but from across the yard, he saw me. He'd been watching my every step.

"Don't bother," he said. "I tried—it just smells like dirt."

***

Dad stood on the back deck in his *Kiss the Chef* apron, flipping hamburgers (homemade—his specialty) on the barbecue.

"Let's all stay home together tonight, kiddos," he suggested.

Isaac grunted, then shrugged (which I think meant "Sure" in teen-boy speak). Normally, Isaac would object to unscheduled family time, but we'd been seeing a lot more of him since Chelsea died. A lot more of him, and a lot less of Mom. It was dinnertime, and she hadn't left her room yet.

"Sure, whatevs," I said, trying to sound less excited than I was. "Are we going to do some fireworks tonight, Dad?"

We all knew (that I knew) the answer to that question already. He probably had a book for us to read about firework-related deaths (and other associated misfortunes).

Book Title:
Liable to Lose a Finger—or Your Life:
Fireworks and Other Fun Things You Shouldn't Do

"*Ha!*" Isaac said.

"*Ha!*" Dad said, mimicking him.

"*Ha!*" I gasped, fake-crying and dragging it out as if I'd been mortally wounded.

Dad clapped his barbecue tongs together, applauding my award-winning performance. Cheeky, but he never said no.

CHAPTER 13

2015—I hate Canada Day

It's hard not to think about Henry on Canada Day. Like a masochist, I find myself playing on repeat that old Counting Crows album he loved while I drive around aimlessly, telling myself this time will be the last. Surprisingly, my therapist condones my self-sabotaging behaviour; she said it's good for me to have an emotional "release" from time to time. She also told me not to worry—I'm not crazy. Apparently, it's hard to forgive someone and move on with your life when you've been robbed of any closure (so the occasional car cry is a small side effect I shouldn't worry about).

Canada Day was the last time I remember seeing Henry happy. He was trying to be strong for us, I think, since our sheepdog had just died. I remember him surprising Isaac and me with an ungodly amount of fireworks, winning us over, being the hero. He'd lit the fireworks under the guise of patriotic celebration when in reality he knew he'd be gone in a few weeks—it was his parting gift. After he left, the sadness I felt was quickly replaced with formidable anger, long before I even knew what it meant to have *daddy issues*. But my therapist says intense anger isn't "productive" and harbouring resentment for so long is *not* condoned (weeping like a baby on your way to the pet store is, though, so that's cool). It's idiotic when you really think about it. So many powerful moves in history have been fuelled by anger, but what's sadness done for the world?

Like every Canada Day, I have plans to see Mom tonight. Like every Canada Day, I'm dreading it. Not because I don't enjoy seeing her, because I do. It's more about the way she pesters me and takes it upon herself to call me out on my "cynical attitude." She thinks she's being clever by peppering her transparent pleas into our predinner prayers. Everyone holds hands, closes their eyes, and bows their heads while she writes me a laundry list of self-improvements: "Dear God, please help Ivy have a more positive outlook on life. She has so much to be happy about. She's smart, she's got a good job, she's beautiful. And most of all, God, please help Ivy find a boyfriend. Oh yeah, and thank you for these hot dogs. Amen!"

She isn't only concerned about my attitude—she has some serious disdain about my all-black wardrobe too. Normally, her nitpicking wouldn't bother me, but tonight I plan on bringing someone along with me, and I still want him to think rainbows shoot out my ass. It's hard to be my oh-so-charming-self when sarcastic witticisms aren't welcome at the dinner table, and my jaded (but hilarious) outlook on life has been banned from our after-dessert tea. I know my playful cynicism upsets Mom more than it should because she thinks I'm depressed, and she blames herself (and *that* summer). She claims I was never the same after he left: "You were never again the happy, cheerful, colourful Ivory I loved to be around," she said. She tried so hard to protect us from what happened. She tried so hard to pull us out of it unscathed. I remember her drilling it into our heads that Henry had left *her* and not *us*, yet somehow, she didn't end up with any of the abandonment issues—I did. She constantly reassured us it wasn't our fault, that we had nothing to do with it. But I knew it wasn't our fault. How could it be?

His inability to cope with all the stress *that* summer caused him to act irrationally. (What was it, sixteen years ago now? Damn, I feel old.) *Irrationally, irrationally, irrationally*—that was the word she used over and over again. "The pressure was too much, and he acted irrationally," she said, as if his decision to ditch our family was akin to my decisions the week before my period. She was too gracious about it when it happened, too kind and understanding. That's what was most *irrational* about the whole situation. But she didn't let it ruin her life; she said God helped her let go of all of her anger and bitterness (and I should ask Him to help me let go too). Most importantly, she wasn't lugging it around like a carry-on suitcase that won't fit into the overhead compartment. Unlike me, she's successfully stowed it away—she's healed. I'm happy for her, truly I am. She got back on her feet, started fresh, remarried.

As for Isaac, he'd managed to turn his tumultuous, drug-filled years after Henry left into a burgeoning musical career. If he was carrying any bitterness around with him, he'd at least learned how to spin it into gold—a modern-day Rumpelstiltskin. Who'd have guessed he'd be the more successful one? I have to remind myself it's not a competition, though, that he's my best friend (which isn't really saying much—Rosie, my Japanese fighting fish, is also a contender). And he's the only person I've truly let myself care about in the last sixteen years. There's no room for jealousy, only gratitude—gratitude for all the ways he continues to support me in my life emotionally, and at times, financially.

Tonight Mom's going to meet Jason. We've been together almost (a record-breaking) twelve months! A full year! It's impressive. I've waited this long to let Mom meet him because she always gets so hopeful when I introduce her to the new men in my life. I hate seeing her disappointed when it doesn't work out, so I wanted to be sure. Mom will be *sure* about him the second she meets him. Not just because she won't have to pray for him (he has so much to be happy about—he's smart, he's got a good job, and he's undeniably beautiful), but because she's *sure* about every man I bring home to her. She's made it very clear she wants grandbabies, and the pressure to reproduce is entirely on me. We've pretty much given up on Isaac because he's nomadic (and his swimmers are probably perpetually stoned). The last boyfriend I brought home told me Mom had interrogated him while I was in the bathroom. She asked him if we planned to have babies and told him we should get a move on "before Ivy's eggs shrivel up like grapes in the Tuscan sun." It made me laugh, but I'm not big on tattletales, so I dumped him the next day. And when I shared it with my therapist and she *didn't* laugh, I dumped her the next day too.

I told Mom if I was single by the time I was thirty-five, I'd find a donor and get artificially inseminated just to make her happy. If she'd been able to handle being a single mom of two insufferable teenage ingrates, I'm sure I could handle at least one small bag of potatoes.

Tonight, I'll make sure to throw on a splash of colour so Mom doesn't make the *funeral* comment again.

CHAPTER 14

Friday, July 2nd, 1999—20 days until my birthday

I don't know where the whole morning went. It felt as though someone accidentally hit the fast-forward button. When Isaac got home, having him near me finally stopped my unravelling. He helped my world slow down for a second.

I followed Isaac as he shimmied under the fence into our next-door neighbour's yard. Before Bob moved in, a family of eight had erected an impressive tree house at the back of the lot, and Bob never used it—not even once. After we'd spent years longingly staring at it from a distance, he finally let us have it, telling Dad he was a lifelong bachelor who'd never have children to banish there anyway.

The tree house was a ten-by-ten-foot square structure with windows on every side and a cute semicircular hobbit-like door that I painted green. It was a home away from home, an escape for when trekking to the Pretty Place wasn't feasible. I'm sure Bob thought he was doing Dad a favour, giving him a place to lock us away in when we were bad. But I was the one doing all the locking. I put a padlock on the little door when I started keeping valuable things in the tree house. It was the level of security I needed after being grounded for something Mom read in one of my journals she'd broken into. Now I locked away the journal where I kept my most private (and sometimes offensive) thoughts, using the tree house as a way to maintain as much privacy and dignity as any teen could expect while living with a very nosy mother. I was gracious enough to share the extra key with Isaac; he wouldn't care to read my diary even if I left it under his pillow.

"Can I come, Issy?" I asked, trying to catch up with his faster and longer strides.

"Sure, if you stop calling me that."

"Okay, I'll stop," I lied.

I loved to annoy him as much as I loved that he was letting me tag along. He pulled his key chain out from his front pocket and let it dangle on the long silver chain attached to his studded belt. *Very "in" right now*, I thought as I followed him up the crooked tree house ladder. The key ring was filled with so many foreign-looking keys, it was likely that most didn't have corresponding locks. I could tell it made him feel cool, authoritative even—as though he had the keys to the city, when really he just looked (and sounded) like a janitor.

He fumbled around trying different keys before he found the right one, then crouched down so low to fit inside the door, he looked to be crawling in on all fours. The tree house had started to feel smaller with every year that passed and every inch we grew. Maybe it wasn't ten by ten feet at all—it had just felt that big the last time I was there. He sat on one of the chairs we'd fashioned out of milk crates and slid the other toward me with a robotic ease that told me he went there with guests more often than I'd realized. He wasn't just being courteous—it was a reflex.

"What do you do when you come here? Something tells me you don't come to write in your diary," I said.

"Nah, but what I do is just as therapeutic," he said, reaching into his pocket and pulling out an Altoids tin.

He took off a thick blue rubber band (stolen from a head of broccoli) and opened it slowly, careful not to lose any of the precious contents within. I thought he was using the tin as a wallet (a creative repurposing I'd seen other boys at school do), but when he opened it all the way, a strong smell of skunk wafted out. It wasn't until a tiny leafy bud dropped to the ground that I put it together: there was some "green" in there, but it definitely wasn't money.

"Oh," I said nonchalantly.

I wanted to sound cool and not at all alarmed. I knew Isaac drank sometimes, and I guess I assumed he did other things too (not cigarettes, because he said his voice was his money-maker), but I felt foolish for not recognizing the *real* reason he smelled funny all the time—he was a stoner.

"Yeah," he said as he pulled a rolled joint out from under a lighter.

It looked exactly like the fake marijuana cigarette Constable Briggs had brought in to our grade five class during our D.A.R.E. (Drug Abuse Resistance Education) session. I remember the sense of conviction I'd had after the program. I vowed my conviction was unwavering and that I'd never succumb to peer pressure. I knew marijuana was a gateway drug with the potential to ruin my life, but as I stared at a real joint for the first time, I had to believe sibling pressure was more powerful than peer pressure.

"I'm not gonna give you any, Ivy—I am definitely not going down for that one."

I laughed. "Obviously."

"It just makes me forget about all the shit that's going on. Mom's got me sleeping with one eye open, and Dad's just a liar. It's stressing me out, man."

"I know, I know." I felt it too.

He put the entire joint in his mouth, completely coating it in saliva before slowly pulling it out of his pursed lips as if he was savouring a Cyclone Popsicle. I couldn't hide my disgust; I'm sure it was all over my face. *Why had I even considered sharing something so nasty?*

"It's called 'baptizing.' It helps it burn more evenly. You'll learn one day, I'm sure."

He turned the moist joint around in a circle as he lit it, watching the thin paper burn in a perfect ring of fire. I wasn't a big fan of Johnny Cash, so I didn't want to validate his overrated music by singing any lyrics to "Ring of Fire," but I had to at least acknowledge the song before I moved on.

"Uh, no, I won't," I said, abandoning the plan I had to sound cool. "That's gross!"

"D.A.R.E. did a number on you, eh?" he teased.

I laughed to confirm his suspicions. Despite the inevitable distance that had grown between us, he still found me pretty predictable. He was right—D.A.R.E. had done a number on me. I'd even kept the #7 pencil the police officers gave to our class at the end of the lesson. Sometimes I'd actually use it too, but only in times of desperation when every working pen in the house disappeared somewhere along with one of everyone's socks. The pencil had TOO COOL TO DO DRUGS written on the side. But the more you sharpened it, grinding it farther and farther down, the more drastic the change to the messaging. After a few uses, the pencil read COOL TO DO DRUGS, then DO DRUGS, and finally DRUGS. It was a hilarious oversight that might have been a bit of a symbolic foreshadowing too. As the years passed, a lot of the kids in my class went from being *too cool to do drugs* to just . . . *doing them.*

"It's okay if you never try it. It just calms me down, ya know?" Isaac took a big pull from the joint and held it in for a long time—impressively long (he-should-be-a-better-swimmer long). He exhaled and went on, visibly distraught and presumably stoned. "Ugh, I dunno. I feel like Dad's about to leave Mom for that lady at his work. Shit is completely screwed up—I don't even wanna deal."

His bogus accusation made him a walking billboard for D.A.R.E.—weed clearly made people delusional.

"What do you mean, Dad's gonna leave Mom for a lady at work?" I asked. I wanted to hear all the delusional details before he got so stoned he couldn't remember his own name and started making even less sense.

"Mom asked me not to say anything to you because you had so much going on with Chelsea and stuff. But yeah, she thinks he's been seeing someone—you know, with all the late nights and shit. There's a lady at his work, the brunette we met at the Christmas party a couple of years ago . . . Holly or something. Remember?"

"Yeah, I remember Holly. She gave us the treat bags and was super nice. There's no way, Isaac. Do you believe it? He's just stressed!"

"I dunno, man. It makes more sense when you consider Mom hasn't come out of her room in forever. It's not just about her job—it's gotta be on top of that."

With the way he was talking, I'd probably have to escort him down the ladder so he didn't break his neck and die (Constable Briggs had said dying was a common side effect of marijuana use). But at the same time, he'd made a good point. Mom had been increasingly distant, and I just assumed it had everything to do with Sternwood. It hurt a little to know she'd shared things with him she hadn't shared with me. I thought I was the only one who kept two vaults in my head to store Mom and Dad's secrets—separately because they often kept them from each other. They shared more with me than I knew was appropriate, and sometimes I felt like their inexperienced couples therapist. I was happy to do the job—I just didn't know Isaac was on the payroll too.

"Bad things happen in threes, Nonna said," I whispered as I stared at the glowing ember dancing around in his hand. As it moved, the ember left a mesmerizing trail of light in the air that reminded me of the sparklers we'd used at Robyn's last Victoria Day celebration.

"Shit! I think I'm accidentally getting you stoned here. Open the windows!"

He swung around and opened the window behind him, and I opened the window behind me. I pictured the smoke billowing from each side of the tree house as smoke coming out of an angry giant's ears.

"Yup, I feel weird," I confirmed.

"Sorry! Don't worry, it's not a gateway drug. I don't think so, anyway," he said, laughing and play-punching me in the shoulder.

Get out of my head, I thought. It was hard to tell if I was feeling weirder from the weed or from the possibility that Dad was cheating. We sat in silence for a few minutes, or maybe an hour. Both deep in thought, or just stoned. Nothing was clear to me in those moments.

"Hey, you!" he yelled suddenly. It startled me back to life. I'd been so deep in thought, I'd almost forgotten he was there. "Honestly, no matter what happens, we'll be okay. I'm sure this crap with Mom is going to clear up soon, and whatever happens with Dad, I have to believe they'll work it out, okay? And even if they don't, we've got each other, and we can take care of ourselves."

Did he intentionally use song lyrics to trigger me? I hummed the opening verse to "Hey You" by Pink Floyd as tears welled up in the corners of my itchy, dry eyes. I tried to stop the tears from overflowing. They were conflicted as they streamed down my face, as if one eye cried for my imploding family and the other cried in appreciation of Isaac's unexpected compassion.

"I'm glad Mom and Dad had you—even if you were an accident," he said, laughing a bit too hard. I'd known he was going to say exactly that—he'd become pretty predictable too.

"I was *not*, Issy!"

He kept laughing, and I smiled, knowing he'd achieved his goal, and I'd achieved mine. I couldn't remember a time when things had felt so effortless between us. It was as if we weren't just siblings destined for a lifetime of hollow exchanges and forced interactions—we were friends. He put his lighter back in his tin and threw the rest of the joint into a coffee can he had hidden under the milk crate.

"Seriously though, we're cool. We got this. Now let's go wash up before they get home, or we could just go for a swim. Does the trick—every time," he said.

As he descended the ladder with ease, I wondered how many times he'd been stoned around me without my having a clue. Or how many times he'd gone for a swim, claiming to be working on his "bod" when really he was washing off the stench. I wondered about Dad and the secrets he kept outside of my vault and about Mom and the secrets she kept with her alone inside her bedroom. I started to spiral emotionally again, but this time I was also physically spiralling as I missed a step, swung around the ladder, and tumbled two feet to the ground.

CHAPTER 15

___

Friday, July 2nd, 1999—
Later the same day—20 days until my birthday

I dried off after my swim, moving around the deck, chasing the
fleeting warm spots on the wood as the sun began to set behind the
trees. I wanted to go change before Dad got home and spritz a little
perfume on myself to make sure I didn't smell of anything illicit. Oh
my God—is that what Nirvana meant by "Smells Like Teen Spirit?"
It's all starting to make sense to me now.

My mind grew more suspicious with every minute that passed after
sunset. Before when Dad was late, I'd picture him at a desk with his
briefcase doing something *financy* on a computer. But after talking to
Isaac, I found it hard not to picture him at dinner with Holly what's
her face.

We were back to living in the Stone Age; Mom had unplugged
every phone in the house again, and we were following strict instructions to only plug them in if we were making a short outbound call
(no dial-up internet either). Before I went upstairs, I used the living
room phone and called Dad on his work line. Of course there was no
answer. I would have called his mobile phone next (to see where he

actually was), but he lived permanently in the eighties, and his aversion to new technology continued to be a massive inconvenience in our lives.

On the way to my room, I noticed my painting of the Pretty Place hanging in the upstairs hallway. The hall that led to our bedrooms was a safe zone in the house for artwork, certificates, poems—anything we felt was display worthy and frame ready. We called it the Marshall Showcase Wall. For the most part, only Mom and I hung anything up there, but Dad framed his first aid and CPR certificate, and Isaac let Mom frame the lyrics to the first song he ever wrote. When I'd left the painting to dry on the dining room table, I wasn't even sure I'd finished it yet. The painting was something I was doing in mourning—consoling myself over the death of our pup. What gave anyone the right to share it without my permission? It felt like an invasion of privacy, but it must have meant Patty-Poo had been *up and at 'em* while Isaac and I were hiding out in Bob's tree house. I hoped she was on her way to the kitchen for some much-needed munchies when she saw the painting because I hadn't seen her eat anything since June (melodramatic, I know). She'd taken the day off but was still locking herself away like Sleeping Beauty banished to the left-wing tower; she hadn't come out of her bedroom since June either.

I changed into a big black Pink Floyd T-shirt Isaac had given me, threw my wet, mangy curls up in a hairclip, and stopped in to see Mom on my way back downstairs. Her room was in a state of unusual disarray, almost as bad as Isaac's. I thought I'd gotten my fondness for cleaning from her, but looking at her room, you'd never know it. There were clothes discarded in piles on the floor (Laundryville must have been relocated), thick dust on her desk, plates filled with old food, and worst of all, a cluttered nightstand. So cluttered, it was giving me palpitations. I wouldn't have been able to be anywhere near my room if I'd let it get so disorganized. My doctor said it was okay I was so finicky about certain things—I was just a *particular* kid, I guess.

Mom was sitting on the bed, putting makeup on using the antique vanity mirror Nonna Perruzza had given her for her birthday, the last birthday Nonna was alive. It bothered Aunt Sam that she'd given it to Mom and not her, but it was something Nonna wanted to keep in the family, passed down from one daughter to the next. Aunt Sam had a terrible illness; I can't remember the name—endo-something. Mom had it too, but she had Isaac and me before it got really bad. Aunt Sam let it progress too far and had to have her uterus removed. It was common knowledge she'd never have children, but she claimed she'd never wanted them anyway. Mom said she treated Isaac and me as if we were her own as a way to cope; becoming sterile in your late twenties is traumatic (whether you admit you want kids or not).

"What are you doing, Mom? That's a tabletop mirror, not a bed-top mirror," I joked.

I was pleased to see the curtains drawn, letting in the evanescent early-evening light. It danced around the beautiful detailing of the mirror's solid silver base, reflecting swirls of soft light onto the walls. I looked at her eyes in the mirror's reflection, and for a second, I thought they were my own. Our eyes were eerily similar, and Mom said her hair had been the exact same colour as mine when she was my age. It was hard to understand why someone as beautiful as her would ever admit to having looked like me, but she seems overjoyed when people say we look like sisters. Isaac was Dad's little carbon copy with his light-blue eyes and espresso-brown hair. The contrast of their colouring garnered a lot of attention (sometimes it felt as if they were prettier than me).

I grabbed the mirror off the bed, careful not to catch a glimpse of my reflection in it. I'd held it many times before, but I was still taken aback by its weight. The delicate vine design on the mirror's frame and base made it look so dainty, though its heft made it feel anything but. I put it back on Mom's vanity and flopped down on her half-made bed.

"No, no, hon, I like the light here on the bed. Natural light is always best, you know!" She never missed an opportunity for a beauty lesson.

"Okay. Sorry, Mom," I said, reluctantly placing it back on the bed and taking a (less comfy) seat on her vanity stool.

"Your father and I are going to go out for dinner—just the two of us. Sorry we have to miss game night again."

She stared at herself intently as she spoke with words that sounded impossibly distant. It was as if her reflection was talking for her from somewhere inside the mirror—somewhere in a land far, far away. Had she been looking anywhere other than her own face, I would have thought her expression disdainful. The makeup was scattered all around her, but she hadn't used any of it, and the darkness around her eyes was more purple than I'd ever seen it—though I'd rarely seen her without her war paint on (Dad called it that, but I thought it sounded a bit violent). The mirror reflected a small circle of sunlight onto her cheek like a spotlight, and there was something so wholesome about the naked skin underneath. Her bare face made her look younger and resilient, but it made her look more vulnerable too.

"That's okay—we don't mind. Is it all right if I plug the phones in to call Aunt Sam tonight?"

"Sure, Ivory. Just hang up and call her back if you hear any weird clicking, okay? And you know what? Keep one phone plugged in for the night while we're out. We're just going to Pog's Place, but I want to be able to get a hold of you if something happens."

Pog's Place was the only restaurant on the Island. And except for one convenience store (not at all a convenient distance from our house), we had to go into town to buy food.

She rubbed the knuckle of her index finger around her mouth, eyes locked on the mirror, caught in her own gaze.

"Mirror, mirror on the wall, who's the fairest of them all?" I chanted. "Do you want me to give you a makeover?"

I couldn't count the number of makeovers she'd tortured me with over the last three years. I was subjected to the primping before every school dance and special occasion. It was partly because she thought it was fun female bonding, and partly because she felt I was an extension of herself (and likely wished this particular extension cared more about her appearance).

"I think I'll just go like this. It's better to be less recognizable, when I think about it."

She wasn't just another pretty face. I hadn't even considered the importance of anonymity with what was going on at Sternwood. Her co-workers knew she lived on the Island, and I'm sure the last thing she'd want was to run into them—or into any danger, for that matter.

She smiled, collected her makeup, and put it back into her pink, sparkly makeup bag, the one I'd gotten for my last birthday and vehemently despised. Sometimes I felt she was more of teenage girl than I was (and if Dad and Isaac were prettier than me, that basically made me an ugly little boy—awesome).

"Did you happen to frame and hang up my painting in the hallway?" I asked. My question was rhetorical, but I could tell by the look on her face she hadn't picked up on that.

"No, but I noticed it there when I went to look for you and Isaac out back. It's beautiful. I can't believe you painted that all by yourself! It looks professional, sweetie."

She got up and placed her hand lightly on my shoulder—so lightly, it almost hovered. It was strange to feel her apprehension; she usually backed up her words of affirmation with hugs of affirmation (not *hovering touches* of affirmation). But maybe her hand had fallen asleep, and she didn't want to touch me because of the uncomfortable pins and needles sensation she'd get. That was about the only thing I could think of to explain her weird hover-hand.

"Hmm," I said, "I didn't frame it. Maybe Dad did."

It was hard to believe—but so was the thought that Isaac, not Dad, had destroyed Chelsea's doghouse. Lately, Dad had been full of pleasant surprises, and I wasn't complaining.

Mom disappeared into their walk-in closet and came out wearing a form-fitting red dress—a dress I'd heard Dad say "hugged her in all the right places." It was promising to see they were making an effort and having a date night. Stress often manifested most visibly as distance between them. It had been a long time since they'd gone out alone together, and as their unofficial marriage counsellor, I believed it was good for them.

I heard the garage door opening and ran downstairs to greet Dad. I waited to hear Chelsea scamper to the laundry room to greet him and had to remind myself (again) that she was out in the backyard . . . indefinitely. He was carrying a bouquet of flowers; I heard the paper wrapping crinkling before he walked into the kitchen. It was a sound I used to know as well as the pitter-patter of Chelsea's claws on the hardwood floor. At one point, he got Mom flowers almost every week, but it had been a while since I'd seen a thoughtful display of affection sitting with us at the kitchen table.

He didn't seem agitated, so I didn't feel uneasy. He saw me smile as I looked down at the olive branch in his hand.

"Mind throwing these in a vase for your mother? I wanted to cheer her up."

He passed them to me before I could respond. As a creature of habit, he needed to go and put his briefcase on the piano bench.

Nonna Perruzza had been a florist, and she'd taught Mom and me a very specific way of preparing flowers for a vase. Like the vanity mirror and my superstitious beliefs (bad things—threes), she'd passed down an aptitude for flower handling to me. I tried my best to cut the stems of the pink and orange gerbera daisies on an angle under a steady stream of lukewarm water, but the stems were thick and unruly. *Why did Mom pick such difficult flowers as her favourite?* My favourite flowers were trilliums. Isaac told me they were illegal to pick because they were Ontario's provincial symbol, but I'm sure he was lying just to scare me. When I was younger, he told me that Snap, Crackle, and Pop from the Rice Krispies commercials lived in stoplights so they could switch the colours and direct traffic. He also told me that jet planes came out every morning to leave a trail in the sky that turned into clouds, and that without jets, we'd never have any rain (and I believed him until grade-six science class). Now I take everything he says with a grain of sand.

***

"Well, do you think I should come to stay for a few days, or what? You know I've left you guys, like, twelve-thousand messages, right?" Aunt Sam asked. She sounded distraught from the other end of the phone line, so I tried to be vague about Mom's situation (though my understanding was vague too). It seemed my casualness didn't alleviate her concern; it just added to the frustration she felt from being kept in the dark. She went on before I could answer either question. "Do you think you're in real danger? What exactly happened to Chelsea? Did Isaac tell you he emailed me last week? What does your dad think?"

She finally paused to let me answer, only because she had to catch her breath. I hadn't been speaking, but I had to catch mine too.

"I don't know. I think he thinks we're okay, or they wouldn't have gone out to dinner tonight. Since Chelsea died ... well, was killed ... we're just keeping our eyes open, kinda thing."

"I'm so sorry that happened, Ivory. No one should have to lose a pet that way. And Patty—I mean, your mom—she thinks you guys were ... targeted?"

"I don't really know what she thinks. She mentioned it may be connected to what's going on at Sternwood, but we aren't sure. She took today off, and I know she doesn't want to go back there."

"She told me about some weird stuff happening with her boss, Stan, at least a month ago. I guess it's gotten worse. Has she been sleeping? Maybe I should come out there, eh?"

I didn't know how much Mom had shared about the Sternwood situation, the money, the *inconsistencies*. I didn't want to tell Aunt Sam just how much worse it had actually gotten—not only with her work, but the marriage too.

"I think she's sleeping. Not sure what else she'd be doing in her room for twenty-four hours a day. She doesn't look like herself, but she wasn't wearing any makeup when she went out either, so I'm not sure."

"No makeup? Get outta here! That's not like her at all. I should come out for a few nights, shouldn't I?"

"No! Aunt Sam, we're totally fine. Seriously, *do not worry*! I just wanted you to know why the phones weren't plugged in and stuff. Seriously though, we're all good in the hood!"

"Don't say that, honey. Aunty Sam actually lives in the hood, so it's not funny." I laughed (it was kind of funny). "Just tell me if she gets worse, like, if she stops eating too, okay?"

"I will. I promise," I said, "I got this under control."

I wondered if Mom's aversion to eating was already at reportable levels, but it was hard to tell; I was used to her limiting her calories during bathing suit season.

"You know, honey, I've been through this a few times too. We Perruzza ladies are just really . . . sensitive, you know? I'm sure when things get better at work, she'll bounce right back. And if Henry isn't around enough, tell me. I'll be there in two shakes of a lamb's tail. Love you, Ivory."

After I hung up, I realized I hadn't been listening for the clicking noises Mom told me about. Even if I had, I likely wouldn't have heard anything over myself and Aunt Sam anyway. There hadn't been a moment of silence in the entire conversation—we'd been catching our breaths the whole time.

CHAPTER 16

Saturday, July 3rd, 1999—19 days until my birthday

Robyn's planning a trip to Ghost Road with her older sister, Sadie, tonight. It's this stupid dirt road that's super dark and heavily forested. It's of little use but has a big story. And of course, it's the one place on the Island I'm technically not allowed to go.

Ghost Road ran parallel with ours, only it was six kilometres north toward town. There were no houses on it, so it was only really used as a shortcut to Darley Road. But still, people came from unimaginable distances to park their cars with their lights and their engines off. Sitting. Waiting. Sometimes they saw it—sometimes they didn't. Legend had it that fifty years ago, a deranged motorcyclist went speeding down it so fast, he missed the turn onto Pine Point and drove right into the barbed wire fence across the street. Decapitated, discombobulated, and probably a bit disoriented, he'd return every night at midnight, searching for his missing head. I wasn't one to challenge the authenticity of ghost stories, but it all sounded suspiciously similar to the tale of Ichabod Crane to me. The only difference was that the horse was subbed out for a motorcycle, and the rider's head was missing—not loyally riding shotgun.

I'd been to Ghost Road with Robyn a few times, but only twice as late as midnight, and only once did anything notable happen. At exactly 12:08 a.m., we'd seen what we thought was a single headlight, materializing out of nowhere, dissipating before it reached us. It was terrifying, bone-chilling even (though it was winter and the heater in Sadie's car was broken, so maybe I was just cold).

I remember coming home from Robyn's the next day and outing myself for breaking curfew, too excited to contain what we'd seen. Despite the palpable thrill we got from our first ghost encounter, Dad felt obligated to debunk the myth with an unsolicited science lesson. He started with a physics lesson about light, and how two headlights appeared as one from far enough away. Then he moved on to geography class. He grabbed his map bag from the front-hall closet and pulled out the biggest map he had of Durham Region and the surrounding townships. He wanted to show us Stilt Street, a road about forty kilometres in the distance that ran in line with Ghost Road. Ultimately, that meant the good people of Blackstock Township were innocently driving up and down Stilt Street, unknowingly lending their vehicle's lights to the overactive imaginations of thrill-seekers far and wide. It made me laugh to think they'd probably driven out to the Island to see the phantom light too—first having to leave its place of origin. Who knows? Maybe Stilt Street was their own version of Ghost Road, but I hoped they came up with a better legend.

Before Dad put the map away, I'd made sure to mark an X where I estimated the Pretty Place to be, so if Robyn or I ever spontaneously combusted, it could live on in someone's memory. When Dad asked what the X stood for, I told him that was where I'd hidden my buried treasure. "We're paying you too much in allowance then, kiddo," he said before walking out of the room, bubble-bursting destruction in his wake. Just like that, the one interesting attraction on the Island was demystified, and another little piece of our childhood had fallen victim to the truth.

But it wasn't the fake ghosts or even being out after curfew that made Mom and Dad ban me and Isaac from ever going to Ghost

Road. It was what had happened seven months ago to Shannon Fallie, a sixteen-year-old girl from town. On New Year's Eve, Shannon was taken to Ghost Road to be raped and beaten, then allegedly (you have to say "allegedly" until it's proven) left for dead—discarded like a piece of garbage in -15°C weather. The lady on the news said her assailant had likely tried to beat her to death (to leave no witnesses), and when she woke from a five-day coma, she couldn't remember what had happened—so he'd succeeded either way (allegedly).

It was *undoubtedly* the biggest, most devastating thing that had ever happened on the Island, and the community hadn't really been the same since. Now cops patrolled the road to take anyone under the age of eighteen home and to let their parents know where they'd been hanging out. But that never made sense to me—if Ghost Road *wasn't* an attraction, Shannon wouldn't have been found so quickly. If Stephen Bursey hadn't jumped out of his big truck to take a piss, who knows what would've happened? Hell, Shannon probably would've been left out there until Kujo found her and brought home one of her limbs, thinking it was a stick. Stephen's no hero or anything, but I did think there was some merit to letting the Ghost Road tradition continue.

I found it hard not to obsess over the case, trying to solve it as I did with all the mystery novels I read. I didn't want to get wrapped up in the details, but I thought a lot about the things I couldn't make sense of, the things that just didn't add up. Whoever left Shannon out there had to have been an out-of-towner—someone who didn't know Ghost Road was a busy place at night. This was hard to reconcile with the fact that the case was never investigated outside our little town. It must've meant the police suspected someone we knew—that or they believed the assailant wanted her to be found. But then, why beat her up so badly? Mom said it was an "act of fate" that led the kids to Shannon that night, and I should just leave it at that. But I read too much to believe in silly things like coincidence or fate; every story is written with intent, just as every crime of that magnitude is committed with at least a little calculation.

Eventually, I had to let it go and respect it wasn't (yet) some sensationalized case on *Unsolved Mysteries*. It wasn't a remote story coming to us via the television from hundreds of miles away—it was real. And not *one-headlight real* either. Truly real. No physics lesson could explain it away (though we all wished it could). The victim would walk the halls of high school with me next year; we'd both be sophomores, and her reason for being held back would always be far more devastating than mine. I think the closeness in our age is what freaked Mom and Dad out the most. Their fear of Ghost Road itself was an illogical placement of blame, and they were just trying to protect me, but as Isaac said, we could take care of ourselves.

***

"Get in," Sadie yelled as she came to a rolling stop at the end of my driveway. Her beige 1984 Honda Civic shared a birth year with me, but I could confidently say I was in better shape.

We puttered away from my house before anyone could notice that our mode of travel wasn't the heel-toe express. I was supposed to tell Mom and Dad whenever I planned to be in a car with someone, but I didn't want to lie about going to Ghost Road, so I chose an omission instead.

"Gary said him, and his buddies saw the ghost light twice last week!"

Sadie was in serious need of one of Dad's science lessons, but I knew Robyn didn't want to ruin the fun for everyone, so we'd vowed to keep it between us and play along.

"Sweet! That ghost must really be missing his head these days. I mean, who wouldn't be? Am I right?" Robyn asked as she turned up the radio.

The newest Red Hot Chili Peppers tune was playing on 94.9 The Rock. I wasn't a fan, but it was better than Sadie's typical choice,

Britney Spears. She flew down Pine Point, driving more recklessly than Mom did when she was late for Sunday service. Nothing scared Sadie, not even Pine Point's lack of street lights or its pothole epidemic.

"Hey, if you don't slow down, we're all gonna be full of *scar tissue*," I teased.

Without missing a beat, Robyn jumped in. "Yeah, I'm just trying to sit on the passenger side of my best friend's ride *without dying*. You dig?"

We burst into a fit of giggles. Robyn laughed so hard, she went full snort attack on us. Sadie rolled her eyes and pulled the latest TLC album out from her overhead sun visor. She knew us (idiots) well enough to know we'd want to listen to "No Scrubs" after Robyn's sample.

"I want to grab a pack of cigs," said Sadie.

She passed Ghost Road and turned onto Island Road, driving away from town toward the convenience store. It was actually called the Island Corner Store and added "corner" to the list of lies right next to "convenience." As we passed the casino, I noticed a fire-engine-red Toyota Supra from the corner of my eye. It looked like Dad's car, even though he often boasted of its rarity. Dad had gone to meet Doug in town, so I knew it wasn't him, and he could've taken Mom's car. This meant it was Isaac—my interest was officially piqued. He had a fake ID, and I wouldn't have put it past him to supplement his (lack of) income with gambling. He'd been pinching pennies all summer because he wasn't working so he could focus on his music, very much to Dad's dismay.

"Thank God they don't card here," Sadie said as she hopped back in the car. She was in and out faster than I could finish my thoughts about my newest unsolved mystery.

"Can you drive slowly by the casino parking lot on the way back?"

"I was going to go back down Darley, but it's cool. Why, though?"

"I thought I saw Dad's car there. I just want to check the licence plate so I can bribe Isaac with the info."

"Smmaaart," Robyn said, turning around to wink at me.

"Don't get any ideas," Sadie warned.

She drove by the casino (slower than we'd be going if we'd taken the heel-toe express), and there was no mistaking the plate. MONIGUI, it read—as ostentatious as the car itself. I couldn't help but laugh every time I read it, thinking it sounded more like a Native tribe than Dad's career choice.

"*Aha! It's him!*" I cheered. "Can we go home now, though? Otherwise, he'll know I went to Ghost Road, and the two bribes will just cancel each other out." *Oh, the intricacies of sibling rivalry.*

"Sure, whatever . . . the ghost thing probably isn't even real anyway," Sadie replied.

Her ignorance sounded even more foolish than her questionable taste in music. Robyn turned back to look at me again, cautiously so Sadie wouldn't see her eyes. "*Of course it's not real,*" they whispered. And for a moment I didn't resent Dad for bursting the Ghost Road bubble. For a moment I believed that ignorance wasn't really bliss at all.

***

Isaac walked in the kitchen looking as confused to see me as I was him. He was wearing checkered pyjama shorts and a plain brown T-shirt decorated with at least twenty moth-eaten holes. As always, his bedtime attire screamed fashionably well worn, bordering on homeless.

I sat perfectly still, head up, shoulders back—cleared of a crime I hadn't committed (and wasn't being accused of anyway). So what if I'd escorted an underage girl to a store to illegally buy a substance I'd watched kill Grandma Marshall? Wasn't that still better than potential date rape on Ghost Road?

"Oh hi," we both said in unison.

"*Jinx!*"

"I thought you went out."

"*Double jinx.*"

It never seemed to get old.

"I thought you were at the casino," I said, showing my cards before I even had a play.

"Huh? The casino? What are you talking about? I can't get in there."

"I thought you took Dad's car, because I saw it there when we went to the store."

"Sure, like you weren't going to Ghost Road. I saw Sadie pick you up. Real discreet." He laughed. I'd have to work on my low profile if I was ever going to be a private investigator.

"Weird. I guess Dad met Doug there instead of in town or s-s-something," I stuttered.

I could see Isaac's thoughts materializing like a dark, angry cloud above his head. I hadn't meant to, but I knew I'd accidentally added to his delusional adultery theory. I was the moisture vapour to his nimbostratus rain cloud (take that, jet planes, and thanks, grade six science class).

"More like he's meeting Holly there while Mom sits alone upstairs, worried sick about all the shit she has going on. He's a real class act."

When it rains, it pours.

I looked at the flowers on the kitchen table—the visual symbol of one man's love for his woman. I had a picture of Mom in my head: smiling, fresh-faced, doing a spin in her pretty red dress. Surely those weren't images associated with a failing marriage.

"What did you do tonight?" I asked. I needed to change the subject before the rain cloud set up shop above my head too.

"I was supposed to see Jessie, but we were chatting on MSN, and I told her I didn't feel like it, and she went all *talk to the hand* on me. Can't say I'm too disappointed," he said with transparently fake indifference.

As he finished his thought, the doorbell rang like a bell sounding the end of recess. It was 9:37 on a Saturday night, and try as I might, I couldn't think of one reasonable explanation for anyone ringing the bell so late. I also couldn't come up with one reasonable explanation for Isaac answering it so late when Dad wasn't home and Mom's lights were on, but she wasn't home either (if you know what I mean).

"I hope the front door is locked," I said, though I doubted anyone heeded Mom's warning to lock the doors in preparation for the millennium crazies. I felt scared and, for the first time in my life, unsafe too. Normally, someone protected me from the unknown. Chelsea was fat, but boy, could she run. And Dad was small, but he had his black belt in karate. Isaac was probably stoned, and all I could think to do was grab a utensil from the drawer beside me.

"A fork, Ivy? Really? Come on, the knives are right beside it! A *fork?*" It was clear we were unprepared for any kind of attack, but at least I was prepared for a late supper. "Take a chill pill, man. Just stay here."

I let out a breath I'd been holding in (since I saw Dad's car at the casino) and traded in my weapon for a more practical choice—a steak knife.

Isaac sauntered out of the kitchen with the same nonchalance he'd had about Jessie, so maybe it hadn't been an act—that, or marijuana eliminates your urgency as much as your self-control.

Three days later (it seemed), he returned unharmed. He was holding a plastic Radio Shack bag; its contents clinked together like broken glass at the bottom of a garbage can. I arose from under the table where I'd been hiding and prepared myself for some not-so-good news.

"What the heck is that?"

"Broken glass," he said. He had a sly look on his face that was simultaneously annoying and calming. *Obviously, he's not too concerned,* I thought as I put my dinner tools back in their respective homes.

"Why in God's name did someone ring the doorbell to give you a bag full of glass?"

His smirk turned to a full-blown smile, and my calm turned to full-blown annoyance.

"It was Jessie!" He laughed hard, trying not to be too loud and wiping tears away from his sunken, bloodshot eyes. But his containing it only made it more contagious; forbidden laughter was better than regular laughter (even if you didn't know what you were laughing about). He reached in the bag and handed me a piece of carefully folded peach stationery.

Isaac,

I made this for you and was going to give it to you tonight before you bailed on me for the second time this week. I know you don't want to go steady with me anymore, so you should have just said that.

Jessie

P.S. Your band sucks.

Inside the bag were the broken remains of what appeared to be a jar and at least fifty little pieces of folded paper. On each slip was an attribute of Isaac's that Jessie claimed to love:

+ Your cute and messy hairdo

+ Your love of animals

+ Your raspy voice (you're better than U2)

+ Your gushy poetry

I sat in awe as I read the teeny-tiny love notes, baffled that he'd been able to make someone notice those things about him, let alone love them (and then hate him enough to take them all back). He laughed it off while I let each whisper of adoration meant for him jump off the paper and whisper disparaging things to me. Every compliment I read reminded me of every compliment I'd never received. He wasn't even three years older than me, but it felt as if he'd experienced a lifetime more than I had—he'd travelled the full heartbreak cycle with multiple girls, while I hadn't even travelled to first base. Experience was everything, and I was going to stay a virgin forever if I didn't find a guy to break a jar over ASAP (not, like, physically, because that would hurt).

He grabbed the papers from my hands and the bag from the table.

"Stop! It's dumb! Jessie thinks she loves everyone. I'm going to throw it in the pit. Wanna come?"

"No," I said curtly, trying to hide my disappointment. I poured myself a glass of milk and sat in silence at the kitchen table. I spied another little love note—the one Dad left sticking out of the bouquet:

I LOVE YOU, PATTY. FEEL BETTER SOON :)

It was written in all caps (boxy and rigid—his signature style) so you'd know he'd written it and not the florist. He'd left a plate of food covered in plastic wrap on the counter for Mom, and he'd brought four days' worth of newspapers up from the bottom of the driveway because he knew she liked to read them. Even though I was drinking milk (cow—dead—doornail), I felt as if I was surrounded by love again instead of death, which was actually like being surrounded by life (I'd done a full 180). I'd never been in love, but I imagined it was the most vulnerable you could ever be. And if feeling terrifyingly vulnerable all the time wasn't what it meant to be alive, then I didn't know what was.

CHAPTER 17

Sunday, July 4th, 1999—18 days until my birthday

Mom didn't go to church today. The news seemed to have the same effect on everyone. We were scared. We were worried. She never missed church unless she was really unwell, and even then, she'd watch a service on television.

Mom came downstairs and found Dad, Isaac, and me trying to make her pancakes, fumbling around the kitchen like three blind mice. Even under her heavy housecoat, I could see the weight she'd lost in the last three weeks. It warranted a mention (though it seemed to fall on her ever-growing list of *concerning unmentionables*).

Her hair was pulled back off her face into a ponytail that looked foreign on her head. I'd never seen her without her curly blonde bangs hiding her "larger-than-average" forehead. Her skin was paler than average too, especially for the first week of July, which added to her overall gaunt look. It had become clear—tangibly clear—that it was time to take her more seriously.

"Where did you go last night, Henry? I really needed you to be home with me and the kids." She looked around at the terrible mess we'd made with good intentions. "Nancy emailed me Friday. I could read between the lines—things are escalating, and they'll be tying up loose ends soon enough." Her conviction grew with every word she spoke. It was as if the fear she felt gave her the strength she needed to stand there and speak without falling over.

"I was meeting with Doug in town, hon—I told you. Come here, sit down. The pan-blobs are almost ready."

The ease with which he told a lie caught me off guard. It was like the time Aunt Sam accidentally told me that Dad was Santa Claus. I wasn't expecting it, but at the same time, I wasn't entirely surprised. Dad was a man of many things—a jack of all trades, a safety freak, a mediocre cook—and until now I'd always thought he was a man of integrity. So many times I'd witnessed him tell the truth when a lie would've saved him from a night of tiring discord. "How many beers have you had, Henry?" Mom would ask, with a sharpness of tongue that told everyone in the room that one was one too many. He'd never reduce the number or claim he was sober, even when sobriety couldn't have been disproved. "All a man has in this world is his word. Never forget that," he'd say over and over again by the light and warmth of his other backyard companion, the fire. I'd never correct him or remind him I wasn't a man; I just let him take pride in a lesson he obviously felt was more precious than my inheritance.

I stood over the stove with a spatula in my hand, surrounded by disaster, listening as he demystified a different kind of lore. Another piece of my childhood had fallen victim to the truth, only this time it was revealed that there'd never really been any truth. His dishonesty permeated the air, leaving a tension thicker than our lumpy pancake batter.

Isaac turned his head toward me with such intensity, I was surprised one of his dental fillings didn't fly out and hit me in the face. I met his angry eyes with a nod. Relenting. Acknowledging. Maybe he was right about Dad. Maybe Mom was right too, and the stress of her crumbling marriage on top of a work-related legal fiasco was just too much for her to handle. Everyone had such wonderful timing in our family. Might as well just keep piling it on. If Nonna was right that bad things happened in threes, I needed to calculate how many bad things that was for four people.

Twelve.

Twelve bad things would happen to our family in total. *Great.* Not quite the reassurance I'd hoped for. Luckily for me, however, two of mine had already happened. Small victory.

"No, I'm not hungry, Henry. And I emailed Stan and let him know I won't be coming in this week. I have the flu." She turned and was gone as quickly as she'd come. Head down, hair up, spirits no better than when she entered. Decidedly, being lied to wasn't the medicine she required.

We sat silently around the table, sulking like the chairs were the day this summer from hell began. The feeling I'd had that day was the "discernment" Mom said I had in abundance before most kids learned how to tie their Velcro shoes. It was like the common sense that wasn't so common. I could read a situation, discern the unspoken, and predict the unpredicted. That early summer day, the ominous shadows I noticed in our house were actually *fore-shadows.*

It was as if the Marshalls were playing a precarious game of Kerplunk, and every second day Dad was carelessly pulling another straw out from our weakening foundation, taunting the marbles to fall, leaving no winner in his selfish game.

"Not like your mother not to go to church," he said, finally breaking the silence with a statement we'd all been sharing without words. "Can't say I really understood the whole church thing. It's all a load of crap to me, but I went because she said it was good for you kids." It felt strange to me that he'd offer some never-before-shared honesty on the tail of an unsettling lie. "To be honest with you guys, I've considered myself an atheist for some time now. Patty asked me not to tell you, but I feel you're old enough to know what I am."

A liar? I thought, or could a man's integrity remain intact if the lie was told for the betterment of the recipient? I thought about the mystery books I've read, the weaving of lies and truths, the victims and their assailants. One thing they're unanimous about is that you're innocent until proven guilty. I had to give Dad the same benefit of the doubt I'd given so many fictional characters I'd imagined with red hands. I had seen his heart, I had seen him bare his skin as a broken, angry boy. I had seen him at his most vulnerable . . . and even then, he was good.

"I knew that," Isaac said. "I know you're a stupid atheist, and I know you're cheating on Mom. Ivy saw your car last night."

His words pierced Dad's chest like the exploding shell from a shotgun aimed to kill.

I gasped, searching the space in front of me for some air. It felt as though the kitchen had taken flight into the atmosphere. Isaac had just flung open the door with his accusation and the oxygen had been sucked out, leaving us no option but to jump.

"You're wrong, Isaac." Dad's voice was low, reverent. "I might not be perfect, but neither is your mother. I have my own stuff going on, believe it or not. I did meet someone in town, and on the way home I stopped at the casino. So sue me. With how things have been lately, I think I deserve to blow off some steam. I'm doing the best I can."

His eyes started leaking—it must have been leaking, since I'd never seen him cry before. Not even after Grandma Marshall died. I looked at Isaac, hoping he felt somewhat satisfied with Dad's explanation, but his fierce stare told me he was adopting more of a guilty-until-proven-innocent attitude.

"I met with Stan, your mother's boss. He and I exchanged emails last week, and it seemed better to speak in person so I could really feel it out eye to eye—man to man."

Guilty.

"I didn't want her knowing," he went on, incriminating himself further. "I didn't want her to think I was going there to fact-check. I know she has reason to be concerned—there's been a lot of bad business tied up in that company—but she's just not as tied up in it as she thinks."

Until.

"Come on, Isaac—don't you know me better than that? You too, Ivy."

Proven.

"I would never, ever, be unfaithful to your mother. We may not agree on many things anymore, but I think we agree on that."

Innocent.

I thought about the cow, its eyes rolling back in its head as the last breath left its body. I thought about the way running was difficult when I was weighed down by remorse. I thought about harmless intentions ending in pain and regret. I thought about Dad's story, and I made up my mind.

I looked at Isaac, then to Dad, then back to Isaac. The similarity of their eyes was uncanny; they shared that same stunning feature, but today they shared nothing else.

Isaac.

Dad.

Both equal parts man and equal parts boy, both equally certain of the truth that lingered around us, both knowing the other was wrong.

CHAPTER 18

Wednesday, July 7th, 1999—
15 days until no one cares that I'm 15

For four days now, the persistent July sun has been rising and setting aimlessly without making its way through the tightly closed blinds in Mom's room. Dad sleeps in the family room to give her "space" while she keeps strange hours in the night. His absence and the absence of light in the room is making it feel more like a basement dungeon than a second-floor master suite. The door rarely opens, if only to slide in a tray of inedible food.

The weatherman on Channel 16 said we should expect some rain in the next few days, but today the sky was radiant and flawless. The air smelled clean and fresh with just enough humidity to make you feel comfortable, even in the early-morning shade. It was one of those perfect days where the outdoors seemed to exist only to bring you joy, and I couldn't take the thought of Mom missing it.

I'd stood outside her door for a few minutes before I mustered the courage (and patience) to venture into her room unaccompanied and uninvited. I needed a good reason, both compelling and somewhat urgent, to get her outside. Occasionally, I'd get letters from a friend-turned-pen pal who I'd met while visiting Dad's family in Ireland. Her letters had slowed in recent years, but I still visited the mailbox sometimes just in case (especially in the weeks leading up to my birthday). It wasn't much of a reason—but it was something.

Reluctantly, Mom agreed to join me on my walk to the mailbox (it was *her* rule to leave the house in pairs, and I tactfully reminded her of that). We walked silently, our slow strides in unison, breaths alternating, and arms swinging dutifully at our sides. We were a mildly motivated machine, somewhat committed to the end goal like the little engine that could . . . but didn't really care to. I didn't mind that we didn't talk as we normally did; I was just happy to be out in the world together, sun beating down on our bare shoulders, our curls looking like little brass Brillo pads to the birds flying overhead.

She waved to a car that sped past too quickly for me to see who it was. Everyone knew everyone on the Island—waving was our unspoken obligation. I tried not to notice as she adjusted the strap on her top and pulled down her shorts, which had bunched awkwardly at her thighs. I'd rushed her to get ready for fear she'd change her mind, but I felt bad as I watched her, obviously uncomfortable in her clothes. It was the first outfit not topped with a housecoat that I'd seen her in since she emerged from her closet, twirling in her red dress. Guilt and the crimson colour lingered in my mind like a drop of half-dried blood, smeared and then stained. To me the dress was akin to the heart she wore on her sleeve, matching in colour, futilely serving the same purpose. If only the sun could cure her ailments the way it so effortlessly did in cartoons—banishing clouds and making flowers sprout in a matter of seconds, healing everything it touched.

The mailbox was jammed full, and for a second I believed it was early-arriving birthday cards sent by my overzealous (foreign) family members. I was disappointed to see no international postage, but I did see a turquoise envelope with Aunt Sam's writing on it. I should have known our phone call would lead to a thoughtful note; she always knew the best ways to cheer me up. Mom handed it to me as we began our walk back home. She shuffled through the remaining pieces of mail, flipping one behind the other, announcing each bill more quietly than the one before. She stopped when she got to a thicker letter addressed to her, Dad, and Isaac.

"I expected his diploma to come in a bigger envelope. I'm going to be angry if they folded it," she said with more spunk than I'd seen in her in days.

She tore it open (with no regard for the other names on the envelope), and as we stood there, halfway between the mailbox and our driveway, she added, her voice fading, *Son's a high school dropout* to her now lengthy list of concerning unmentionables.

I read from over her shoulder (with no regard for the names on the envelope) and learned that the letter was the fourth time the school had attempted contact. Isaac's impressive initiative to retrieve the mail was beginning to make sense. So was his indifference to our unplugged phones and his insistence on a buffer year before college. Even still, a bomb like that always drops eventually. *What was he thinking, keeping it from us at a time like this?* Or maybe keeping it from us at a time like this was *exactly* what he was thinking.

"Did you know about this?" Mom asked as she sped up, walking toward our driveway with new purpose.

"Of course not, Mom. I had no idea. He tells me nothing."

Her shoulders and spine were still curved, looking brittle and weak, and she shuffled her feet as she walked, but her appearance no longer mirrored her spirit. Isaac was going to get it—and I didn't want to be home during World War Three in case there were any civilian casualties.

***

It had been a while since I'd gone to the Pretty Place on my own, and I felt a sense of nostalgia that came from entering it the same way I'd discovered it. The walk was only about ten minutes (give or take), but it had a funny way of feeling longer or shorter depending on why I was going. I grabbed a handful of wheat and pulled the little dusty beads off the sheaf, collecting them in my hand. I'd often find myself fiddling with plants if they were within arm's reach, especially if something was invading the safe spots in my mind. There was something so appeasing about the sweet, earthy scent of a young leaf freshly plucked from a living tree or plant. I'd rip them off and fold them up, taking satisfaction in the sound of every healthy crack, seeing how many folds I could make before the leaf turned to green mush. Sometimes I'd tear them into a million pieces, throwing them in the air like organic confetti, left with a gooey residue on my hands—the sweet-smelling blood of Mother Earth (sacrificed for my boredom). For every leaf I'd kill, I'd try to balance my negative karma by taking a helicopter off a maple tree and burying it in the soil, hoping to start a new life. Even if one seedling survived, it would right all the wrongs I'd ever done, all the leaves I'd ever wasted. That made me feel better about it, like it being okay to litter as long as it's an apple core, because there was the smallest chance your sin could produce fruit.

I was counting on the Pretty Place and its surroundings to mend the little pieces of myself that had torn apart since the summer began. I'd thought the months before high school would give me time to transform, time for all the remnants of my former self to be washed away by the baptizing waters of Lake Scugog. But instead of a summer filled with transformative preparation, life had been saving up all of the hardships my heart could bear to graciously gift them to me for my fifteenth birthday. And I wasn't sure the Pretty Place could heal all of that.

I followed the painted rocks in toward the core of the forest. Though I needed no trail or reminder, I didn't want to take from the rocks the only job they had. The leaves of the willow tree near the water were growing strong now, the branches still woven together from the swings we'd made when Robyn and I last came. The water was cool, glowing with the familiar (but elusive) gold colour I wasn't able to portray in my painting. Everything was far more spectacular in real life than I'd been able to depict, but that wasn't surprising. No one could capture the true essence of the Pretty Place—some things just weren't meant to be captured, and life had taught me that lesson (the hard way) more than once. The first time was after I'd held a baby toad captive in my Polly Pocket dollhouse. I'd thought it would appreciate a tiny mansion, a house fit for a toad king. Instead, the toad dried up and died from the heat of the direct sun. I was too young to know that toads needed water and soil and to be moist at all times. I was too young to know that not everyone or everything longed for something more beautiful than what they had—sometimes you can be content with dirt and mud, and sometimes you can only survive in darkness.

I thought I liked being scared. I'd never say no to a scary movie or travelling through the Dark Forest (if I had to) alone at night. I thought I liked being sad too. I'd listen to sad songs on repeat, and if a beloved character died in the book I was reading, I'd read the chapter no less than twice. I'd called myself a *tortured soul*, and I used to think it made me sound interesting and unique—something someone would notice one day and write on a tiny piece of paper and put in a tiny broken jar. But the more bad things I tracked against the twelve, the more I realized I only *thought* I liked those feelings because I never truly understood what they were. Self-inflicted sadness and fear without real danger are just little boosts of adrenalin that remind you you're still alive. But *real* fear and *real* sadness—these are things I would never choose to repeat.

I took out the journal I'd grabbed from the tree house before I stole away to the back fields. I wanted to do a formal tally of the three bad things that were plaguing each member of our family. Isaac not finishing high school was definitely one of the twelve, and although I knew they were all inevitable, I'd hoped for smaller struggles. My doctor had told me that whenever my mind got too busy or I became overwhelmed with details, it would help to make lists so I could organize my thoughts the way I did my drawers:

Bad Things List:

1. *We accidentally killed a cow*

2. *Mom's in danger (Sternwood)*

3. *Chelsea died*

4. *Dad may be cheating*

5. *Dad lied about being at the casino*

6. *Mom's a recluse*

7. *Dad sucks at his job*

8. *Isaac's a beauty school dropout*

$$12 - 8 = 4 \text{ bad things left}$$

I wished Nonna was still alive so I could ask her about this bad-things-happening-in threes business. Like, how would you know if something were bad enough to count as one of the three? Or what if something really good happened? Did that erase one of the bad things? I needed to know the magnitude of that number, four. Four meant that if we wanted to spread it out evenly, everyone could have only one bad thing left. That seemed fair. I hope it worked that way—one bad thing each didn't seem so overwhelming. I grabbed the turquoise envelope from my backpack, the letter from Aunt Sam I was saving for when I was alone. Cozy against the fallen trunk of a yellow cedar, I felt myself relax for the first time in hours, letting out a breath I'd been holding since Mom opened the eighth bad thing.

***

I'd dozed off, sitting upright with Aunt Sam's letter still unopened in my lap. I was startled awake by a clumsy June bug that had flown into the side of my head (they're the Valley girls of insects). I could tell it was almost dusk by the angle of the light peeking through the trees and the coolness in the air. The trek back would take at least forty minutes, and I was feeling sluggish, in no rush to return home to the war zone.

Outside of the forest, the sun was moving quickly, setting with conviction. It was that time of day when you could look directly at it without hurting your eyes, and I watched as it fell down the sky toward the edge of the earth like heavy rain on a windowsill.

A shuffling noise came from the tall grass in the distance. I'd been on high alert since Jessie rang our doorbell, but I tried not to panic and grabbed the nearest sharp stick I could find. Sometimes the wind made unsettling noises, playing tricks on your ears the same way the dark played tricks on your eyes. *Nothing to be scared of,* I reminded myself. *Nothing wrong with a little grass shuffling—probably just a mouse.* But it wasn't the wind, and it wasn't an animal. It was a man—a man holding an animal. Maybe a goat, maybe a deer, maybe a fox. I was right to think there was nothing wrong with a little moving grass; it's *what* moved the grass that could be concerning. I stopped, lifeless, frozen in place as if the gym teacher had just called out "red light" and I was fixing to win. I held my breath and thought about all the statues I'd ever seen, but no matter how still I was, I'd lost the game before it began. The man had heard me and feverishly scoured the open field between us, searching for the source of the noise (not the wind—sorry, bud). We locked eyes as the last bit of light fell behind the trees and off the earth—an untimely departure.

He put the animal down and waved in my direction. Neighbourly waving must be an obligation that extended beyond roadways. I stayed still as he approached, his face finally coming into focus . . . it was Junior.

Green light!

I walked slowly away from Mount Everest, cautious, trying to gauge his outrage as we neared one another. For a second I forgot he didn't know we'd killed his cow, and the only tension between us would be from Chelsea's death and Dad's beating (the evidence of which he still wore on his face).

"I wanted to tell you I'm sorry, Ivy. It . . . I . . . it was never meant for your Chelsea. Those German shepherds are always causin' me and Pop so much trouble. They're the ones who should be paying for it, not you."

My mind flashed back to the moment I'd noticed him there. He and the creature in his arms had looked like a silhouette, black, with light glowing all around them. *Was it a dog?* And where was it now? It was only a few minutes later now, but we stood talking in complete (uncomfortable) darkness. I looked back toward my house—my little way of saying someone would come looking for me if I didn't get home soon.

"What were you holding there? When I first saw you," I asked.

I was pushing the boundaries of what I knew to be politely inquisitive, but I didn't care. He owed me an explanation (it could be his penance). He shifted his weight from one leg to the other, clearly uneasy in his shit-stained coveralls.

"It's a calf. Err, it *was* a calf. It's dead now. Had a vet up to the farm last week, and some of my cattle have that Johne's disease. It got that one young."

We kept our heads down, each looking at the other's dirty shoes, anything to avoid eye contact.

"Okay. Well, I better get home. Sorry about your face."

"I had it comin.'"

He turned and ambled away, walking toward a path that would lead him straight home, either forgetting the calf or purposely leaving it behind. I wondered if it was some kind of sacrifice he made to the farm gods, or if our conversation had just rattled him as much as it had me.

I lifted my nose to the star-laden sky, breathing in deeply, searching for the scent of death in the air. There was nothing. No smell, no morbid confirmation, only the familiar aromas that told me I was standing in a field—at night (alone). The calf must've died recently, then (fresh death). I thought about going to look at it to make sure it was actually a calf and that it was actually dead. Instead, I walked back home, going the long way around, basking in the new truth. If his cattle were sick, not only was his act of revenge unlawful, but also completely misdirected too. And because we hadn't actually killed that cow, Chelsea's death was much less my fault. Small victory?

CHAPTER 19

Friday, July 9th, 1999—13 days until I'm 15

At 2:19 p.m. the front doorbell rang while I was sitting on the
back deck. I heard it only by chance because Isaac left the kitchen
door ajar, letting every ladybug on the Island take up residence in
our solarium.

Before opening the door, I checked the peephole—a security feature
Mom insisted on while Dad pointed out its futility on a door we never
(used to) lock. A man from Sternwood was standing on our front
porch—a guest about as welcome as the grim reaper. Unlike during
the night of Isaac's big jar scare, Mom came down from her room,
standing out of sight on the stairwell, listening as I braced myself for
another uncomfortable interaction. The man didn't *look* like a criminal,
but I knew the best crooks were the ones described as "unassuming"
in the books I read. He didn't look like a businessman either, not the
way Dad did. He appeared less rigid in his wrinkled khaki pants and
short-sleeved yellow button-front shirt (the bouquet he held helped
soften his look too).

"Stan told the team that Patty was under the weather. He wanted
me to personally deliver these flowers and tell her to get well soon," he

said, making the little get-well-soon card on the arrangement redundant. "Is Henry home, by chance?"

Nice subject change, arsehole. You aren't getting any info outta me, I thought as I reached out and accepted his Trojan horse.

"No, he isn't. And thanks, she's fine—really."

"Just let her know we're thinking about her, okay? And to give us a call when she's ready to come back in. No one's *mad* at her like she told Nancy. We just want her to come back in one piece, is all."

His gaze fell to the welcome mat as he stepped back, away from the front step. I slammed the door without saying another word. *One piece? How many pieces was she supposed to come back in? What the hell was that supposed to mean? If I had my way, she'd never go back there again—in any number of pieces!*

I stood staring out the peephole, gripping the flowers so tightly, I had to say a quick *thank you* that they weren't thorny roses. I watched as the spy got into his car and drove away, making sure there was no funny business on his way out of our lives. And I hoped no one waved to him as he drove back into town.

I knew Mom was still on the stairs; I could hear her. Isaac and I had learned the exact foot placement required to use the stairs without making a sound, not a single creak, but I guess she didn't need to sneak around the way we did.

"Mom, I know you heard that. It's okay, he's gone."

Looking at her, I realized I hadn't seen her in almost two full days. She looked frailer, paler, and if it were possible, as though she'd lost even more weight (I tried not to be jealous).

"Do you believe me now, honey?"

She sighed as she stood up in her hiding place, gripping the railing as tightly as I held the flowers, but neither offered us any support.

"Of course. I always believed you. Always. Tell Dad you're not going back there."

She came down the final four stairs, meeting me on the landing. I remember laughing in history class when I learned that women originally carried wedding bouquets to overpower the stench people had in the fifteenth century (inevitable when you bathed once yearly). Standing as close to Mom as I was, I was thankful to be holding the bouquet upright and close to my nostrils.

I stepped away as politely as possible while she stared at the flowers in my hands as if they were pig tongues. They weren't her favourite, but they weren't *that* bad. Her sudden burst of energy surprised me as she tore them from my grip, wafting even more fifteenth-century stink in my direction. *She couldn't possibly be putting them in a vase, could she?*

No, no, she wasn't—she was putting them to death.

I watched in awe as she mutilated the flowers, beating them on the piano bench, white carnation heads flailing in the air like kernels being heated to popcorn. Sweat beaded on her brow as every precious petal was lost, fluttering to the ground, casualties of an unfair game of *he loves me/he loves me not*. I had never seen my mother act so violently, and I found myself stunned—still like a statue for the second time in two days.

"Whoa, Mom. Okay, you killed them—you killed them dead."

She stood breathless over the remains, staring, surveying her success.

"Sweep it up for me, will you, Ivory? And bring it out to the firepit and burn it all, okay? Thanks, hon."

I didn't argue, pushing down my disdain for her hypocrisy. I'd been cleaning up my own messes since I got my first kitchen playthings, but as I watched her gather her energy before each step back upstairs, I realized she couldn't clean it up even if she'd wanted to.

***

"I'm taking your mother to the doctor's tomorrow. This stuff with Isaac isn't making it any easier for her to sleep," Dad said audaciously, as though he'd forgotten the part he'd played in her recent bout of insomnia.

I didn't feel like keeping him company by the fire tonight, but I didn't feel like being alone either. The temperature had dropped to the teens, and the dew on the grass made my feet feel as if I'd gotten a soaker. Sliding my bare thighs onto the cold bars of our old patio chair, I knew my jean short shorts were a foolish choice, and I envied Dad in his frayed Nautica sweater.

"So, what's the doctor going to do, then? She'd be better if she just flat out quit work and you guys . . . you know . . . figured it out."

"We're working on that, but I don't think that will be enough. She needs some sleeping pills or something. I dunno—I'm not a doctor. That's why I am taking her to one."

I gauged how approachable he was by assessing his alcohol consumption, the same way I analyzed his mood based on musical choice. His curt response told me he hadn't yet drunk enough rye to calm his nerves—it was best to wait before I told him about our afternoon visitor.

"Isaac told me he isn't going to finish high school—that he wants to be a full-time musician. You know what that means?"

I shook my head. I genuinely didn't know.

"It means you're basically my only kid worth givin' a damn about 'cause you're the only one who's gonna amount to anything." Disappointment floated off every word, fuelling the fire we sat beside. I wondered what the fire looked like when he made it while he was happy—but I don't think he ever did.

"That's not true. How would you know? People make a living as musicians. People *you* listen to."

I thought about all the musicians he admired enough to play them for me. The rock 'n' roll gods I only knew because of him. If anything, Isaac's chosen vocation was largely because of Dad—not in spite of him. He'd taught us about the importance of music before we even knew to care. He'd shown us that Peter Frampton could make his guitar talk, that John Lennon could still matter outside of the Beatles, that "Smoke on the Water" was wildly overrated, and that it was okay to listen to James Taylor (as long as no one was within earshot). Mom loved music too, but Billy Joel's *Piano Man* and Fleetwood Mac's *Rumours* were eventually referred to as "secular albums" and replaced by Christian worship CDs. Sometimes I'd still hear her listening to Supertramp, though—I think they fall somewhere in between.

I could tell Dad's aversion to Isaac's decision was as much about Isaac as it was about himself. Were his lofty sneers hiding a hint of jealousy? Dad had taught Isaac to play the guitar, but Isaac had surpassed Dad's capabilities before he started high school. Dad would only sing in the concealing steam of his shower, but Isaac took to the stage the first chance he got. Maybe Isaac's guitar, microphone, and amp were sore reminders of the things Dad had traded in for a suit, shined shoes, and a briefcase.

"That's not real life, Ivy. *People* don't make a living doing it—you have about as much chance of winning the lottery. Isaac is going to be a high school dropout who can play the guitar—nothing more."

It had always been Mom cultivating our inner artists. She wanted for us what she'd never had. She wanted passion to guide our career paths. And Dad wanted our career paths to be guided by financial security—something he'd never had growing up either. I could see the importance of both, but I knew the real lottery was the one you'd win when you were paid to do what you love. *Couldn't we have it all? Or at least some?* I'd have to pick my college major in a few years. My science grades had already crushed my hopes of becoming a veterinarian (and after my fine work with Chelsea, I wasn't sure I could stomach the idea anymore anyway). But my passion for reading had pointed me toward a more obvious choice: becoming a detective. Or publishing detective books. I'm not sure what kind of money you make as a detective or a publisher, but at least I knew I'd enjoy it.

I tried to sympathize with Dad as I stared at a rogue white petal on the glowing cinder block at my feet, the only petal that had survived the massacre. *Good for you,* I thought. *You made it away with your life—not once, but twice!* Now that was bravery, true perseverance, and I had to admire Isaac and his bravery too.

"I'm sorry you feel that way, Dad, but Isaac's really talented, and you know it. Forgive me for saying it, but right now we have bigger fish to fry." We both knew I'd continue to push the limits with my attitude as he continued to pour himself premixed drinks from the pitcher next to him. Tonight my bravery came from knowing he'd likely forget this conversation in the morning.

"What could be more important than my only son's future?"

"Only son?" I repeated.

I'd meant to only think it, but it beguiled me—I'd never heard him refer to Isaac that way before. Of course, he was his only son, but there was something so disarming about the way he pointed it out. I hadn't thought about the unique bond a father and a son would share. Perhaps it made sense of the way they blamed one another for every bad quality they saw they had in common.

Isaac had pressures on him that I didn't; Dad never tried to persuade me to take advanced math or go into finance the way he did Isaac. Maybe it was those very pressures that were pushing Isaac toward a different way of living. You didn't have to commute an hour and a half to pick up a guitar, and I could see that being all the persuasion he needed.

"What about the future of *all* our lives? What about the fact that some man came to the door today and told me he just wanted Mom back *in one piece*? What about the future, or lack thereof, of this family? Aren't these things a bit more important than Isaac's decision to be the next James Hetfield?"

I threw in the Metallica bit in case Isaac was eavesdropping from his open bedroom window. After two days of self-sentenced solitary confinement, he surely needed a morale boost.

"Okay, calm down. There's no need to get carried away. I told you we're handling . . . it," he said. He was trying to calm me down while a hint of panic danced with his words. "What man came to the house today? Why didn't you tell me earlier?"

I was glad to finally hear some urgency in his voice. I and the flower petal shouldn't have had to be alone in our fight for our lives.

"I wanted to wait for the right time. He came by this afternoon. I recognized him. I think he's, like, Stan's right-hand man kind of thing."

I searched my brain for how I'd know that but came up with nothing.

"Okay, what did he look like?"

I searched my brain for those details too, hating that I'd fixated more on his clothing choices than his physical attributes.

One point for a career in publishing.

"Um, he was, like, a foot taller than me, I guess, and he was wearing a yellow button-front shirt and khaki pants." He glanced over at me, waiting for more—waiting for something useful. "And I think, um, light brown hair and brown eyes." I hoped he wouldn't detect my uncertainty; brown on brown sounded like a default choice.

"A foot taller... really? That would make him, what, six foot six?"

I laughed; defaulting to brown eyes and brown hair was the least of my problems.

"I meant to say half a foot."

He nodded. "You're probably right either way. It would have been Rob, Stan's right-hand man."

One point for detective.

The sun had set earlier, and from the corner of my eye, I could see fireflies glowing in the thick pines beside us. It was easy to mistake a runaway ember for a firefly, but I'd gotten good at distinguishing the different-coloured glows. The arrival of the fireflies usually meant school would start again in five or six weeks. Sometimes they came earlier if the summer had been a hot one. But if they came earlier, that meant there'd be no Indian summer, and I liked those better. Even if it meant the actual summer months weren't as hot, summer weather in the fall was still exciting—like a surprise birthday party you pretended not to know about.

"What's wrong?" I asked. *Other than everything.* I couldn't see his face, but his breathing sounded angry.

"Nothing. It's fine. I'm just surprised he came to the house, is all. What did you say to him?"

"He asked me to give Mom some flowers and to extend well wishes. Oh, and that he just wants her to come back *in one piece!*"

I repeated it *again*, and this time I emphasized each word as if English was my second language.

"Hon, that's just a saying. Don't read into everything so much." He was trying to make me feel like a bull's tit, and I didn't like it one bit. If anything, I was the glue holding this broken family together! *You should have some respect*, I thought—and *only* thought, because he wasn't quite drunk enough for me to make such a bold claim out loud.

"I know you care about us all and you want us to be okay. And I know I've made some mistakes, Ivy, but I'm doing everything I can to fix them. I promise you, I'll protect this family until the day I die—even after, if I can. I'll come back as a ghost, and you can just meet me on Ghost Road, and I'll protect you from there."

We laughed while he prodded the wood with a stretched-out coat hanger, and I pictured him as a ghost meeting me on Ghost Road in his ghost car.

"Grab the radio and put on Q107, will ya?" he asked. I quickly (and as always, obediently) got up and walked over to the shed, tripping on the front wheel of our wood-loading wheelbarrow. "It's on the shelf right inside the door—if you make it that far," he teased.

I turned the radio on, and it teased me too with the closing bars of "Ziggy Stardust." I hated knowing I'd just missed a great tune. Dad had taught me most of what I knew and loved about classic rock, but our mutual taste parted ways at David Bowie.

"Ivy, don't think I don't know what you're thinking."

About David Bowie?

"I'm glad I taught you and Isaac about music—I just didn't expect it to ruin your lives." He finished off his drink before going on. "I want you to know that everything I've ever done, I've done it for you guys. Sure, I would've loved a job in the music industry, but what kind of life would that have given you kids?"

"It's fine, honest! I love my life!"

"Well, you'll love it even more when I hit it big at the casino. We'll get an in-ground pool and a Porsche and a new puppy too!"

"That would be amazing, Dad."

He smiled and glanced over at the fence right around the spot where Chelsea had escaped. For a second I wanted to ask him if he ever thought about her, if his heart sank when he walked by the empty patio stones or the place in the laundry room where her bowls used to live. I wanted to know if he had nightmares about her, waking in a cold sweat as I did—but when his eyes bounced back to mine vacant, I knew the answer was no.

CHAPTER 20

Saturday, July 10th, 1999—Today is the greatest day

The Smashing Pumpkins are certainly not known for their uplifting music, but sometimes I like to start my day with the lyrics from "Today." I figure all I can do is ask the universe for a perfect day, and the worst it can say is no!

When Mom and Dad returned from her appointment, they seemed hopeful, as if one of the straws had been carefully placed back under the marbles in our game of Kerplunk, as though things were finally beginning to mend.

"Let's have lunch as a family," Mom yelled, hanging halfway out of the solarium door.

"Sure, Mom," Isaac agreed (for the both of us). He hurriedly pulled himself up the ladder, his neon swimming trunks gurgling as the water drained down his slender calves. "Ivy, let's dry off and see what happened at the doctor's."

I hadn't realized they were all on speaking terms again, but the heightened concern in his voice reflected their sudden reconciliation.

"She already seems better, doesn't she? She hasn't eaten with us in days!" Blood rushed to my (already sunburned) cheeks with a flash of heat. I hadn't noticed Mom was back outside setting the table. I felt embarrassed to be caught speaking about her as if she weren't there—as if she were the child, and I was the parent.

"I'm sorry, honey. I know I haven't been myself lately, but the doctor told me I'm going to be fine. The headaches are just stress related, and so is the insomnia. He gave me something that should have me back to normal in no time."

She folded the napkins for the cutlery, corner to corner like little paper tacos. Isaac looked at me with wide eyes and one eyebrow raised—he didn't know about the headaches either. How could we have had no idea the migraines were back? Were we that self-absorbed? I'd been so focused on alleviating the cause of the stress, I'd forgotten how important it was to also treat the symptoms. I thought of all the times Mom had nursed me back to health, through all the broken bones and careless injuries. She had a special soup and a special song, even for a case of the sniffles, and I hadn't brought her a single Advil! If I knew one thing for sure, it was that I wasn't parent material—not like she was, anyway.

Dad was puttering around in the kitchen, prepping food that was more complicated than the hot dogs and hamburgers we were used to. Our poolside feasts were normally low fuss and high satisfaction (kind of like our summers used to be).

"Chicken on a bun!" he said proudly as he emerged from the kitchen holding Nonna Perruzza's serving platter. "Mom's and Ivy's favourite!"

His excitement made Isaac and me smile big toothy smiles that for a split second almost made us look related. In the unflattering, direct midday light, I could see that his moustache was really starting to come in—another thing that made us look related (I'd have to make the joke before Dad did, to show him who's boss).

"I heard you playing in your room this morning, Isaac. It was lovely. You should leave your door open so I don't have to stand on the bed to hear you through the vent." Mom laughed, but everyone knew she was being serious. I pictured her in her white nightie, standing precariously on her tippy-toes, stumbling around on the mountain of decorative pillows. The image made me feel guilty . . . or maybe it was sad. Sometimes I had trouble telling them apart at first, the same way it's hard to tell if something's really hot or really cold the first moment you touch it.

The world seemed to pause, silent all around. It was as if even the birds had stopped flying to watch Dad's reaction to the mention of their son's rebellion through music. Their *only* son.

"Yeah, what were you playing? It sounded good," he said, casually putting the chicken on the hot grill of his pristine barbecue.

Wow, I thought, *this family is full of surprises!*

Isaac's big toothy smile made its second appearance inside of an hour—that had to break the record set back in '96 when we got our big trampoline.

"Thanks, guys!" he said, sounding less bewildered than I knew he was. "Just a little tune I wrote—just noodling around, really."

The cicadas sang their monotonous song, buzzing loudly in the trees, their volume matched only by the sizzling sounds of our cooking meal. The barbecue's propane fumes competed with the fresh smell of the cucumbers Mom cut up for our salad, and the sun's warmth blended seamlessly with the balmy breeze that blew south from the lake. I closed my eyes, listening, smelling, feeling, but most importantly, remembering to appreciate my surroundings. I promised God I'd not take *normalcy* for granted ever again.

"What are you doing, Ivy? Wake up and pass the mayo," Isaac ordered.

He'd ruined my moment, but I didn't care. I didn't open my eyes, not right away. First I had to tell everything around me one thing: "You've won," I whispered. "We've won."

The Marshalls were going to be just fine.

***

Ding-dong!

The jarring sound pulled me out of seventeenth-century Scotland and back into the nook in the front bay window. *Jeez Louise, that doorbell's really earning its keep lately.* Ensuing silence filled the air, a space once filled by Chelsea's uncontrollable barking. Now when the bell was pressed, the memory of her faded howls rang out in my ears—further proof of Pavlov's law. Mom had given us strict orders not to open the door after the flower incident, but I could see Robyn through the peephole. I opened the door.

"Hi," she said, squinting accusingly. "Where have you been lately?"

We were matching in our clothing (but not in attitude), both in linen shorts and a plain white tee. We were almost twins, if not for our polar-opposite hair. Her elegant chocolate locks draped distinctively down her shoulders, while my vanilla (perpetually tied-back) curls wouldn't be able to pick my shoulders out in a crowd.

"Nice outfit, stalker," I said, and she looked down and smiled. "And it's been, like, four days, so cut me some slack." Four days was a long time to not see Robyn, especially in the summer; her disapproval was warranted. "You know things have been weird at home. A guy came by the house the other day, and honestly, I get why my mom's been freaking out all summer. He said they just wanted her back in *one piece!*"

Her eyes softened to empathetic. "Was that some kind of warning or something?"

It was nice to talk to someone who knew their ass from a hole in the sky.

"I think so. But I'm not sure. I think Dad's taking care of it. He's known Mom's boss a long time too. I'm pretty sure they played college rugby together or something." I shrugged and moved aside, waiting for Robyn to come in the house. "Apparently, when he said he was meeting Doug, he was meeting Stan. *'Oh, what a tangled web we weave.'*"

"Like sand through an hourglass, these are the days of our lives," she giggled. She easily picked up what I was putting down, yet somehow continued to miss my invitation to come inside.

"Do you want to come in, or what?"

She looked down the street toward her house, then stepped back. "I think Cindy would prefer that we don't hang out here, or my house really—you know, with everything going on." She stepped back again, awaiting my reaction.

"*What?* Are you crazy? Why would you tell your mother?" I was incensed. Was it time for another contract signing? This time regarding confidentiality?

She sat down on the stone steps at the base of our porch, wrapping her arms around her curled-up legs, assuming the fetal position— more like the *sorry* position. "Iv, I didn't say a word! Honest. She's just been hearing things from the neighbours. Patty emailed Sharon's mom or something."

Sharon was an older girl we weren't really friends with (no one was). She lived near Sunrise Beach, and her mother was a lawyer.

"Great—just great!" I said.

The Marshalls were a hospitable but private bunch. Those we let into our home were welcomed with open arms, fresh swimming towels, cold beers for the men, iced tea for the girls. People knew who we were, but it wasn't as if we were revered, and we certainly weren't heading up any local committees either. Mom and Dad mostly kept to themselves, sharing little of our personal lives but never missing an obligatory road wave. Our clothesline didn't air our dirty laundry—it only air-dried our pool towels. That our hardships had made their way to the neighbour's gossipy grapevines infuriated me. I had to change the subject before my eyes exploded with angry tears, but Robyn beat me to it.

"How's Isaac taking it all?"

The subject change didn't change my urge to cry, but it did help me redirect my anger.

"He didn't finish high school, eh?" I said with unabashed candour, blatantly motivated by one thing. "Still like him? A high school dropout?" And for the first time, I took pleasure in his blunder.

She gave me the side-eye the way she did when we were playing Crazy Eights and she was pretending she didn't just pick up the queen of spades.

"So he's doing a victory lap, then?"

Big victory for her, I thought, annoyed she didn't even try to deny that she liked Isaac.

"No—he's just straight-up dropping out to pursue music like he's the next Steven Tyler or something." I hated Aerosmith, so that one was to hurt Isaac—should he be eavesdropping.

The empathy in her eyes now turned to adoration. "Good for him, I guess, following his dreams." She sighed. "Oh, and I don't *like*-like him. Gosh, Ivy, come on," she said, with about as much conviction as a hung jury.

"Whatever—I don't care," I lied. "Let's go see the Candy Lady, then, since we aren't allowed anywhere else." It was neutral ground and something we'd been neglecting all summer. She'd be thrilled to see us.

CHAPTER 21

July 2017—I . . . feel . . . weird?

I feel kind of weird about it. Realistically, I should feel weirder than I do, but I've never had a predilection for virtue. If I asked Isaac, he'd say it was okay, wouldn't he? He'd discarded the old notebook as if it were kindling—literally. He was going to use it to start a fire. I'd saved it, thinking there'd be some embarrassing poems, real blackmail-worthy stuff, ya know? But the pages are laced with gold, of course.

So yeah, when I was approached and asked if I had anything of Isaac's to sell, it came to mind. Print publishing isn't exactly a secure profession; I've been downsized twice in the last three years. The prospect of having a nest egg—hell, even a safety net—was enticing.

Honestly, it's still so hard for me to wrap my head around the fact that some poor schlep will pay money for a book of Isaac's unpublished and otherwise forgotten poems. Isaac! My Isaac? Really? I guess I'm just too close to him—I can't see the forest through the leaves.

I recognized a few lines from the poems scattered throughout his songs, but none of the songs that went platinum. Who knows, maybe Jason was only with me for the bragging rights.

It would be nice if someone paid me for *my* childhood gibberish. I guess mine would come in the form of some bad abstract paintings. Is there a market for those? Probably not. I could try to sell my journals, maybe. I can just see the headline now:

SAD AND DESPERATE SISTER OF ISAAC MARSHALL
TRIES TO SELL HER OWN POSSESSIONS, FINDS OUT
THEY'RE WORTHLESS

Isaac started writing his thoughts into lined Hilroy notebooks years before Mom encouraged me to find some kind of creative hobby (so he was better because he had more practice, right?). He needed no encouragement—it was second nature to him. He never locked the books up like a deranged squirrel hiding nuts in the tree house—the family just knew to leave well enough alone. After Dad left, Isaac brought a bunch of them out to the firepit to burn, and that's when I stole one. I remember the big chunks of paper floating up above the fire; the ash would keep burning in the air before it turned grey and lifeless. It reminded me of a firefly or the moments before a shooting star fades and disappears.

The pages are worn now, not from age, but from use. I've read the notebook more times than I can count. If I had to count, I'd probably say at least twice a week for eighteen years. How much is that? I'm in publishing—I'm not a mathematician.

I've tried writing it all out onto new paper, but the words don't sound the same in my head—I can't hear Isaac's voice anymore. I can't picture him writing, crouched over his desk, or stoned, sitting on a milk crate. I can't see him sharing it with his bandmates, seeking validation in his work. I can't hear him humming new melodies alongside the words or ripping the pages out in frustration. I stood to gain a few thousand bucks from the sale, but without the stained and wrinkled pages, the words might as well have been written in a language I didn't understand. Maybe that's what people mean when they say they've sold their souls. They've sold something that means everything to them, and in doing so, lost everything. Is their blood money really worth all they've lost? I'm sure the richest people in the world would say yes.

We come and we go
We are loved and loathed
We are bought and sold
Disappointment won't show
Because you sold your soul
In fear of getting old

That was from the first Post Thrills album, and it's one of my favourite songs of theirs, although horribly overplayed. My favourite *poem* of Isaac's is near the end of the book I took, and it's my own little secret. You can see the writing grow more sombre as the pages turn. This page was rippled when I got it; so were the pages that followed. Maybe from a spill, maybe from spilled tears—the true source I'll never know. Even though the words from this poem never made it into any of his songs, the feeling I get when I read it—that feeling is in all of them.

"Die Young"

You always said you'd die young
You'd live your life, you'd have your fun
There'd be no way to fence in the ocean
Drugs and sadness—your killing potion
And the only thing that you'd refuse
Were chances and help and a worthy muse
You'd swear you loved her, your baby girl
You'd kiss her head, her every curl
But wherever you went, wherever you turned
The sadness it followed, it cut, it burned
Hidden deep behind blue eyes
Forced to believe your own damning lies
We never stopped believing no matter how hard
she fought
We'll never start believing you'd end it all with one shot

141

I think it's about Kurt Cobain, but I've never been sure. Isaac's writing was moving even back then—he was before his time. Now you can say the same about his songs. They're moving to me and (strange to think) hundreds and thousands of other people too. It's not as though the Marshalls invented those emotions, but I still feel as though almost every song was written about or for us. I can hear it. If not in the lyrics, then in the bassline—if not the bassline, then in the violin. I hear Mom. I hear Henry. And no matter how hard I try not to, I hear *that* summer.

CHAPTER 22

Tuesday, July 13th, 1999—Everyone just leave us alone!

Three nights with those sleeping pills, and no one's sure if Mom's feeling better or worse. I don't think she'd even be able to tell you. I told Dad it's not about the sleep—it's about the danger we're in, and no pill is going to fix that. He said he's looking for a second job, and as soon as he finds one, Mom can quit. I think he's just saying he's job-hunting to excuse the fact that he hasn't been home for dinner for the last three nights. I continue to feel a distance, expanding and sometimes contracting, on and off, depending on Dad's mood. Things are volatile again (understatement), despite the spark of hope that pulled up a chair and had lunch with us on Saturday.

Mom was turning out to be quite a popular woman for someone who (I thought) didn't keep many friends beyond Nancy, Doug's wife. When the doorbell rang for the thousandth time this month, I hoped to see Aunt Sam staring back at me through the peephole, holding her slumber bag and her famous double-fudge cake. Instead, it was two women from church, both in their Sunday best (even though it was

Tuesday). I suppose house calls called for pastel dresses, kitten heels, and curled hair.

I tiptoed backwards from the door, closing my eyes, hoping the churchgoers couldn't hear me avoiding them.

"I see you in there, honey. It's just Marilyn and Liz from Living Light. We want to say hi to Patty!"

I knew who they were, and I knew what they wanted (neither detail compelled me to open the door).

Ding-dong!

That brat Marilyn rang it again! If Mom had been sleeping, she certainly wouldn't be for long. I opened the door begrudgingly. The inward gust of wind managed to change my scowl to a welcoming smile—as if I was opening the door with a new personality.

"Hi, ladies. What can I do for you on this fine, sunny afternoon?" I didn't recognize myself among the trite pleasantries.

"Oh Ivy! Hi, dear! Where's Patty? We've come to say hello, see how she's doing."

"She's not here right now, actually. Out and about, you know." I smiled.

It was hard to ignore the change in Marilyn's body language as I spoke, her chubby arms folded on her chest, head cocked slightly to the side. *Too bad, so sad—no Patty for you today, ladies,* I thought. I continued fake-smiling as I slowly closed the door.

"Well, her van's still here, dear," Marilyn said, pushing the door open with one finger, impervious to the weight. "The garage door is open!" She must be the brawn in the operation, and I guess Liz could qualify as the beauty.

Right, garage open. Okay, I hadn't thought it through. Why wasn't lying as easy for me as it was for Dad? Sweating through my sundress, I formulated what I hoped was an intelligent response. "Yeah, well, she walked!"

"She walked where, dear? To town? That's four hours at least."

Damn, who were these women? The Patty police? I was out of

ideas and moments away from resorting to name-calling when I heard
Mom walking up behind me. She gently cupped my elbow and put
her other hand on the small of my back, as if to tell me everything was
all right.

"Sorry, ladies. I told Ivy I was going for a walk earlier. She must not
have heard me come back! Come in, come in." Lying seemed effortless
for her too, even though her energy reserve was being fuelled only by
tea and baby cookies.

She ushered them in and promptly locked the door behind them,
motioning to them to go into the living room. I nodded a few times
and walked backwards out of the foyer, hands folded behind my back,
looking like an idiot (and probably a bit like a baby seal). It was my
turn to eavesdrop from the stairs as the gaggle of ladies cross-exam-
ined my mother. Their intentions were good, but I couldn't fight my
intense desire to protect her. Even the houseplant on the landing was
starting to look like a threat.

"Patty, honey, are you not well? When we didn't see you at worship
practice, we tried calling, but we couldn't get through." It was the first
time Liz spoke; she was quiet, reserved, and sweet.

Mom cleared the phlegm from her throat; obviously she hadn't
been doing much singing lately. "Things haven't been good, no. It
started with some trouble at work—bad stuff—and now . . ." Her
mumbling was too difficult to hear from my balcony seating.

"It's okay, love. Come here."

I heard Marilyn move closer.

"Where are your tissues?"

"Under the table there." Mom's voice was breaking. I couldn't see
her, but I could hear the tears rolling down her face like thunder
without lightning. I was surprised by her honesty, by her willingness
to share with these women. Crying was a *behind-closed-doors* kind of
activity, something I'd learned by observing both parents at funerals.
I could count on one hand the number of times I'd seen Mom cry in
front of Dad.

"What can we do to help? We'll send Brad over with some meals, for starters."

"Oh, it's fine, it's fine. I'll be quitting my job this week, and I'm praying the stuff with Henry just . . . works itself out."

There was silence—I hoped it was because they were nodding their giant hairspray-burdened heads.

"Some days I just feel like the devil is wrapping his claws around me, pulling me down to the pits of hell. I should have come to church on Sunday. I just wasn't feeling well. The stress is hard on my body."

Silence again, hopefully nodding.

"He'll protect you, Patty. Just trust Him—He's hearing your prayers."

"Thank you, Liz. I really needed to hear that today. Thank you guys for coming by."

The conversation ended so abruptly, I didn't have time to run back up the stairs and out of sight. In fifteen seconds flat, they rounded the corner of the living room and saw me patiently waiting on the steps like a child caught awake past bedtime.

"Walk us out, will you, Ivy? Your mother should go get some rest."

It was more of an order than a request—the adults in my life were full of those. "Sure," I said, stretching my arms and rubbing my eyes. I opened my mouth wide and gave my best fake yawn as though I'd just woken up from a peaceful catnap . . . on the stairs.

Outside, Marilyn steered me away from the house, one hand on my back and the other firmly gripping my elbow (as if to say everything was *not* all right).

"Where are your mother's keys?" she asked with hushed urgency.

I shrugged, thinking, *How should I know?*

"I want you to find them and hide them, okay? She shouldn't be behind the wheel in that state."

Liz nodded in agreement. Confirmed: this was a noddy bunch.

"And tell your father the congregation's here to help in any way possible. We're just a phone call away. Your mother has the number.

Your family is in our prayers, sweetie." Liz leaned in and hugged me gently with her lower body at least a foot and a half away from mine, the way you do when you're not quite sure if you have permission to touch someone.

"Thank you both. I really appreciate your concern," I said as they got into Marilyn's car. And I meant it, I genuinely meant it. Maybe when I'd opened the door to them, the welcoming smile wasn't a fraud—I just hadn't realized its authenticity yet.

The silver sedan backed steadily down our driveway as Liz reached over and tapped the horn to say one last goodbye. I listened to the crackling pop of the gravel—sounds I knew so well. It was the same crackling pop that marked Dad's arrival home from work each day, but for some reason, it sounded different. Higher in pitch (or happier) somehow.

***

The phone was ringing, which could only mean one of two things: Mom felt safe again, or Dad really was job-hunting. Both options were promising. By the time I got the headset to my ear, a conversation was already under way. The detective in my blood stopped me from hanging up right away before hearing who it was—the first phone call in weeks was (kind of) a big deal. It was Dad, and I knew Doug's accent immediately; he was the only Texan I'd ever met.

"Yeah, I left it plugged in and waited for you to call me back. I don't want to talk about stuff on work email anymore," said Dad.

I pressed the mute button and curled back up in the reading nook; if things were getting juicy, I wanted to be comfortable and ready to reassume my prime (fake-napping) position.

"Okay . . . well, how are ya? Why weren't you at work today?" asked Doug, more as if it were a transaction than a genuine concern.

"Booked it off. Had other things to take care of," Dad snapped, as though he thought Doug's questions were transacted in accusation.

And why shouldn't they be? Dad hadn't even told us about his so-called day off, and he'd certainly made himself scarce while the cheer committee rolled in. *Thanks for the help, Papa Henry.*

Doug let out a long sigh—no, a breath. He was smoking. "Henry, you better know what you're doing. I can't cover for you forever. I got my own family to think about."

"I know, and you know I appreciate it. It's a mess. I got Patty here thinking I'm Bill Clinton, and she's not sleeping much. Stan's been asking about her. Sent Rob over to the house on Friday, and I didn't appreciate it one bit. My poor kids ... they don't know what to think." Silence came from the other end of the receiver. *Do people nod while they're on the phone too?* "I'm just trying to deal with one mess at a time."

He wasn't asking for anything, but every word was pleading.

"Jesus, Henry—why didn't you tell me things were gettin' so bad for y'all?" There was a pause, then a clicking sound that took me a second to place. Either Dad was lighting a candle or Doug was having another cigarette. "Just tell me next time you're gonna be away. Ashley was rummagin' around in your desk lookin' for the Clark file, and I didn't know what to tell her."

Ashley was Dad's assistant. She was like Chelsea in human form—overweight and underintelligent. The mention of her name didn't affect me, but I wasn't sure what I'd do if Holly came up.

"Ugh, that moron! I told her I was leaving the Clark file and all the other working files in a pile on her desk!"

"Quit fightin' it, Henry. Move to computer filin'. That's what it's here for—so this kind of thing doesn't happen."

The quip made the conversation less heavy but not light.

"I'll be back in tomorrow. Patty's gonna quit. Don't tell Nancy just yet. I'm figuring out the money stuff—just trust me and keep covering for me if you can." Again he was pleading, and it was hard for me to hear him like that. It was as if the pride I'd normally hear in his voice wasn't audible over the telephone.

They hung up without saying goodbye as people do in the movies.

I put the phone under a pillow to press the *off* button (this wasn't my first rodeo). I closed my eyes and resumed my fake-napping position, making a mental note to think of other ways to look inconspicuous. Dad sat still for a while before running upstairs to what was now being referred to as "Mom's bedroom." It gave me time to digest everything I'd heard. I needed to decode the conversation; so much of it was confusing. Why did Mom think Dad was the president of the United States? Why did Dad care so much about Rob coming over? What was Doug covering? Why was Ashley such a dummy? So many unanswered questions, so much to think about, but I could feel my second pretend nap of the day turning into a real one.

CHAPTER 23

Friday, July 16th, 1999—6 days until my birthday

I couldn't bring myself to look at Dad after his conversation with Doug. The way he sounded, imploring Doug to support him in whatever was going on. It was as if he had the weight of the world on his shoulders and his knees were about to buckle. I'd take pride and arrogance over humility and vulnerability any day.

"Try bringing a slice up to your mother, Ivy," Dad said, defeat still lingering on the tail of every word. We all knew tonight would mark the third missed game night in a row, but no one cared.

"Why me? She doesn't answer the door when I knock."

"Yesterday she told me she only wanted to see you from now on. Just open it and go in. She'll be happy to see you, I promise."

He smiled and looked down at his drink, his trusty companion. He'd had a rye and ginger beside him at all times since the phone call. If I were Doug, I'd be worried that he'd found a new best friend.

"Okay, Dad," I sighed, accidentally spitting a piece of pepperoni back onto my plate.

I quickly surveyed the area, not wanting to draw any attention to the spit-up. Both Isaac and Dad saw, but neither poked fun at me.

What was this strange world I'd found myself in? Not even one joke about my disgusting eating habits? I had to look outside to see what colour the sky was here. I tried again. "She's not going to eat it, but if you insist. I'll bring her tea too!"

Success! All my food remained securely in my cheeks.

"Good girl. You're a good daughter."

Good girl? This disarmed me the same way his comment about Isaac being his *only* son had. He hadn't called me a good girl in years, and I hated myself for being so hard-hearted, for seeing his softness as weakness. But as with Isaac's affinity for music, Dad was the one who'd taught us that way of thinking.

When I was four, I broke my leg. I was young enough that the wound healed quickly and without complication, but the break caused a different kind of wound, a deeper kind with a scar that wasn't visible. We'd been skating on Lake Scugog, wobbling around on the uneven ice, and Isaac had fallen a handful of times. But he already knew the rules: no crying unless you were a wuss. I fell once, and the waterworks began. I cried loudly, begging Dad to take the skates off, but he told me I was drawing too much attention to us—that I should be like Isaac and keep skating, that big girls didn't cry. When the crying wouldn't stop, he reluctantly took me to the hospital, where we found out I had a broken tibia, a spiral break, and I had to have a cast all the way up my leg to my hip. We don't talk about the way he was that day or the way he's always been. I've grown to appreciate the hard lessons he's taught me. He may have raised us as if he had two sons, but I was better because of it. Anything Isaac could do, I could do too. If he had to load wood from the shed to the garage, so would I. If he had to mow the lawn, I'd clear the brush. If he shovelled the snow, I'd laugh from the front window (it's a man's world, after all).

Dad broke the silence before it became the fourth person in the room with us.

"You can take my car—I don't care," he said as if relenting to something, but I wasn't sure what.

"Really?" Isaac said.

Dad kept his mouth closed as he chewed. "Mhmmm," he said, then swallowed. He'd been taught proper table etiquette—his elbows always remained politely at his side, his food politely in his mouth. "It would be too hard for you to take a bus all the way to Wasaga with your guitar, and we can't find your mom's keys."

(Oops.)

I'd forgotten about Isaac's first away-gig in Wasaga. He'd mentioned it at the beginning of the summer, but he knew better than to bring it up again—he was treading lightly. It was hard not to be jealous when the high school dropout was rewarded with a weekend getaway while I and my straight-B report card would be left here watching *Jeopardy!* reruns with Dad.

"Well, thanks, Dad. I really appreciate it," Isaac replied.

I finished my pizza and grabbed two slices for Mom, placing them on my used plate (to avoid making more dishes).

"Ew!" Isaac yelped, putting his hand up in my face. "Don't do that—you basically threw up on that plate!"

Everyone laughed, and when I looked up through the dirty, slanted glass of the solarium, the sky was blue. Greyish and kind of dark, but blue nonetheless.

***

I turned the knob slowly, thankful the lock mechanism had been removed because Mom had stopped obeying the no-locks-at-night rule (in case of a house fire). She was lying disconcertingly still on the bed, her feeble hands folded together on her chest. She looked sound asleep—only her eyes were wide open.

The room smelled musty and stale; the window hadn't been opened in days. It felt as if I could see the air and I was cutting through it as I walked. Nothing had moved since the last time I'd come in. The food was still on the plates that scattered her dusty dresser, the laundry bin still overflowed, and her nightstand was still overwhelmingly clut-tered. I counted four half-empty glasses of water, two Bibles, a note-book, three pencils, Nonna Perruzza's mirror, her makeup bag, and an orange bottle of prescription sleeping pills (that I was beginning to believe were placebos).

"Hi, Mom." I approached with hesitation.

Was she sleeping with her eyes open? I'd seen Chelsea do it before, but dogs had three eyelids. My heart hurt for a second when I thought about Chels, but not as much as it hurt for Dad on the phone or Mom lying broken in front of me.

She didn't reply. I guess humans could sleep with their eyes open too. *Good to know*, I thought as I started to moonwalk out of her room, desperately trying to ignore my inclination to tidy up. I put the pizza on the ground in the hall and went back in. I just had to clean a bit. I wasn't sure I'd be able to sleep if I didn't, and she'd do the same for me—in a heartbeat.

Gathering the plates, I was horrified by the rotting food, not only by its smell and the recently opened fly hotel, but because it was proof she hadn't eaten anything since our barbecue on Saturday.

"I've had such a terrible headache, honey, for days now. It must be another migraine."

She startled us (me and the flies).

"Well, Mom, what do you expect? You're not eating. You're not sleeping. Why aren't the pills helping?"

She rolled to her side, facing her nightstand, away from me. The back of her head was matted with curls that hadn't been washed or combed in days. I could see her reflection in the mirror, but today her eyes looked nothing like mine. They were blackened and glazed like the glass eyes of a porcelain doll.

"I don't trust them. They make my stomach feel sick. If I could just get this headache to go away, I'd be fine."

It wasn't just her eyes that looked different; her voice wasn't her own either. The tone was strange. Breathy. Hollow. She'd mentioned wanting to be less recognizable when she went out to dinner with Dad last week, but she'd taken it too far—I wanted my mom back.

"Dad said you can quit soon! Does that make you feel better about everything?"

She shrugged.

"And the church ladies came by. That was nice, right? They're praying for you. And Dad's been around a lot more lately. That's a good sign too, right?" I lied.

I hoped that every shred of positivity I could share would uncover a piece of her I could recognize. Maybe a little part of her was still left in her smile. But I wouldn't know, since nothing I said brought her any joy.

"I know you don't understand, Ivy, but it's hard to trust anything anyone says, especially your father. I haven't shared with you what's going on between us. But if you knew. . ."

I did know. Well, I knew what she thought she knew—what she'd told Isaac—but no one had confirmed it.

I sat nervously at the very foot of the bed, not wanting to take up too much space and give her a reason to ask me to leave. I'd gotten used to the smell in the room, but I hadn't gotten used to looking at the woman who was lying on my mom's side of the bed.

"How many days haven't you slept now, Mom?"

She turned and looked straight at me. The eye contact startled me almost as much as her speaking when I thought she was asleep.

"Why? Did your father ask you to ask me that? I told him I didn't want him back in here. I'm sick of the interrogations. I'm not telling him anything, and I'm fine. I sleep . . . on and off."

She was out of breath by the end of her claim; speaking with such persuasiveness was arduous for her. She dropped her heavy head down onto her pillow as if the weight of the world had left Dad's shoulders to rest on hers. Our conversation had exhausted her. Maybe now she'd finally sleep.

"Mom, just focus on getting some rest. Everything that's stressing you out will blow over—I promise. In a few weeks, you'll look back, and it'll be like none of this ever happened."

I left the room feeling better—and painfully unaware of how much truth would be found in those words.

PART TWO

157

CHAPTER 24

Saturday, July 17th, 1999

1:45 a.m.

There was no pulse. I checked ten times—I knew I was doing it right. The jugular, the wrist, it didn't matter . . . there was nothing.

CHAPTER 25

Friday, July 16th, 1999

7:02 p.m.

Isaac packed his bag and boogied out of the house like a bat outta hell, leaving me alone to do all the dishes. The uneaten food I'd brought down from Mom's room triggered Dad, not only because he hates waste, but also because it crushed his plans to pretend everything's still okay.

"Unacceptable—completely unacceptable," Dad said. "She's somehow gathered the strength to move the desk up against the door."

He stomped through the kitchen to the dining room (bar). His steps grew louder and heavier, keeping a rhythm that was beginning to sound like the bassline of "Moby Dick"—the Led Zeppelin song, not the whale. He'd given me the oh-so-endearing nickname Fairy Flat Feet, though today it seemed to fit him better.

"Are you sure? How could she move a desk on her own? When I was up there, she could barely lift her head."

"Of course I'm sure. What can I say? She's strong when she wants to be."

He wasn't using the tiny cup he normally used to measure his liquor, so I tried not to notice how much he filled his glass (as Mom did). I tried not to keep track of how many he'd had too (as Mom did), but I'd unintentionally counted (as Mom did). Five drinks so far.

Isaac had picked a perfect time to vacate the premises. It was getting weird at the Marshall residence, and I wasn't exactly sure what role I was meant to play in all the chaos.

"What should I do? How can I help? I'll do anything I can." My offer was as empty as it was useless.

"Honestly, hon, right now there isn't much you can do. I think it would be best if you just went out for the night. Would Cindy mind if you stayed there?"

"No, of course not," I lied. It was getting easier to lie every time I did it, but I guess you could say that about anything that challenged your integrity (maybe next time I stole a five-cent candy from the corner store, I wouldn't cry the whole way home).

I turned on the kettle and took out Mom's favourite mug, the one with *Footprints in the Sand* on the side—I wasn't giving up on her so easily.

"You're a good kid, you know that?" he said again.

He stood beside me as I leaned on the kitchen counter, waiting for the water to boil as though the impending hiss was a countdown to my freedom. His left hand gripped his drink tightly while his right hand rested lightly on my head. Although his touch was gentle, and his hand not much bigger than my own, it felt unexpectedly strong, as if at any moment he could crush me to the ground like a pop can. It was the second time in one night he'd told me I was good. Two times in one night—now *that* was a first. His words may have been slightly slurred, and hell, he probably didn't even remember saying them the first time, but there was a sincerity in his voice I wasn't going to tarnish with analytics.

I smiled and grabbed the mug. "You're a good Dad, ya know that?"

He smiled back and took a big, long sip of his rye and (no) ginger.

7:36 p.m.

Tonight probably would have been my first-ever *Jeopardy!* victory against Dad, but he'd gotten one thing right—Mom's door was barricaded with their solid walnut desk. I didn't always choose to see the glass as half full (especially if it was filled with rye), but in my books, her having enough strength to move a desk on her own was a good thing.

"Mom, come here. I have a cup of tea for you," I said in my loudest whisper. I waited a few seconds before pushing the door open a crack to look inside. Dishevelled, she appeared suddenly, as though she had been standing silently beside the desk the whole time.

"Where's Isaac?"

"He's in Wasaga for that big gig."

"Oh good. Where's Henry?"

"He's downstairs."

"You should go out—you shouldn't be here," she said as her eyes darted up and down and all around me. She was making me feel as if I were three raccoons standing on each other's shoulders dressed up in a trench coat.

"Yeah, I'm going to Robyn's. I know when I'm not wanted."

She closed the door without saying anything else. I stood listening, expecting to hear her move the desk to let me in or at least take the tea from my hands. Instead, I heard her go into the bathroom and slam the door.

"Goodnight to you too!" I yelled.

I left the rejected tea on the floor with the rejected pizza and walked dejectedly down the hall to my room. The heavily garnished showcase wall felt counterfeit as it shamelessly boasted our family's accolades and accomplishments. The framed report cards, poems, certificates, my painting—none of them were fraudulent in themselves. But the happy "togetherness" they projected—that was what felt fake.

I tore my painting off the wall and threw it at the linen-closet door, watching with satisfaction as it fell, the glass shattering into pieces. The Pretty Place had done nothing for me lately except offer false hope—hope that going there would make some kind of a difference. All the bad things were blurring together, one into the other, which made it hard to know where one of my three bad things ended and the others began. I wanted to trace back to the beginning, to pinpoint exactly when everything started to go wrong. But the last few weeks had felt like a tangled web of never-ending shit, and my disorganized thoughts were beginning to make me feel just as I'd felt when I looked at Mom's nightstand ... nervous.

***

8:42 p.m.

"Let's go out, then," I pleaded with Robyn. I hated the desperation in my voice as much as I hated it in Dad's; pleading was becoming our family's go-to tactic.

"Okay, okay," she said, pulling her housecoat closed around her. It had been raining on and off all night, the air was cool and damp, and she wasn't prepared for a late-night front porch rendezvous. "I'll ask Sadie if we can go for a drive or something. Just stay out here."

I didn't have to be upstairs in the hall with the pizza to feel rejected—it was following me everywhere I went. The trouble we were in was making me a pariah with my street friends the same way being held back a year had with my classmates. I wished Mom hadn't emailed Sharon's mom or had at least paid her so that confidentiality was assured; I'd remind her to involve Dad next time she was feeling litigious.

"She said we can go to Ghost Road if you want," said Robyn,

emerging from the side of the house (more discreet than from the front door). "She's just gotta get ready."

I nodded.

"Is everything okay at home? Do you feel safe?"

I nodded again. I didn't know how I felt or if everything was okay at home, and I didn't know how to communicate that—I just knew I needed to get away for a few hours. I sat cross-legged on Robyn's front lawn, elbows resting on my knees, clammy hands holding up my unwieldy head. Tufts of brown grass stuck to the inside of my thighs, and the newly cut blades prickled the ticklish spot behind my knees. It had been so long since Dad had mowed our lawn that the smell of freshly cut grass had become foreign to me. It wasn't just what took place between the four walls of our home anymore; the dysfunction we felt had started to over-flow into the open. It angered me to think about how much of our lives we unintentionally shared through the panes of our neighbour's window. Mom's side of the garage constantly ajar but always occupied. Dad's early departures and late returns. The missing doghouse and non-existent barks. The unkempt yard and overgrown ditch. The greening pool and vacant clothesline. All of these things, innocuous by themselves, together told the external piece of a crumbling interior.

Robyn sat down beside me, our bare legs close enough to share body heat. I'd thought shorts and a sweatshirt would be warm enough for mid-July, but a chill was radiating through the deepest parts of my insides. I couldn't tell if it was the dampness in the air or the water on my face, but I was beginning to feel engulfed, everything around us moving toward me. The trees and the houses were leaning in on me while the ground beneath me leaned away. I was sinking from the weight of a world that had finally come to crush me too.

Robyn reached over and grabbed my hand, "It's going to be okay, Ivy, I promise."

I held on to her tightly, knowing that at any moment the earth could collapse from under me and her grasp would be the only thing keeping me alive.

CHAPTER 26

Friday, July 16th, 1999

11:26 p.m.

Sadie kept her lights off and dropped me off at the end of my drive-way; Ghost Road had been a bust. I couldn't go home yet, so I walked across the street to the empty lot.

Since we'd moved in, the lot had been vacant, waiting longingly for a lavish home all its own. I daydreamed about what might become of the lot; I hoped for a new neighbour, a cute boy, or a celebrity who'd build their summer home on it. Whenever I'd wonder out loud, Dad would tell me not to jinx it. If a house was built there, we'd lose our direct view of the lake, and to him, being able to see the water was as good as living on it. Isaac and his friends were doing their part to ensure its vacancy by hosting "small gatherings," and they were getting sloppy. The open space was decorated with an array of discarded party items, bottles, and cigarette packs.

I took my sandals off and walked along the polluted shoreline. At the base of the dock was a limp, yellowing sign that warned, Use Dock At Own Risk—as if using a dock, especially in the shallow, muddy waters of Lake Scugog, was somehow perilous. It was a man-made lake, and like our Viceroy home, something you'd make with open space and a whole lot of gumption. The lake would've taken years and years of hard work, shovelling, and excavating, playing the role of Mother Nature. But if Mother Nature had wanted a *real* lake to exist around a *real* island, she'd have made it herself. She really was a force to be reckoned with, wasn't she? So much of the dug-out earth has fallen back into the lake now; only half of its depth is left for water. She's merciless—sometimes I think I can feel the Island sinking back into the mud too.

It wasn't raining anymore, but the air felt as if it was goading the rain, daring it to come back down. I'd learned about pathetic fallacy last year in English class, so I knew that if this day had been fictitious, I'd be breathing a sigh of relief because relief from rain would mean relief from sorrows. The earth was no longer crying, so I didn't need to cry either. The sun would rise high in the sky tomorrow and our family would be saved! But right now the sky was cloudy, murky like the lake, and only a few devoted stars made their way through the clouds. *Thank you*, I thought as I found the Big Dipper despite the obstacle. Dad had taught us about every constellation and how to find one by finding another like a treasure map, one clue leading to the next. Light pollution on the Island didn't exist; he said that was the reason we'd left the city. "If you can't see the stars above you, what's the point of living?" he'd asked Isaac and me, at the ripe ages of ten and seven. Neither of us had a good answer back then, and even today mine would be nonsense, but something told me Isaac would know exactly what to say.

I knew I couldn't stay on the dock all night, no matter how much I wanted to let the waves rock me to sleep. I'd wanted to wait until every-one was asleep before I went home, but the light in Mom's room was still on and I couldn't wait any longer. I started my walk back toward the house, and in that instant—as though she'd heard me—the light turned off and the entire house was left in complete darkness. From across the street, it almost looked abandoned again, the way Dad had found it before he made it into the beautiful home it was now. Strange how the absence of light can so easily mimic the absence of life.

***

11:58 p.m.

Practising my stealth moves, I crept into the family room without putting on a light or making a sound. Dad's current "bed" was still folded up and piled neatly on the armrest of the couch, the same as it was that morning. I opened the brown curtains that hid the sliding glass door (I'd broken), and a cloud of dust wafted into my face with such force, it felt like I was walking through a cobweb.

Acchoooo!

I'd plugged my nose, but it was too late; I'd blown my cover before I could investigate Dad's whereabouts any further. Exposed and teary-eyed, I searched the backyard for signs of a fire that I knew would be built entirely out of whisky and misery. The shed light was on, but other than that, the backyard was as dark and nebulous as the front.

If Dad wasn't on the couch and he wasn't by the fire, I hoped it meant the upstairs ban had been lifted and he was finally allowed to sleep beside his wife, in a bed not intended for sitting. I followed the invisible footprints up the stairs, the ones that marked the spots that didn't creak.

The pizza and tea I'd left were still sitting all alone in the hall, crying quietly as I passed. My eyes and my ears were playing tricks on me again, and there wasn't any wind or animal to blame—only darkness. I turned on the hallway light and my reality materialized around me; I hadn't been hearing things—I'd just been wrong about who the tears belonged to. Mom was crying somewhere inside her room. The door was open just enough to see that the desk had been pushed away but not put back into place—as though she wasn't yet sure the threat had cleared and was expecting it might return.

There weren't two voices coming from the room. I listened closely, waiting to hear Dad's consoling murmurs alongside her sobs, but her sobbing was only getting louder, stronger. She was distressed and alone; like oil and water, they didn't go well together.

I let myself in, following the sound of Mom's cries as if they were a little trail of painted rocks—they were working cries. They led me into the bathroom, where she was sitting in their four-seater Jacuzzi. There was no water in it, but she sat there crying as though her tears would eventually fill it up. A bathtub was a safe place during a tornado, but beyond that I wasn't sure what kind of solace it was offering her. The bathroom was in worse shape than the bedroom had been earlier. The garbage can beside the toilet was filled with items that should have been on the counter, while the floor was littered with things that should have been in the bin. If I'd thought the nightstand was unbearably crowded and the food plates unimaginably putrid, I'd have to invent a new adjective to describe the filth that surrounded her.

"Mom, what are you doing in there?" I tried to strip my voice of a reprimanding tone.

Her head turned toward me slowly, revealing her blackened eyes, still empty and glossy like eyes on a china doll. My heart moved up, pounding in my throat, and for a split second I was worried she'd be doing the reprimanding.

"It isn't safe. It isn't safe."

She pronounced each word deliberately as though each was a full sentence, and in hushed tones because the danger was right outside the door. Her voice had taken on an eerie quality that made me feel awkward and uncomfortable; it was like having a conversation with a stranger.

"Why? What happened? Where's Dad?" I moved closer, offering her my hand to get her out. She looked toward the door and then right through me as if I were a ghost. She started to respond, but the answers weren't directed at me; she was having a conversation with a stranger too. She sat unnaturally still, only moving to look up at the ceiling, then back (through me) to the door. Her words were jumbled, hardly audible, and at times she was speaking in broken Italian (the way she and Nonna used to when they argued in front of us).

I moved closer, reaching into the tub to hold her hand in mine, hoping the contact would affirm my presence. Her hand remained limp and lifeless—it wasn't just her eyes taking on doll-like qualities. I had to look in the mirror behind me to make sure I wasn't invisible.

"Mom?" I said again. The pleading had returned to my voice.

Closer to her face now, I began to understand her more clearly. She was talking to God, or an angel, or at least someone *up there*. The destination offered me some comfort, but the strange little voice in which she delivered the message gave me goosebumps. Not in a good way as Aretha Franklin did, but in a bad way—like hearing a growl, but not yet seeing the creature it's come out of.

"Please protect them. Please protect them, please. Forgive him, God," she whispered over and over again. Her prayer had turned into a chant—resounding and repetitive but still ambiguous. *Forgive Dad for what?* I hopped over the edge of the tub and sat across from her, taking in all that was left of her. Her whole body, her frame, her foundation—a shell of who I used to know—looked broken in the white nightie with stained brown cuffs and yellowed armpits. She'd been wearing it for days. Side by side, her feet were longer, her hips were wider, and her head sat up taller than mine, but the woman across from me looked like a little girl, slight and unintimidating in her dirty pyjamas.

"Let's get you showered and changed," I said as I moved in closer to her, bracing myself for more rejection. Instead, she ignored the suggestion, continuing to give no indication she knew I existed. She turned her head toward the window and began chanting again, this time more feverishly, tears streaming down her face.

"Please, God, keep them safe, God, protect them." Sobbing, she let tears fall into her lap, her arms wrapped tightly around herself as she rocked her concave shoulders away from the tub, then back. Away, then back. A belt of light skin at the base of her ring finger drew unwanted attention to the absence of her wedding band. The finger was exposed, and the pale skin underneath looked delicate and supple, telling of nineteen years of ceaseless protection. It was troubling to see her for the first time without it, but the band of white on her hand concerned me much less than the red that speckled the rest of it. She looked hurt, maybe cut, or in some parts scabbed. I started to think more seriously about her choice to be in the bathtub. What were her plans? To fill it to the brim and slide peacefully below the surface? To leave the world with an accident as an alibi? I tried not to panic, but my mind raced to places I was shocked it hadn't been before. Her despair had deepened, grown so grave. Why hadn't I considered that the hardships in her life could start to feel insurmountable? Why hadn't I considered she might hurt herself? Until six weeks ago, Patricia Marshall was the strongest, most pulled-together woman I'd ever known. Save for the occasional quiet period, she was always happy and well-adjusted with a clean house, dinner on the table, and a front-row seat to Sunday sermon. The thought that things could get this bad had been as distant to me then as her voice was now.

"Mom, are you hurt? Are you going to hurt yourself?" She finally looked at me as if I was a tangible being—not one she recognized, but an opaque one nonetheless.

"Never!" she replied. "I told you it wasn't safe here. When did you get home?" Her question seemed genuinely addressed to me. Maybe she truly hadn't seen me until just then.

She looked down at her shaking hands, squinting, trying to focus her eyes, as though they were hands she did not recognize. Uncomfortable and cold, she shifted her weight, tucking her bare feet underneath her while she scanned the bathroom, seeing it for the first time too. She appeared to have just awakened from a trance and was as perplexed about her location as I was.

"Okay, I'm safe, Mom. Don't worry, I'm safe, and you're safe, and Dad and Isaac are safe too. What happened after I left? Why are you in here?"

"No," she replied.

She rubbed her temples, moving her fingers in deep clockwise circles, the pressure and intensity indenting purple Os on her translucent skin.

"We're just going to get you one of those sleeping pills and an Advil for your headache, and you can go to sleep, okay? You stay here. I'm going to find Dad."

I swung open the bathroom door, accidentally slamming it into the (out of place) desk that still sat in barrier-position. My heart stopped, stunned by the loudness of the crash (also out of place) in the otherwise silent room. I looked back to see if I'd startled Mom, but she was having a staring contest with the headrest across from her. I wondered who was a better opponent, the antique radio in the family room, or the cushion? I tried to shuffle my way around the desk, clumsily knocking a glass of rye to the ground. The spill added to the boozy smell that was beginning to overpower the sour stagnation in the air. I could see Dad's feet poking out from beside his side of the bed. *What a drunk*, I thought as I turned back—if my bathroom exit hadn't woken sleeping beauty, I wouldn't be able to if I tried. He'd obviously drunk himself into the kind of stupor you'd wish you'd never wake up from.

In the bathtub, Mom was chanting some kind of prayer or song, back to thinking she had no audience. If only I knew how to turn invisibility on and off, I'd be a much better eavesdropper. I reached down, positioning my arms under hers, preparing to lift her up and out of the bathtub. As though my invisibility switch had been flicked back on, her body language told me she was suddenly very much aware of my presence—and she very much didn't like it. Her limbs flailed violently, thrashing in all directions. It had taken her half an hour to acknowledge my presence, but in a half a second, I'd managed to petrify her. She'd gone from morose to manic. Her strength was remarkable for someone who hadn't eaten or slept in days. I stayed firmly in position, not wanting to hurt her, accepting she'd hurt me. First an elbow to the ear, followed by a blood-curdling scream in the other—I'd be lucky to hear again.

"*Stop. Don't touch me. Why are you touching me?*" She yipped and yelled like a prisoner on death row. I'd thought I'd made my intentions pretty clear; I had nightmares sometimes too, but the prospect of sleep shouldn't elicit this kind of response.

"Mom! Stop!" I pulled my grip in tighter, feeling her hot breath on my shoulder. "I'm just going to take you to bed. Calm down." She threw her limp body down, folding like a cheap suit. It was either her surrender or a devious escape plan, and I hoped for the former.

"It isn't safe out there, Ivy. I'm telling you." Her words were made up of mostly air now, floating to the ceiling and evaporating before anyone could hear them or decide if they were true.

"Then you can sleep in my room. Don't worry, I'll sleep in Isaac's."

She unfolded herself, trembling with uncertain movements, refusing my help as she lifted herself out of the Jacuzzi. I'd never been in the position to care for one of my parents before, and it felt good to be there for her the way she'd been there for me my whole life. For the second time that night, I wasn't going to give up on her so easily. I asserted myself, putting my arm around the small of her back and her arm around my shoulders. If our ankles had been tied together, we'd be doing a three-legged race.

Between wobbly footsteps and near tumbles, my hand miraculously found empty spots on the hall wall to support us as we walked to my room. All at once, the medley of mismatched frames looked crooked, as though we'd had an earthquake and I'd missed it (or maybe the Island was sinking on an angle). I looked proudly to the spot on the wall that should have been vacant from my earlier attack but found my painting of the Pretty Place resurrected, nailed (crookedly) back into place. The glass wasn't broken, and the closet door was unharmed. *Am I dreaming?* I wondered.

Mom collapsed onto my tiny bed, somehow looking even slighter atop it. I opened the window to let in the air she'd been a stranger to for days; it smelled fresh and clean. It was raining again; I could hear a melody of heavy drops beating down on the metal eavestroughs—a sorrowful song God had sent to lull us both to sleep.

"I'm going to grab your sleeping pills and a glass of water, okay?" I gently kissed her forehead as she'd done countless times to me in that bed. Her skin felt cool but salty from sweat, calm but uneasy. Had the rain not come to sing her a lullaby, I would have closed the window to avoid a chill. Instead, I pulled up the covers and unfolded the knitted blanket that waited patiently at her feet.

"How didn't I see it? How didn't I know?" she whispered, staring intently behind me. Her words so quiet and so weak, I wondered if she thought she hadn't spoken them aloud. "He was in on it, in on it," she repeated. "He would have got my kids." The creature had returned in her distorted voice (and her distorted self), so much so that she'd forgotten her *kid* was sitting right beside her. I stopped myself from turning around to look at who she might be talking to, partly because I knew it was no one, and partly because I was scared I was wrong.

CHAPTER 27

Saturday, July 17th, 1999

1:29 a.m.

I was playing chicken again, running quickly through a room with my arms wrapped around myself, not reaching out to feel for the walls. Only this time my eyes weren't closed—the lights were just off and the curtains drawn. I'd snuck into Mom and Dad's dark room many times as a frightened child after a bad dream, but the room had become uncharted territory since then. It was almost as if I'd never been there before and never would be again, though in the light of day, it was anyone's guess.

The nightstand that had once caused me so much discomfort had now become my most important destination. I reached it tripping but unscathed, grabbed Mom's pills, and tiptoed back toward the door, holding my breath as I crept. If I were playing a game of *Mission: Impossible*, my mission (if I chose to accept it) would be to sneak in and out of the room in complete darkness without waking the formidable beast. Maybe not so much formidable as drunk, minding his own business, and sleeping soundly on the floor (on his side of the bed, no less). It was a beginner's mission really—not impossible at all. I would have passed with flying colours had I been able to ignore the responsibility I felt to check on him. Even in his self-induced inebriation, he deserved a little attention.

I parted the curtains and opened the blinds, welcoming the hazy nighttime glow—everything looked better under the light of the moon. Slowly and gently, I kicked the soles of his moccasins, apprehensive like an unexpected guest knocking at the door.

"Dad!" I whispered as I knelt down and grabbed the toes in his slipper, wiggling his foot from side to side.

"Dad?" I said louder.

Nothing.

"Hello, earth to Henry," I yelled.

Nothing.

Not even a grunt.

I squeezed his shin, not moving any closer, afraid he'd wake and reflexively karate chop me in the neck as he did when I jumped out of the front closet, trying to scare him. His shin was rigid and strong like the rest of his body. He was stronger than he looked, but I'd learned that most times big things came in small packages. When I was younger, he'd point to his bicep and say, "Baked potato," then give my flabby arm a pinch, and say, "Mashed potatoes." It always made me laugh—Isaac too.

I tapped the top of his knee three times, smacked it (hurt my hand), and began formulating an apology.

Nothing.

"Up and at 'em, Atom Ant!" I teased, rather pleased with myself.

Nothing.

He better not be playing a practical joke, or this time I'll be doing the karate chopping, I thought. I tried to move his leg back and forth; it was rock-solid like a baked potato, but it certainly wasn't a hot potato. He usually radiated heat as if he had a furnace inside him, especially when he drank, but his leg was colder than mine.

"Dad, wake up. This isn't funny," I said, relenting and crouching down toward his shoulders.

The moon had fallen back behind the clouds, taking its dull light with it. I reached for the lamp on his nightstand; I wasn't playing *Mission: Impossible* in the dark anymore—I was trying to figure out what the hell was going on, and I needed light to do it.

Nothing.

It was unplugged—along with everything else in our house invented after 1878.

Breathe in. Breathe out. Breathe in. Breathe out.

I reminded myself of the basic necessity of living while voices I didn't recognize argued in my head. The rooms in my mind had grown crowded and noisy, and I could hear panicked orders being yelled down every hall. *Light, you need light!* one voice said again. But I didn't need illumination to know that something had gone terribly wrong. His body was too still, and he looked like a mannequin—a mannequin in need of medical assistance, which meant this was a real-life emergency situation (the kind I'd been trained for).

What's the first step to administering first aid, Ivy? I heard it so clearly, I thought he'd asked me from his place on the floor.

That's easy. Assessing the situation is the first step. I looked around for any potential danger I could remove from the area.

Nothing.

His face was as clammy as my hands were. He had to be unconscious—he'd gotten so drunk, he'd gone comatose. I hovered an inch above his mouth, praying, feeling, watching for his chest to rise and fall.

Nothing.

If I couldn't see the movement, then I should have at least been able to feel his breath on the side of my face. It didn't matter how faint—I just needed to feel it. I put my ear to his mouth.

Nothing.

"Dad, what do I do now?" I asked, frantically searching my memory for a rhyme or a jingle he'd taught us to help in a situation like this one.

Nothing.

A deep thumping filled my ears, so loud, I felt it through my entire body and then through his. I begged God to let it be his heartbeat, but I knew before I asked that it was mine.

A pulse! I remembered. I put my middle and index finger on the spot on his neck that had the best blood flow.

Nothing.

I squeezed his rigid hand in mine, trembling as I desperately searched for the rhythm in his wrist.

Nothing.

Nothing.

Nothing.

My eyes adjusted to the dark, but like an infant seeing for the first time, I couldn't understand anything on the ground around me. Hand cream, Nonna's mirror, a basket of magazines, broken glass, a phone book. The longer I looked at the shaded forms, the less sense I could make of them—the less sense I could make of the entire situation. Adrenalin sped through my veins, lighting a fire in every nerve, every pore. I needed to stop for a second, to breathe for the first time since I'd opened the blinds. The air in the room had grown thick, invading my airways the way the lake had when I'd fallen through the ice. If I'd closed my eyes, I would've thought I was underwater, even though it felt as though I hadn't drunk water in days. My mouth was dry but at the same time salivating, my body was chilled but covered in beads of sweat, and my stomach turned as I began to understand the *real* reason the air smelled like booze.

I ran to the bathroom and missed the toilet by less than a foot, throwing up on the tub's marble stairs. In the stark fluorescent light, I was forced to collect myself, my thoughts, and my brain (which I thought was leaking out my ears).

Assess, clear, pulse . . . CPR?

I raced back to him with new hope, positioning myself over his chest, intertwining my fingers the way he'd instructed. Through his shirt, I found his belly button, then realized I only needed it if I was doing the Heimlich manoeuvre, so I located his xiphoid process but forgot why it mattered in the first place. Pressing down in the middle of his chest for what felt like hours, I talked myself into believing I was accomplishing something. I talked myself into believing that when I stopped, his lungs would fill up with air on their own and warm blood would flow back into his big heart, back into his strong hands.

Why hadn't I checked on him sooner? Why hadn't Mom told me? How long had he been like this? The questions weighed on the back of my neck, pushing my head downward, sucking away every ounce of energy I had left. Nothing was making sense, not even the CPR I was doing on the person who'd taught me how to do it. Anger boiled every liquid I had inside me, gathering and dancing around in the pit of my stomach. There was no use trying to make it to the toilet—I puked what was left of my dinner into the wicker trunk at the foot of their bed. Pizza and anguish coated the clean sheets I'd helped Mom fold weeks ago, before everything started falling apart. When she was the mayor of Laundryville and Friday night game night was non-negotiable. When the doorbell never rang, but if it did, Chelsea barked incessantly. When Mom loved her job and no one ever talked about her coming back in *one piece*. When Dad was always going to stay and we were always going to be a family.

I checked his pulse again and again and again. I knew I was doing it right, but I kept getting the wrong answer. I could put him on his side in the rescue position—that would help. *But help what?* He said to do it when there was a risk of someone choking on their own vomit, but that seemed more likely with me than him.

I thought about everything I'd ever read, every book that talked about the loss of warmth subsequent to the loss of life. I didn't understand why he'd been this way for so long. *Why hadn't the ambulance come and gone? Why hadn't anyone tried to save him?*

The phone on his nightstand sat propped up in its cradle, but like all the other phones in the house, it hadn't been plugged in, and it hadn't been charging. No matter how many times I pressed the on button, the dial tone was as absent as Dad's pulse.

It didn't feel real—maybe it wasn't. In the dark, my mind tricked me into thinking he looked peaceful, that, relegated to the floor as he'd been many a drunken night before, he was just sleeping off a hangover. Or maybe I was having a nightmare—a really bad one. In the morning I'd wake to find it was just a dream, that the whole summer had just been a dream.

This wishful thinking consoled me long enough for the adrenalin to slow its journey through my veins. As soon as it was gone, I missed it—real life was too hard without its help. Like an addict approaching withdrawal, I felt the severity of my situation escalating with every second that passed. Suddenly, I was aware of pain again. Something sharp was poking into the back of my thigh—I'd sat on a piece of glass. It had sliced far into my flesh and I'd bled mercilessly before I even had a chance to notice.

Rest—Elevate—Direct pressure.

I grabbed the pillowcase from Dad's pillow and tied it around my leg. He'd taught us how to take control and remain calm in an emergency situation, how to perform first aid even on ourselves. He'd taught us so well, yet somehow I wasn't able to save him, and the proof of that lay irreversibly cold beside me. Understanding just how catastrophic my failure was made the room lean in on me again. I was spinning, then crashing, then silent as someone came into the room and cupped their hands over my ears.

CHAPTER 28

Saturday, July 17th, 1999

2:10 a.m.

I'd fainted. I'd left. I wasn't sure where I went, but when I looked at Dad's lifeless body beside me, I wanted to go back. I reached over and tried to find a pulse—again.

Nothing.

He was dead.

He had been dead long enough for his furnace to shut off, which meant he was dead when I first walked in. He was dead when I saw his feet poking out from beside the bed. He was dead when I called him a drunk and a formidable beast. He was dead.

I thought about earlier in the night, how I'd disobeyed his orders, spending time with Sadie and Robyn at Ghost Road. Was he dead when I was there? Or when I was sitting on the dock, musing mindlessly while critical moments passed? Moments when, if I'd been home, I could have saved him. Moments when I would have methodically carried out everything he'd taught us, only not in vain. I tried not to think about what happened in the hours after I left, what unexpected guests may have arrived, what struggles occurred, what decisions were made.

2:15 a.m. My watch told me the first thing my eyes had believed in hours.

I reached for the sleeping pills I had left on the ground next to his feet, my hands still trembling uncontrollably as if his body was chilling the entire room. I walked down the hall, reminding myself how to put one foot in front of the other—the same way I'd had to the night we ran away from Junior's farm. That animal's death, even Chelsea's, felt like nothing compared to the death that was filling the room I was trying to walk away from.

I knelt down beside my bed, pill bottle tucked securely in my palm. Mom's eyes were closed shut, tightly scrunched together like a drawstring bag. If she wasn't sleeping, she was definitely making an effort to. Even as she rested, expending no energy at all, she looked weak and frail, helpless and exhausted. As much as I needed her, she needed me more.

"Mom!"

I focused my eyes on things around me that didn't hurt me when I looked at them. Floral wallpaper. Sponge-painted headboard. White side table. Sheer yellow curtains. Hardwood floor. My room's mundane decor kept my mind momentarily occupied, saving me from the intense feelings of disorientation I was trying so hard to avoid.

"Mom, wake up." My voice, like Mom's, had become unrecognizable. I was standing in my own room, but I wasn't inhabiting my own body.

"Is he okay?" Her eyes flashed open, sparkling like black beads in the glare of the night light.

The top of my neck throbbed, pulsating into my skull. I dropped the pills to the ground, steadying myself on the box spring. A thorny numbness was taking over every inch of my body. I knew I wasn't dreaming, but I stuck my thumb in the gash on my thigh just to be sure.

"You knew something was wrong with Dad? Why didn't you tell

me? He isn't okay," I yelled. The affliction in my voice astounded us both.

"He was in on it. He was part of the danger. I protected you," she whispered calmly.

"What did you do, Mom?" I held firm to the box spring, unsteady even on my knees. No amount of support could brace me for the answer I didn't want to a question I wished I'd never asked.

"I don't know, I don't know, he'll be fine in the morning," she mumbled.

"You just said you had to do it to protect us."

"I told him to leave. I knew he was in on it. I knew he was looking to take you kids too. He just needs to leave." Her voice was growing stronger, and the conviction in it scared me. At least, I thought it did. But like the parallel of hot and cold, love and hate, in that instant, I'd been mistaken; it wasn't fear I was feeling—it was anger.

"Mom, he's not okay. He's gone. Do you even understand what you've done? He's gone!"

Saying it aloud finally made it true, and I collapsed to the floor and let myself feel it, crying fierce tears of sadness, anger and guilt, frustration and fear, and other feelings I had never before needed words for. The pain had been dormant, desperately waiting for my brain to catch up to what my eyes had seen. Waiting for my heart to accept that ignoring it wouldn't prevent it from being true. My body heaved and convulsed, moving in a way I'd never felt it move before. I was wailing like a siren, a grievous sound I'd never heard myself make before. I was becoming a version of myself I'd never known, but it was okay because I'd rather be that version than who I really was—a girl whose father had been killed in the room down the hall, a girl who'd let it happen.

"No no no no," she repeated. "No no no no no."

She said it again, not in disbelief but in disagreement, chanting as she moved her finger around her lip, tracing it as she used to when I knew her. I grabbed her hand away from her mouth, flinging it to the bed.

"Not no, Mom—yes. What did you do?" I tried to breathe from my nose, afraid my thrashing heart would fall out of my mouth as I spoke. I could feel it in my throat, in my ears, in my feet, and in my hands. I could feel it trying to burst out of every weakened spot in my body. I dug my thumb into my thigh again, deeper this time, opening the wound wider and soaking the pillowcase through. The pain was real—there was no denying it—and at that moment, physical pain was the only thing I wanted to feel.

"He was trying to drug me to make it look like an accident. He'd been meeting with Stan. Don't you see, Ivy? He was in on it."

"In on *what*, Mom? *WHAT?*"

"He'll be okay tomorrow, Ivy. He'll be okay tomorrow."

She said my name again, but it brought none of the comfort it had in our former life; it only sounded sinister, like the foreboding words of an imposter. I didn't know what to believe. I'd spent so much time focused on the danger culminating outside our home, I'd never considered that it could be coming from within it too. I grabbed the pill bottle from under the bed: *Eszopiclone. Take as needed, no more than five nights in a row without consulting a physician.* The label claimed there were thirty pills inside, but the bottle felt light, almost empty. I poured its contents into my hand, the remaining three pills trickling out like the last sands through an hourglass. It had only been a week, and twenty-seven pills were gone— the only thing that supported any truth to her words.

"In on what?" I asked again.

"All of it. The money. The gambling. From the very beginning. I just want him to go away. I just want him to be gone . . ." Her voice was difficult to hear over my sobs—difficult to understand through the lack of hers.

I was still trembling, laying on the frigid floor, sliding around from one side of the room to the other, as though the hardwood was lacquered with ice. It was exhausting to be sitting still but constantly moving. I knew I needed to calm down, to assess the situation in a different way, with clearer eyes. I needed Mom to come back to her body too, to tell me what to do next. Crawling up onto the bed between her and the wall, I put a sleeping pill in my mouth and swallowed it hard, without water.

"Mom, you have to take this. We have to sleep."

"I just want him to go away . . ." she muttered. She opened her mouth and let me put the last two pills on her tongue, swallowing and closing her eyes with no water, no discomfort, and no objection. I wasn't sure how long it took for them to start working, but I heard her breathing change before I could even feel the warmth of her body through the sheets.

She was able to turn off her mind, but my bones felt as if they were trying to free themselves, to break out from under my skin while the darkness wept into the empty space they left. I willed my breaths to mimic hers, to settle into a normal pace. I knew I'd eventually calm my body, but my mind was unruly and relentless as it raced down a vicious path of possibilities. In one night, my entire life had come undone—so much for saying, "Change doesn't happen overnight," because it undoubtedly did. When your mother kills your father, it's not a milestone with a slow progression. If anything, I felt I'd aged ten years in the last ten hours. Only with my eyes closed and my body unmoving could I muster enough energy to understand the magnitude of what was going on—of what those ten hours truly meant. By next week, Mom would probably be in jail, and Dad would be in a cemetery. And I hadn't even begun to let myself think about Isaac—what I'd tell him, how I'd explain why I wasn't there, how I'd let it happen. We were orphans now. Five days before my fifteenth birthday, we'd become orphans.

Outside, the sky continued to lighten, turning a muted grey as the sun came up behind a thick blanket of clouds. If not for the dreary skies (proving that, once and for all, pathetic fallacy was real), the sun would have been all the way up in the sky by the time the sleeping pill finally took effect. Reluctantly, my mind surrendered, letting my body drift in and out of a shallow sleep filled with harrowing images of a nightmare that was so much more—it was our new reality.

CHAPTER 29

Saturday, July 17th, 1999

4:32 p.m.

After I opened my eyes, it took my brain a few seconds to remember what had happened. I should have cherished that time more, but I didn't know that those fleeting moments would be the last in which I ever felt normal.

Mom slept beside me, snoring and oblivious as if nothing was amiss. I watched as her chest slowly rose and then fell, rose then fell. Air effortlessly filled her lungs, a feat I'd never thought to appreciate until I'd watched a chest lie still, broken after the air had forsaken it.

It still wasn't bright outside, but I hated that there was any light at all. Light made it harder to ignore I was alive when it exposed every painful thing around me.

I didn't move. I didn't want to wake her, and I didn't want to start the clock on the day we had in front of us. *Who should we call first? Do you call 911 when the person's already dead? How will we tell Isaac?*

Would Mom go to jail for life if we made it look like an accident, or if it was self-defence? Why would he try to harm her?

My mind started to feel crowded again, my thoughts moving so quickly, everything around me was moving in slow motion. It was easy to feel dizzy when what was outside your head couldn't keep up with what was inside. If I didn't organize myself and bring them together at the same speed, I'd be sick. Mentally, I began to write my to-do list for the worst day of my life:

1. Wake Mom

2. Go see Dad

I stopped. The back of my throat ached when I thought about waking Mom so she could look at Dad, so she could see what she'd done—I just couldn't do it. She was too weak, and she'd never be able to understand the consequence of her actions, regardless of intent. I wiggled myself free and left her to sleep peacefully in my bed (one last time). Hopefully, she'd be dreaming dreams that reality hadn't seeped into. When she woke, she'd be in a life as confounding to her as the single bed she'd slept in. Maybe that was the reason she'd seemed so against sleeping in the first place—she understood that everything could be much worse in the morning.

In the hall, I thought morbidly about the newest certificate we could frame for the wall. Not even death could stifle my dark sense of humour. I used it to distract myself, a tactic I'd inherited from Dad, a thought that now offered a unique sense of comfort and a new kind of pride.

With closed eyes and a broken chest, I stood outside my parents' bedroom door, trying to envision the sharpened details of a scene that even in the dark had been too vivid for me to process. I tried to picture what Dad might look like, but my imagination came with limitations I knew I was lucky to have. In broad daylight, all the uncertainties would be clarified, all the mysteries would be solved, all the blame would be laid, and all our lives would be changed.

Even if I'd been able to imagine the disturbing way he looked, skin mottled and waxy, I never could have prepared myself for the smell. In the hall, it was just another summer day at the Marshall residence, but a foot inside the door, it was clear the room had borne witness to a heinous tragedy. It didn't smell like a dead deer or the limb of a decaying goat—no, those smells from the back fields had done nothing to prepare me for the smell of human death. The stench wasn't enveloping yet, but it was distinct. It was a mixture of stagnant morning urine and the unassuming smell of tartar scraped freshly from your teeth. It reminded me of both those things if they'd been trapped in our meat freezer during a power outage. Sitting, rotting, mouldering—with a lingering hint of rye. These were the smells left over from a man whose aftershave used to enter a room before he did. These were the smells that I knew would never leave their room.

I looked to see if his moccasin-wearing feet still jutted out past the foot of the bed, half expecting they'd have come to life in the night and moved as the painting of the Pretty Place had. Other than the new smell, everything was exactly as I'd left it. Vomit still soiling the sheets in the trunk, the phone still broken on the ground where I'd thrown it, browning drops of blood (his or mine) still on the floor where they'd fallen.

All the puzzle pieces I'd seen in the forgiving light of the moon were fitting together, against my will. There he lay, undeniable in the daylight—the darkest image I'd ever seen.

He was wearing his classic bedtime uniform, plaid pyjama pants and a plain grey T-shirt, stained and strained under his expanding skin. He must have come upstairs to get changed before bed. His wallet and the book he'd been reading sat neatly on his nightstand; he'd wanted to sleep beside her again. On the dresser was another cold tea, sitting atop yesterday's paper. He didn't drink tea, so he'd brought it up for her—an unlikely act of kindness coming from a man she painted as nefarious. Unless she was right, however, and the tea had been maliciously prepared to disguise the taste of exactly twenty-seven sleeping pills.

The broken cup that had pierced my thigh sat distant from the other shards of glass that had once made it whole. They rested at the base of the wall, which appeared to be their breaking point. Mom's vanity mirror lay awkwardly inches from Dad's head, miraculously unharmed but obviously misplaced. His body had changed since I'd been with him last. The stiffness I'd mistaken for strength had dissipated, as if he'd finally relaxed. His skin was discoloured and blotchy, no longer his own. Kneeling down to look more closely, I could see that the surface of his body touching the ground had turned navy blue, almost bruised. With nowhere else to go, all the blood inside him had obliged the rules of gravity, pooling underneath.

I continued to scan the room, deliberately overlooking the details I knew would make Mom's actions irrefutable. *Would the rules of plausible deniability still apply?* I wondered, though I wasn't exactly sure what it meant. I hoped I'd be able to absolve her of guilt, that I could deduce a different story. Maybe he'd slipped or choked, or he was the one who intended to take the sleeping pills. But there was nothing he could have slipped on, no evidence of asphyxiation, and no signs he'd taken his own life.

What there was, which I could no longer ignore, was blood on the swirling floral decoration of the antique mirror's base. What else was there? A deep welt and fatal dent on his left temple. An unquestionable sign of a struggle, then a fall. And a husband who had tried to get into bed with a wife he hadn't known he'd made an enemy of.

My heart broke as I mentally played out the devastation. I pictured him moving the covers, trying to calm her, cautiously sitting down in their bed beside her. The mirror, which usually sat atop the vanity, had been visiting the nightstand in recent days. An unlikely but viable weapon, she'd reached for it, grabbing it tightly with all of the strength left within her. She bludgeoned the man who'd once slept there beside her. A man who was beside her at the altar saying, "I do." A man who was beside her for the birth of her two children. And now the man who was beside her in death.

I'd never know if her intention was to kill. I'd never know if I could have saved him had I been there. What I did know was that his involvement in the danger Mom felt would remain contested. It was hard for me to look at him lying helplessly on the ground and see anything other than innocence. It was hard for me to look at him at all. I grabbed the fitted sheet from their bed and floated it down over his body, immediately feeling a tension in my chest release. Not being able to see him made it feel less real. Not being able to see him let me pull air back into my collapsed lungs. I took another sheet from the wicker trunk, a top sheet this time, and using all the strength I'd regained from my short rest, I rolled his body onto it, holding my breath, pretending I was folding up an old Persian rug in our basement. Again, a small string of tension released in my chest and I could breathe in more deeply, giving my brain a tiny bit more oxygen, extending my life a few seconds at a time.

The cut on my thigh hurt on and off (when I stopped spinning long enough to remember). The wound reminded me of itself at the same times I was reminded I was human, like when I was thirsty or had to pee. Normal things (human things) that never seemed to happen in movies when someone was dealing with a dead body. The damp pillowcase had suppressed some of my bleeding, but Dad wouldn't have been pleased with the cleanliness of my half-assed wrapping job. I grabbed Mom's pillow, stripping the case to use as my second (hopefully cleaner) bandage. The room had been achingly silent, other than the sound of my laboured breathing, until the pillowcase revealed itself as a half-assed hiding spot. I stood aghast as a collection of pills fell to the ground at my feet, the pitter-patter to the floor like summer hail, unexpected and perplexing. I recognized the circular blue ones as the sleeping pill I'd taken the night before (and I didn't need to be Rain Man to know that if I'd counted them, there'd be twenty-seven). The others, orange, yellow, and pink, created a colourful mosaic of pills I'd never seen before. Pills that at the very least told a story of neglected wellness, and at the very most of attempted murder.

I collected the pills in my hands and brought them to the toilet, flushing what I realized afterwards to be valuable evidence. Everything I did went against everything I'd read or seen on TV about proper protocol for a situation involving death. But I didn't care. I didn't care to call the police or whoever I'd call because the moment I did, the moment they came to collect his body . . . that was the moment I'd lose them both. At least right now they were both in our home, under one roof, while I cleaned the bathroom and moved the desk back. At least I could still feel them near me, one tucked cozily in my sheets, the other wrapped tightly in theirs. At least I wasn't an orphan just yet.

Mom continued sleeping soundly in my bed, safe from the carnage that awaited her. Had she been awake, I would have asked her about the other pills she'd been hiding in her pillowcase, the mismatched circles and tiny squares she'd hoarded like a prized marble collection. There were a lot of questions I needed to ask, a lot that hadn't been explained even after I'd looked more closely in the light. I needed to know why—I needed her to tell me. *Knowing why won't bring me back,* I could hear Dad saying, muffled through the sheet that cocooned him. Knowing why wouldn't stop Mom from going to jail. Knowing why wouldn't make me feel better either.

***

I had to talk to someone. I needed to hear a voice I recognized. Downstairs, I searched for a working phone and found that the one in the living room was still in the cradle where I'd returned it after eavesdropping on Dad's call with Doug. Without the foggiest clue about what I'd say if she answered, I dialed Aunt Sam.

"Hi, honey. I was getting worried when I hadn't heard from you." Her inflection was distinct. It was the first thing that felt truly familiar in the last twenty-four hours.

"Yeah, sorry. We've been really busy!"

"Did you get my letter, Ivory?" she asked, sounding concerned.

I'd forgotten all about it after I fell asleep in the Pretty Place. It was still in my backpack.

"I totally forgot to open it. Sorry!" Every word I spoke had a battle behind it. I fought the urge to cry, and I fought the urge to confide in her.

"It was important. You guys weren't answering my calls, but I wanted to tell you something about your mother you should know." The comfort I'd felt from her familiar voice began to disappear with each sullen word she spoke.

I paused, scared for her to go on, forgetting that no news would be worse than the news Mom would share with her in the coming weeks.

"What do you mean? What do I need to know?"

Aunt Sam was the bringer of cheer, not the bearer of bad news; this role was new and strange for her. She was as hesitant to continue as I was to listen. "Sweetie, sometimes your mom has . . . episodes. Here and there since we were kids. She'd stop sleeping, eating, and would get paranoid. She'd always pull herself out of them, though."

Tell me something I don't know.

"I know, Aunt Sam. We're dealing with it."

"It's more than that," she said, breathing in long and deeply as if she needed extra air to finish delivering a punchline. "When I say paranoid, I mean delusional—she gets really wrapped up in things, things that may or may not be real. It helps to just bring her back down to earth, though, ya know? Remind her of the things that *are* real—things that are right in front of her."

"I don't understand what you mean." I knew I sounded childish. But I needed to hear it again to know what it meant, to process what it could mean for all of us.

"Honey, what I'm saying, and what I should have said to you when you called me a few weeks ago, is that your mom may be sick. Mentally.

She might take something for it, but she's never really wanted to talk to me . . . or anyone . . . about it."

Like the daylight that pieced together the details of how Dad died, I was scared her words were beginning to piece together the details of *why*. It had been in front of me the whole time—I just couldn't see it. This truth had been hidden behind the shadows in the scarce light of the moon too.

Tears soaked my cheeks, coming together on my cracked lips, pooling under my chin. I tried to cry quietly, to act normal and maintain the facade that we were okay. But the thought that Mom may have killed him out of delusion—that it was all a mistake—was more unnerving than any of the other options. It eliminated our ability to make it look like an accident or self-defence—it eliminated the possibility she'd live the rest of her life outside of a jail cell.

"Don't cry, Ivy. It's okay—she'll pull herself out of it. She always does." She spoke with credence, but it felt like a lie from where I sat, in the house that harboured the truth. Mom hadn't pulled herself out of it; she'd only pulled us all in with her.

"Okay, thanks for telling me. I have to go now!"

I hung up so I could cry as hard and as loudly as I needed to without the fear of sharing too much.

Mentally.

Sick.

The words made me feel (physically) sick.

Sick . . . mentally. Was that what they called people who didn't want to eat or sleep? I'd read *One Flew Over the Cuckoo's Nest*, but Mom wasn't anything like the characters in that book, and surely she wouldn't be checked into a place like that.

I thought about the turquoise envelope, the information concealed within that so badly needed to be read. The answers it had to questions I hadn't yet needed to ask. I thought again about how I could have prevented it—something that seemed even more preventable now with the information Aunt Sam had intended to share. Like the moment I chose to leave Chelsea off the chain, I had inadvertently caused another death by leaving that envelope unopened.

The sun was lowering in the sky, a reminder that time wouldn't wait for me to come up with all the answers, that time wouldn't wait for me to deal with it my own way. With each hour that passed, the situation got worse and more difficult to explain. I practised my explanation, what I would say happened, why I'd let him lie there for hours, and I started to feel as though I was in the future looking back, telling a friend a story I'd made up. A story I'd taken too many liberties with, a story I could pretend had a happier ending than the one I was living. I started formulating alternative endings as if I were in a Choose Your Own Adventure book:

- He died of natural causes in his sleep.

- He died of terminal illness like his mom.

- He didn't die at all. He just left and never came back.

Each ending to my adventure less painful, more idyllic than the one before, any of which I'd sacrifice everything for. There was no ultimatum I wouldn't give God or wager I wouldn't make with Him—if only to have my reality be not as tragic, not as hopeless as it had become.

Upstairs again outside my bedroom door, I braced myself not for a putrid smell or a horrific sight, but for heartbreak—heartbreak I'd been putting off for hours.

"Mom," I whispered quietly, a few inches from her ear.

"Why am I in here?" she asked, swaying herself awake. "Where's your father?"

Where's your father?

Where's your father?

Where's your father?

I repeated it in my head to make sure I understood the question.

"Where's my father?" I repeated it out loud to make sure *she* did.

"Yeah, Iv, I'm just so drained. My head hurts."

Longing for sleep, she dropped her head back down to the pillow, closing her eyes before she'd finished speaking.

"He's in your bed," I lied, picturing his feet poking out from beside it. "You didn't want to sleep with him, so you came in here." It was more of an omission than a lie, but an omission that carried a penance heavier than any lie I'd ever told.

"Right. Okay, I'm going to nap for a bit, hon . . . wake me in an hour." Her affable demeanour was so unlike that of the woman I'd slept beside last night, and it was obvious her memory shared few details with that woman too.

I closed the door with no intention of waking her again. I'd let her sleep, and I prayed that when she woke, she'd have pulled herself out of it as Aunt Sam said she would. So far out, she'd be removed from what had happened. So far out, it would be as if it had never happened at all.

CHAPTER 30

Saturday, July 17th, 1999

10:52 p.m.

It dawned on me then, suddenly and unexpectedly, as if my future self intervened to change my fate. I knew what had to be done so we could live some semblance of a normal life. And as if a part of me had descended deep into my mind, I started to see things through distant eyes. The movements I made, the things I saw, the breaths I took— they were all happening *to* me, not because of me. I was existing deep inside myself while a stronger version of myself took control of the life I no longer wanted to be a part of.

I locked my bedroom door from the outside and walked to theirs. Inside, I waited to be overwhelmed by the smell, but it didn't affect me; it couldn't find me inside where I was hiding. I searched the room and the closet for things Dad would have taken with him when he left, filling his carry-on suitcase with his most prized possessions (and some practical ones too). His wallet, his toothbrush, the valuable coin collection his father had given him, underwear, a framed photo of Isaac and me, a pair of old runners, his heartburn medication from his nightstand. I went to gather the cash I knew he kept stashed in his sock drawer (like a bad cliché) and found the drawer filled only with socks. He had no cellphone or laptop, but he'd never go anywhere without his briefcase. I grabbed it from the piano bench and fit it into the luggage with ease.

As if I were bewitched (or possessing some other kind of power), I closed my eyes and found myself in the backyard beside the fireplace, suitcase in hand. I hadn't actively decided to burn it, but the strong smell of gasoline in the air told me it was part of the plan. Dad kept the jerry can in the shed for the riding lawn mower, and under no circumstances were we allowed to use it in the pit. Carelessly, I poured more gas onto the luggage, readying myself with the matches I found in my pocket.

Fuel. Heat. Oxygen.

These, I'd been taught, were the three points of the triangle that created fire; if you had all three, you'd be successful. If you needed it to stop, you just had to remove one. Fuel was the only thing I wasn't sure about; I hadn't been taught a catchy rhyme that confirmed the requirements for burning anything other than wood. But at least I knew that *stop, drop, and roll* would put me out should I catch on fire.

The suitcase sat vertically in the centre of the pit. I moved blocks of wood to the fire, strategically leaning them against his suitcase like a pole holding up a tent. When my hands neared the flame, I couldn't feel the heat, but I knew it was fierce—I could see it dancing in the light that covered the shed, swirling from the top like a spirit leaving a body.

***

I borrowed some manhunt clothing from Isaac, cleared the plates from the hall and my parents' bedroom, and put a new set of sheets on their naked mattress. I threw out the broken glass and blood-stained pillowcase and soaked Nonna's vanity mirror in the sink while I cleaned the vomit off the bathtub stairs.

The white sheet that concealed Dad was the only glaring problem in my otherwise flawless plan. If I was going to have to trek into the back fields with him, he needed to be dressed appropriately too. I searched the linen closet for something less conspicuous and found a dark-green top sheet with no matching fitted sheet in sight. *This set won't be missed,* I thought. The top sheet had been abandoned the same way we were going to be.

***

Water was stinging my eyes. I blinked again to find myself standing in the rain on Tiny Trail. Instead of having to remind myself to put one foot in front of the other, I was suffering from the opposite problem: my limbs were still moving without my permission, letting me know what I was doing only after it was done. Unlike when I'd been near the fire's heat, I could feel soreness in my hands from tightly squeezing the wooden handles of the wheelbarrow I pushed. I'd stopped more than once to rearrange my heavy, unbalanced load. It was awkward, contorted, and hard to contain, but I moved quickly—I could feel an urgency deep, deep down in my stomach. The rain fell harder, angrier, filling in the darkness that kept me company, the darkness that kept me hidden. I'd travelled the path to the Pretty Place so many times before, I could have done it with my eyes closed—and at times, I felt I was.

***

Inside the forest, I was farther away from the situation. I knew there was a meticulously preordained plan, but I was understanding and experiencing it only from a distance. At times I was watching from six inches behind the surface of my eyes, watching as I contemplated the best spot for my load, carefully weighing my options. Other times it felt as though I was overseeing what I was doing from a towering tree branch as another me furiously dug into the soil on the other side of the creek. I was so far away, but I could still feel the blisters forming on our hands with every heave of the shovel. I was so far away, but I could still feel the rain on our sweat-soaked back as we followed the trail back home.

***

My body lay floating, arms out, face up in the pool. The early-morning warmth made the air and the water equivalent in a way I'd never felt before. It was as if every part of me was submerged while, at the same time, I was completely untouched. It was all around me, but then it was nowhere close. It was everything, but then it was nothing at all.

The fire had been refuelled through the night. I watched it burn for hours, too strong to be snuffed out by the rain, too important to give up. It was 6:42 a.m. now, and the fire had finally weakened, all the contents of the pit destroyed save for some coins that were impervious to the flame. I buried them with the vanity mirror on top of Chelsea's ashes. It was the only way I knew how to keep them without really keeping them, and I knew Chelsea would keep them safe.

CHAPTER 31

Monday, July 19th, 1999—Two days since

I felt so foolish, believing every word that came out of Mom's mouth. So foolish for barely questioning even the most outlandish accusations. I'd never had a reason to doubt her before. She was my Mom—she was who'd taught me the importance of honesty and the destructiveness of lies. She'd contacted a lawyer and let the whole neighbourhood know, and for what? Worst of all, she'd thought that Dad coming to bed meant sleeping with the enemy, when the enemy had been in bed with her all along—the enemy was her.

After waking on Sunday morning in Isaac's room with Dad nowhere in sight, I did what I thought was best and asked Aunt Sam to come over.

"So, what, he just left while you guys were sleeping and didn't tell you where he went?" Incredulity dripped off her every word as she sat across from me at the kitchen table. Her strawberry-blonde curls were pulled tightly from her face and she was wearing her signature all-black outfit; it was a funeral-appropriate look (more fitting than she'd ever know). "And Isaac has his car?" she continued, bewildered.

"Yeah, maybe Dad left with . . . someone. I dunno."

"Someone?" she asked, prodding me as I'd hoped she would.

"I dunno. Mom thought he might be—"

"I told you she gets paranoid. Don't think like that. He probably just forgot to leave a note." She pulled her glasses off the top of her head and put them on, scanning the kitchen counters like a detective scouring a crime scene for clues.

I nodded and joined her in her futile search, opening drawers and cupboards, then the fridge (the search equivalent of napping on the stairs).

"He'll show up after work tonight. Don't worry, honey—let's just focus on getting your mom well," she said. She left the kitchen and walked upstairs toward her only sister and the only person she'd ever had to care for. She brought no water, no medicine, no tea, and no soup. She brought no remedy at all, and for a moment I wondered if calling Marilyn and Liz would have been a better idea.

I could hear her shuffle Mom out of my bed and into her bathroom. My throat constricted, afraid they might see something suspicious inside. I'd done a thorough job cleaning, but I'd never be able to fully scrub away the fear. The shower squealed on and water rushed loudly through the pipes, reverberating through the house. Aunt Sam would help Mom in, completely unaware that the hot water was washing away the sins Mom didn't even know belonged to her. Sins that washed over me every time I feigned concern about Dad's whereabouts. Every time I plotted eagerly in my head. Every time I thought about the wagers I'd tried to make with God. Every time I was dumb enough to think my actions had afforded us normalcy. What had I bartered with to hide the truth? What had I given up to save one parent because I couldn't save the other?

"It smells weird in their room, doesn't it?" Sam asked, appearing suddenly (this time her prodding was unwelcome).

"Well, she's been in there for days on end with rotting food and stuff. I opened the windows, so now it will air out."

"Okay, cool. Thanks." She sat back down at the table, drenched from her brief stint as a caretaker upstairs.

"Your mother is a stubborn woman, but I told her I'd rather sleep in a litter box than next to her, and she seemed to respond to that." We laughed hard, both favouring laughter over crying. Her expression changed quickly as she went on. "But she's not well, Ivory. I'm not gonna lie to you—I've never seen her this bad. She doesn't seem to know what's going on. I asked when she showered last, and she couldn't remember. She couldn't remember anything, really."

"Can we take her back to the doctor?" I asked. Mom had to be okay. If she wasn't, everything I'd done would be in vain. She just had to be okay.

"Of course, honey. We'll try to get her in this week once your dad is back."

"We should go soon either way! What if he doesn't come back?" I stopped myself from going on.

Her eyebrows lifted, one higher than the other. She wasn't trying to hide her reaction to my off-putting response.

"Well, it's only been a day since you've heard from him. You know their marriage was in a tumultuous state, honey. He probably just needed a break . . . to reset."

"I know, I know."

"Marriage can be hard," she claimed boldly (with no experience to draw from). "Sometimes people just need a break! But he'll be back. Henry isn't the type to just up and leave. Gotta give him some space, is all." This claim was actually founded on fact. He *wasn't* the type to just up and leave, and it hurt my heart to think about. It hurt, even more, to think about who else the ruinous lie about him leaving would hurt—but in different ways. Mom and Isaac would be hurt thinking the lie was real, while I'd be left to hurt forever knowing it wasn't.

Aunt Sam went to every room that had a phone, brazenly plugging them back in as if she'd decided Mom wasn't just paranoid about Dad, but delusional about everything.

"Mom probably doesn't want those plugged back in, eh? Work stuff going on."

"Well, we need them plugged in case your father calls, don't we? He likely already has." I rolled my eyes, sitting back down so she couldn't see me through the window in the wall. As with the Ghost Road legend, I'd already grown tired of being the only one who *actually* knew the truth. "And we'll just have to see if anything pans out with her job. Hopefully, she hasn't burned any bridges there."

She continued to shuffle around from room to room, tidying and plugging things in. She turned the antique radio on in the family room, letting it emit a loud, staticky fuzz that angered my ears.

"It's hard to get any channels on that old bugger," I yelled through the wall window. I waited for her to turn it off, more irritated with every second that passed. "Can you turn it off, Aunt Sam?" I pleaded. I stood up to see what she was doing, but she wasn't in the family room anymore. I walked quickly to the living, then the dining, then the laundry room—she wasn't on the main floor at all.

Goosebumps lined my arms, forging a path up my shoulders and behind my ears. I wanted to turn the radio off to make the white noise stop, but I was paralyzed with fear—not only because the radio had turned on by itself, but also because with one step into the family room, I could feel the temperature drop, forcing goosebumps down a new path all the way to my toes.

"What were you saying, hon?" Sam appeared in the doorway. "I was just upstairs plugging in the phones. Your mom's sound asleep."

"Nothing. Never mind." I tried to brush it off as if it were nothing; I preferred that to an inexplicable alternative.

"Jeez," she said with a gasp. "Go outside and sit in the sun, Ivory. You're as white as a ghost."

It was a lot easier to find my way to Mom's bed since the room had been cleaned and was back to its familiar self. Mom had been cleaned too, but I knew she needed more time to be back to her familiar self. I lay beside her on the bed, stroking her head slowly, taming her curls the way she had when I was sad or sick.

"Are you awake, Mom?" I asked, hoping the question would wake her if she hadn't been.

She let out a quiet moan, soft and gentle, almost a whimper. She was awake, but it didn't sound as though she wanted to be.

"What if Dad doesn't come back? Will we be okay?"

She turned onto her back and together we stared up at the ceiling. I pictured a giant mirror covering it, reflecting the room back down to us; I imagined what it would have seen three (long) nights ago. Like a sped-up movie scene, I saw it happening before my eyes. Dad falling to the ground. Mom running to the bathroom. I saw me grabbing his feet, rolling him up, cleaning the floor. I wanted to see more, to fill in all the blanks my imagination couldn't handle. But there was nothing left to draw from; the more I wanted to see it, the further it got away. The mirror was cracking, and soon it would shatter into a million pieces, crashing down on us like an avalanche.

"We'll always be okay," she muttered. She rolled over, away from me, and pulled the covers up over her head as if preparing for the mirror to break too. Everything she'd said for weeks could easily be called into question, but not this. This was true and she knew it—she meant it. I'd been waiting on my three bad things, collecting tiny hardships, thinking the adversity was significant. Dad's death had to count as more than one. It was the ninth bad thing anyway, and because there were only three of us left, it absolutely had to be the last one.

CHAPTER 32

April 2018

Today I received my final diagnosis. My glorious, glorious diagnosis. I've been asked to write about how it makes me feel. After three second opinions, I can confidently say that Mom didn't share her mental illness with me, and that makes me feel wonderful! I've been told it's extremely hereditary—as hereditary as her wild hair and wider hips. And what can I say? The resemblance is uncanny. It was a positive thing, but in true therapist fashion, she shared it with me in the same breath as something negative. She believes I've grown obsessed with the idea that I was sick like my mother. Apparently, in our sessions, I speak too frequently about the time in my life when Mom was being diagnosed. A few years ago I was asked to recall the summer Henry left with some kind of fondness and positivity, and now she says I'm obsessed for fixating on it! At first, it was hard for me to even remember 1999. It was a lifetime ago, and most of the Henry-related details are a bit hazy (okay—they're *a lot* hazy). But the memories that remain clear are allegedly feeding into my "irrational fears" about my own mental health. Typical shrink—nothing's ever good enough.

We've learned so much more about Mom's illness since that time, but back then, like most people in our life, we'd never experienced it before—or anything like it. To Isaac and me, her paranoid delusions seemed real; we didn't have a reason to doubt anything that came out of her mouth. Once Henry left and Aunt Sam came to stay, Mom got better and the paranoia stopped. It turned out her paranoia was often rooted in small (sometimes big) truths. How vindicated she must have felt as the web unravelled and she found it had been littered with reality. She just needed a bit of help getting back there—back to the reality we shared. Aunt Sam took her to tons of doctor's appointments, which ultimately led to a short hospital stay as she attempted to get properly diagnosed. And I'm sure it was made more difficult by her struggling to remember things as simple as how to communicate and as complicated as how she'd awakened one day to find her family abandoned.

Eventually, Mom confirmed she and Henry had reached the crux with an impending divorce—a separation wanted by both once they'd accepted their insurmountable differences. They'd grown so far apart, so distant from the person the other had married, and they found no common ground in interests they'd once shared. To Mom, the things Henry did were all evil, and to him, the God who made her believe that didn't even exist. It's hard to say if the probable divorce was the cause or the consequence of her deteriorating mental health. The way she tells it, though, their divorce and her diagnosis were as inevitable as they were mutually exclusive.

Some signs that Mom had a mental illness had been there for years, plainly written on the walls, but our naiveté made us illiterate. To further complicate it for her ridiculously inept doctors, other telltale signs were completely missing, like her not being diagnosed by age twenty-five, or that she was always able to maintain healthy, happy relationships, be a consistent, commendable parent, and hold down a good job. She wasn't the perfect candidate for the kind of diagnosis she ultimately received—she didn't check all the boxes, and she didn't raise all the red flags.

After months of analysis and various drug combinations (a gruelling and protracted process), a chemical imbalance was her catch-all diagnosis, which left us just as confused as she was the morning she woke up after a three-day nap. It would be at least fifteen years after that before enough research speculatively connected her chemical imbalance with her hormonal one. After her endometriosis had forced her to have a partial hysterectomy, she was left in need of synthetic estrogen—her womanhood in the form of a little pink pill. But she'd heard rumours it caused breast cancer and weight gain, both things undesirable enough that she deprived herself of a hormone her body could no longer produce naturally. It was just one piece of an immensely complex puzzle, but it was a piece that might have helped us at the time—a piece that was right in front of any doctor who cared to look.

I've watched for the same pieces in myself since *that* summer, worried after every bad period, late sleep-in, or suspicious thought. I've been constantly on the lookout, never letting it fall too far from my mind for fear it might sneak up on me the way it snuck up on her. In a million ways, I feel imbalanced every single day; I can't imagine what my life would be like if I shared her illness too.

My final diagnosis has proven much less mysterious than hers, though—maybe because science has advanced, or maybe because mental health awareness is on the rise. By the time I turned twenty-five, I'd made peace with the fact that instead of a chemical imbalance, I suffered from OCD in the form of intrusive thoughts. Today I added attention deficit hyperactivity disorder (ADHD) to the list. There's some comfort in knowing these two illnesses can acutely explain so many previously inexplicable quirks from my adolescence. What I didn't like or couldn't understand, I'd gotten used to just blaming Henry for. It took years for me to identify the real reasons I'd get overwhelmed by disorganization, obsess over the number three (it's still my lucky number), or feel forced to sing lyrics out loud against my will. And only now do I know the real reason I was held back in elementary school. In the nineties, doctors seldom diagnosed little girls with ADHD, especially if their grades were good. Apparently, they didn't properly diagnose anyone with anything if the predetermined shoe didn't fit—a shoe crafted as a one-size-fits-all approach to mental illness and a person's symptom presentation. Anything beyond the typical cookie-cutter causality was far too complex for general practitioners back then to understand.

As it were, Mom hadn't just needed sleeping pills and a good meal—and I wasn't just *nervous, sensitive,* or *finicky.* Mom wouldn't have pulled herself out of it, as much as making lists wouldn't cure me. I probably would've been diagnosed earlier had my contempt toward doctors not grown exponentially with every useless appointment Aunt Sam took Mom to. The gross lack of knowledge surrounding mental health sickened me even then at the ripe age of fifteen. And as my contempt grew for doctors, it grew equally for Henry as I thought about the kind of person he had to be to leave a woman in that state. He might not have known she was sick (mentally), but we still believed he left her in the middle of the night like a coward, and when I thought about that being true, it made me sick (physically).

CHAPTER 33

Friday, July 23nd, 1999—Six days since . . .

If I thought things were weird last week, this week has been a whole new rodeo or ball game, or however the saying goes. Aunt Sam has agreed to stay until Dad came home, and Isaac has more or less committed to staying away.

When Isaac got home from Wasaga Monday night, he seemed unfazed that no one had seen Dad since Saturday. "Sounds about right," he said, sneering before he left for the tree house for another "nightcap." Without Dad around, our disobedience levels skyrocketed, while fear of punishment dwindled to almost nil. I'd be lying if I said I wasn't at least a little tempted to take advantage of the situation, but it was because I wasn't feeling well. I just wasn't feeling like myself.

Strange things, inexplicable and unforeseen, were upsetting my stomach. I threw up in the meat freezer downstairs when Aunt Sam asked me to grab a sirloin roast. Then I threw up by the firepit on the way to the shed to get her a pool noodle. Maybe it was the flu, or maybe I'd simply grown tired of being her servant. She waited on Mom, I waited on her, and no one waited on me—not even on my birthday.

On Tuesday, Doug called, and Aunt Sam said he sounded

concerned—really concerned. He asked a lot of nosy questions she didn't have the answers to—like what files from work Dad brought home, where they were, and if he left any instructions for Doug regarding a "repayment."

On Wednesday, work called to see when he'd be back in, first extending the typical pleasantries you'd expect during a health-related absence and then changing their tone when Aunt Sam offered little information and even less reassurance. They asked if they could speak with Mom. Sam was reluctant to put her on the phone, unsure of how she'd handle it (she was feeling a bit better, though nowhere near 100 percent), but Mom insisted it was fine. I could only hear one side of the conversation, and from what I heard, it went about as well as the call with Doug. At one point she said, "Sure, I have nothing to hide," which is something someone only says when they *do*, in fact, have something to hide, or at least if they're being accused of it.

Dad's abrupt absence forced a lot of people in his life to scrutinize their last interactions with him (a.k.a. it was stirring up a lot of shit). But when Mom seemed lucid enough to talk about it, her memory failed her about their last days and conversations together, something I'm sure would plague her for the rest of her life. She didn't remember their last interaction or conversation, but one thing remained resoundingly clear: their final and most definitive argument. It had been the night they went out for dinner at Pog's Place. She'd worn her favourite red dress, picked for (what I thought was) a special occasion, not knowing it would be the last occasion they'd ever celebrate together. It was mutual but still complicated, amicable but still painful. That night, as they sat among the breadsticks, candlelight, and checkered tablecloths, they agreed their marriage wasn't working. I overheard Mom telling Aunt Sam in the family room that they both appreciated that the timing wasn't right and planned to pick up the conversation again in the new year—once I'd settled into high school and Isaac had a better idea about what he was really doing with his life. After that night, she admitted her memory got fuzzy, distant and strange as if she was in a trance she wasn't sure she'd completely found her way out of yet. I had no idea sleep deprivation was so powerful (or so dangerous)—nor had I any idea I'd be part of a broken home before I turned fifteen.

When Aunt Sam heard the news of an impending divorce, she agreed to stay as long as Mom needed. Sam was lucky to have a flexible job as a freelance writer; we'd just have to get better dial-up internet if she was going to telecommute. She didn't know things had gotten so bad in their marriage or that it had been going on for years. I guess she could add marital state to the list of personal details Mom felt it unnecessary to share with her—right up there with mental state. Mom had seen two doctors in the last three days, both unable to tell us exactly what was going on, and both willing to prescribe her something to "help" anyway. It was like Russian roulette for her brain—I just hoped she pulled the trigger on the right medication.

Every time the phone rang, it grew more difficult, almost pitiful, to watch Aunt Sam's hope grow. In the same way tension can suck the air out of a room, replacing it with something thicker, unfounded hope can do the same. It was even more palpable than tension sometimes, filling up the room around me, suffocating me like mustard gas. During the seconds after the phone started to ring and before it was answered, I couldn't breathe, no matter how hard I tried. Without fail, Aunt Sam expected it to be Dad, but she was only met with a myriad of unsettling questions, questions that only confirmed Dad's absence further. He'd owed people money, he'd been messing up at work, they'd planned to divorce. He'd hidden his secrets away from us, and instead of being more deeply concealed by his disappearance, they only bubbled up closer to the surface. With every call we answered that wasn't him, every time his chair sat empty at the dinner table, and every unwatched episode of *Jeopardy!*, Aunt Sam became less certain about her original claim that *Henry just wasn't the kind of man to up and leave.* She'd promised we'd hear from him on my birthday—if not with a phone call, then with his return. By dinnertime, no one wanted to acknowledge he'd made no contact—no one could bring themselves to acknowledge my birthday either.

I was officially fifteen, and I felt like seventy. I was having trouble trusting my mind, my ears, and even my eyes. I felt the way I imagined Grandpa Marshall did right before he went into an old folks' home. *Senile*, Mom had said. I think I was going senile. Like clockwork, the second I found myself alone with my thoughts, the radio in the family room would turn on by itself, sometimes blaring static, other times aptly tuned to Q107. This was peculiar (for a lot of reasons) because I thought its ability to transmit faltered decades ago. Also, most radios require human interaction to come to life, and whenever I'd go to turn it off, it would silence itself before I reached it. Senility wasn't fun.

And it wasn't just my ears I couldn't trust anymore—my eyes were in on it too. When walking down the hall to my room, I kept seeing things (well, *one* thing, really). At first, it was from the corner of my eye, then directly in my line of sight. Every time I walked by the painting of the Pretty Place, the ground shifted. Not below me—it shifted in the painting. It could have been a glare from the glass or maybe my own shadow, but even that didn't make any sense. I'd smashed it on the closet door, and no one seemed to notice or care that it had miraculously mended itself, finding its way back to its original spot (not once, but twice). I'd say that was cause for concern—you know, something worth mentioning. Meanwhile, Dad's framed coin collection left a conspicuous blank spot on the wall, and no one noticed or cared to mention that either. It had become blatantly obvious to me that no one else in the family was gifted with the powers of deduction—no one had even asked about his briefcase.

I'd been waiting for someone to point out the things that just weren't adding up, to point out that something was awry. I waited and waited, but when nothing happened, I realized that I was beginning to experience only the opposite. Tiny truths were solidifying Dad's big reasons for leaving. It was hard to think about, but I guess it wasn't a small victory—it was a huge one.

***

"You've been spending a lot of time up here," I said to the closed door of the tree house. I knew Isaac heard me climb up the ladder—he just hadn't indicated if I was welcome yet. I knocked gently, trying to be polite, uncertain of the shape he was in.

"All right, all right, come in," he bellowed, swinging open the little hobbit door. As one would expect of a hobbit home, a strong boozy scent and a thick cloud of smoke greeted me upon entry. The tree house wasn't just a smoking room anymore, but a personal bar too.

"What is going on in here? You stink, man."

"Life stinks, Ivy. Get used to it!" His words of wisdom were more difficult to take seriously with his slight (but still noticeable) slur.

"I know, I know."

"Do you, though? You don't seem too broken up about Dad. Must mean you're dumb enough to think he's coming back," he said, taking a swig of what looked like water (but his slight slur and subtle sway told me it wasn't).

"You don't know that, Isaac! Aunt Sam said he just needs a break."

"Pfft. Sure, Iv," he said, spitting all over my face. "Convenient timing, don't ya think? Mom's clearly not okay. She's sick in the head."

"You're sick in the head." I couldn't resist an easy rebuttal, one that hopefully kept the conversation at shallow depths. I wasn't prepared to get into the nitty-gritty specifics, especially with an audience unprepared for the nitty-gritty answers.

It had been easy telling Aunt Sam and then Mom all the information they'd needed to assemble the story of what they thought happened the day Dad left. I'd been the gas they needed to get the wheels inside their heads turning so they could formulate their assumptions and cushion their consolations as they tried to make some sense of the bizarre situation. A situation we *needn't blow out of proportion.* A situation that *probably had a logical explanation wrapped up in it somewhere.* He'd forgotten to leave a note. He'd called, but the phones were off. He'd be back soon. He'd just needed a break. But the phones kept ringing, and the logical explanations kept changing. They were now hushed and behind closed doors, and the positive outlook had dissipated. *He's done something illegal, hasn't he? I didn't know he gambled. Maybe he couldn't handle the pressure at work. Do you think he'll file divorce papers?*

It wasn't hard with Aunt Sam or Mom, but with Isaac, it felt different. With Isaac, it hurt more to think about how he'd take it when he found out (he was right) that Dad was never coming back. With Isaac, the smell of vodka on his breath and skunk on his clothing was more telling of pain than the tears I'd seen (and heard) Mom crying. With Isaac, I didn't know what to say, so we sat in silence while the wheels in our heads turned—just in different directions.

"What did he say to you? Like, what was the last thing he said before he left?"

I had to stop the motion in my head and think about his question for a second. When I remembered, I was thankful I hadn't thought about it earlier. I closed my eyes and held my breath for a long time, hoping he couldn't see me or what I was thinking.

"Well, what was it?"

I prayed God would make him move on, forget about the question. But I'd bartered away everything valuable I had left in my life—I was out of favours.

"The last thing he said was 'You're a good kid, you know that?'" I mumbled as the back of my throat started aching. "Then I told him he was a good dad too."

The words reluctantly escaped my mouth, and tears reluctantly escaped our eyes. If Isaac had planned to keep a tough exterior, he'd failed—all of his armour had fallen off now. I'd heard Mom tell Dad alcohol was a depressant, and since I couldn't remember the last time I'd seen Isaac cry, I had to believe it was true.

"He must have known what he was doing. He must have known he was going to leave that night, Ivy. Think about it."

"Yeah, I guess you're right," I said. I liked the way it sounded coming out, and I liked the way it made me feel even more. It felt good to picture him alive and well somewhere else (just not here). "And he took his suitcase, ya know, his briefcase, even his coin collection from the hall wall. No one's even noticed."

"I noticed—just didn't think there was much point mentioning it. I care more about Mom now. Someone's gotta figure out what's wrong with her."

He was speaking normally again, as if thirty seconds of crying had sobered him up.

"She's really sick. Aunt Sam says she's been like this on and off her whole life, just never this bad. She might have, you know, a mental illness," I treaded lightly, having never said it out loud before. If I was right, she'd be the first person I'd ever met with a mental illness, and I wasn't sure how to feel about that.

"Duh, Ivy. What did you think was going on?"

Damn it, Isaac. I shrugged. I wasn't even going to attempt to say what I *thought* was going on. It would be about as useful as telling him that our antique radio was haunted.

"Do you think Mom knew Dad was gonna leave her?"

I had to let myself hum part of Led Zeppelin's "Babe I'm Gonna Leave You" before I answered. Despite the lyrics' sad connection to our shitty situation, the song still made me feel happy. Or maybe it was sad . . . I had to be pretty messed up to get those two feelings confused.

"Really? Singing? Now?"

I didn't hear myself singing out loud—but like happiness and sadness, I mixed up my inside and outside voices too.

"Sorry. I don't know if she knew. Probably. If she did know and he's not coming back, then all we can do is help Aunt Sam get her better because we've only got the one parent now."

I wanted to believe it was true—maybe I *needed* to believe it was true. Every time I thought about Dad being alive, I felt better, less likely to vomit without warning, more capable of sleeping and eating, more capable of surviving.

"Yup, and I'm fine with it," said Isaac, pulling his armour back over his chest.

It wasn't right, but I could get used to the thought of Dad leaving. *It sure beat the hell out of the truth*, I thought as I opened the curtains and threw up out the window behind me.

CHAPTER 34

June 2018

It's funny to think I inherited my money problems from Henry, the man who devoted his life to working in finance. I suppose gambling is the antithesis of financial security, however, and we all had to learn the hard way that Henry's gambling had grown into a serious problem—we were left with the debt, after all.

Even after my diagnosis in April, I continue to obsess about what negative health issues I might have inherited from my parents. If it wasn't Mom's mental illness, could Henry have had a rare bone disease that presented later in life? Was I predisposed to diabetes and heart disease? Would I go grey early? What about male-pattern baldness—was I at risk? It was like I was the only person in the world who didn't have a father to bounce questions off of. *Hey, Henry, I hate cabbage and men. Did I get that from you?* My therapist suggested I write a list of some of the positive qualities I'd inherited from either parent, at least what I could remember. The list goes on and on for Mom, but Henry's begins and ends with musical taste.

A penchant for whisky and making bad choices (with money) were the only other characteristics I could claim to have inherited from Henry. I was thankful neither problem was as crippling for me as they were for him. I don't remember much from the summer he left, but I think I remember *why* he did. I'd been there while Mom and Aunt Sam pieced it all together. It started with the call from his work when his unaccounted-for absence began to raise questions about (unaccounted-for) funds in the (unaccounted-for) books he kept. I remember standing by as his firm's lawyers questioned Mom about our finances—where he kept our savings, if they could have access to our records and accounts. Upon closer inspection, two things became clear: he'd been embezzling money from his clients, and none of it resided in our bank accounts.

Doug, his supposed best friend, folded like a cheap lawn chair, helping to fill in the holes of the investigation in order to keep his job. He admitted that he and Henry would borrow money sometimes from the men who owned the "company" Mom and Doug's wife—I think her name was Nancy—worked at. Henry had gotten in deep, borrowing dirty money from Stan Sternwood in order to win back, at the casino, the money he'd stolen from his clients. An ill-fated plan, given the casino was where he'd lost our money in the first place.

Mom had known there was something going on—she'd known there'd been a new tension at work—but she hadn't known the danger wasn't connected to her—it was connected to Henry. She'd been partially right about the mistress too—it just so happened the mistress's name was Jack. Blackjack. It was the plight of an addict—always chasing their last hit to fix their last problem. But hit after hit, Henry's problems grew larger—at work, at home, and in his marriage, threatening our safety. It was a perfect storm, a hole he dug so deep, he knew he'd never get out alive. At a minimum, he was facing divorce and jail time, or at a maximum, divorce and violence at the hands of his lenders. Owing illegitimate money to a group of legitimate criminals was a dangerous game he played with the devil, but the devil always cheats.

"Spanish Train" by Chris de Burgh is the song that plays in my head every time I think about Henry's gambling problem. It's about Lucifer and Jesus playing poker, gambling with the souls of the dead. If they made a movie about my life, it would be a part of the soundtrack, playing during the montage of Henry's demise. And he'd loved this tune, so it meant (if I'm being honest with myself) I loved it too. We'd listen to it on repeat, and I'd belt it from the back seat of his Supra—the bucket seats I could barely get in and out of. Whenever I got really carried away, he'd turn the volume down, leaving only my squeaky prepubescent voice to serenade him and Isaac. And (if I'm being honest with myself again) he used to make us laugh a lot.

Thinking about the options Henry had that summer, I know that none of them boded well for him or his family. In some ways, I had to give him credit for running away. He wanted to give us more than he ever had, and when it was clear that this desire stood to give us even less, he left. Deep down, Henry had a lot of good in him. It's just easier for me to remember him as the villain—way easier.

CHAPTER 35

Tuesday, August 10th, 1999—24 days since Dad . . . **left**

We rode fast toward Sunrise Beach, our bikes cutting through the muggy air that smelled of hot pavement and pond water. It felt good. I haven't spent much time outside since Dad left, and I haven't seen Robyn in weeks.

"Well, what do you think? Is he coming back or no?" asked Robyn.

She'd wanted to meet at Mount Everest, but the thought of going anywhere near the Pretty Place made me strangely uneasy.

"It's hard to say. I honestly don't know what I think anymore," I replied, swerving to ride over a pothole filled with soft asphalt. It was true I didn't know what I thought anymore, because my thoughts didn't exist. It had been radio silence up there for weeks, and I wasn't dreaming—not even nightmares. My mind was vacant, empty.

"Well, at least Patty-Poo is getting better, right? And you get to see Aunt Sammy more, so that's cool."

Usually her undying optimism perked me up, though for some reason it made me feel as hopeless as my empty mind did. Inexplicably hopeless, like her original suggestion to meet at Mount Everest. I couldn't remember the last time I'd had an independent thought or a concrete explanation for an independent feeling. Strange, strange days were upon us, days I knew were passing, one after the other, sunrise to sunset, but days I felt absent from. Almost as if I was on autopilot, just going through the motions.

"Yup, pretty cool."

"And how's Isaac taking the fact that Henry just up and left?"

Her inquiry didn't rouse even the slightest irritation. *Why had I cared if she liked him, anyway?* It felt so trivial now.

"He seems okay. He's not around much, practising for the Post Thrills' upcoming gigs and whatnot. I can tell he's hurt, but he seems more angry than anything."

"That's fair. It must be so hard," she said.

She was careful not to make too much eye contact, but when she did, her eyes were sad, and her expression was empathetic (I hated it). It had only been a few weeks, but the empathy was bothering me more than anything else. Empathy that came in the form of long sighs, slow blinking, concerned nods, and "I'm so sorry to hear." Usually from people who claimed to know me but I didn't recognize—people who must have been a part of my life before, when I was still capable of the elusive brain activity otherwise known as thought.

"Well, he'll probably come back, and Mom's getting better, so everything will be fine." I heard myself saying it, brushing her words off like a horsefly about to bite. Empathy had a way of confirming situations that hadn't been (fully) confirmed, and that wasn't *fair* in my eyes. There was no conclusion to our story yet, so there didn't need to be any (conclusive) commiseration. Dad could still come back; no one was taking that off the table just yet, except maybe Isaac.

"You're right. Anyway, I'm sure you're sick of talking about it. What else is new?"

"Um, we start high school in three weeks!" I feigned excitement but knew I should've appreciated the subject change. Aunt Sam and Isaac only talked about Mom's doctor's appointments and Dad's departure. I was sick of it—I was sick of everything. I was just always feeling sick.

"Yeah, we do!" she exclaimed as she rode past the path that led to Sunrise Beach.

"Where are you going? That was the turn."

"I know. I just want to ride by Allen's house," she replied curtly. Her cheeks quickly turned pink. It was faint under her swarthy late summer skin, but I could still see it.

"Oh my God, why?" I said, already knowing the answer.

***

"Do you dream much?" I asked, lying beside Mom on her bed.

Lying-down conversations had become the new norm for our family; Mom's bed was her office, and horizontal chit-chat was our water cooler equivalent.

"Lately, a bit more," she replied. I'd gotten into the habit of counting the number of words she'd say at one time, using my fingers like an umpire counting strikes. Her sentences often ranged from one to three words, so a four-word reply was a home run.

"What do you mean, lately? You weren't before?"

"Well, I wasn't sleeping before."

Five words—new record.

"Oh, right. Yeah, that makes sense."

"Why do you ask?"

I was normally the one leading our conversations and doing all the question asking, and while she may have gone down in word count, she got double the points for an inquiry.

"No reason, really. I just can't remember my dreams anymore, and it's starting to freak me out."

"It's probably better that way."

Back up to five—outta the park!

The conversation ended with that—brief, but progress was made nonetheless. Regular conversation wasn't easy for Mom anymore; it had gone from being an unconscious inevitability to a scheduled activity. The doctors told us that the little energy her body maintained should be used to fix her brain, not for being social. She was allowed to sleep a lot if she felt she needed it, but we had to check in on her at least twice a day. As long as she didn't want to sleep "forever," the doctors said to leave her be. I knew no one could actually sleep forever, so I wasn't as worried about it as Aunt Sam seemed to be.

We'd brought the basement TV upstairs for her, but it sat collecting dust on her vanity. She wasn't interested, even when it was on mute; she said it was too noisy. We'd bring our dinners upstairs and eat on the floor next to her bed sometimes too. She'd usually pretend to be sleeping, but I'd seen her smirk at the jokes we told, the really funny ones, anyway. Sleep deprivation and mental sickness could take a lot from you, but it hadn't taken her sense of humour—small victory.

Maybe Mom was right—maybe it was better for me to not remember my dreams (or parts of my reality). It felt good to hear her say something I didn't immediately want to question or refute. I'd expected it to take a lot longer for me to trust her words again after what happened, after I realized how gullible I'd been. I was embarrassed. It was hard to believe someone so *precocious* could be so puerile. But I didn't want to doubt her; I wanted things to go back to the way they were, to be normal (as normal as they could be with Dad gone). I hoped we'd find ourselves there again, in the realm of familiarity, when conversations returned to a vertical position and I stopped calculating her responses like they were math equations. When Robyn's Mom let her come over again and we didn't owe Doug money. When Aunt Sam's visits were short and sweet and she never told me to do my laundry. And, oh yeah, when I could go a few days without feeling sick—that would be nice too.

CHAPTER 36

Friday, October 22nd, 1999—97 days since he left

*At first, the food appeared at our door because Mom was obviously
sick, then because Dad was obviously never coming back. But finally,
the gifts of casserole have slowed. No more cellophane-wrapped dishes
of sympathy lining our kitchen counter—only took three months.*

Tuna casseroles, shepherd's pie, baked ziti, lasagna—they all just
tasted like pity now (and sadly, pity had a way of making me lose my
appetite). We didn't need it anyway—the food or the pity. Mom was
almost better, cooking, sleeping, and showering unprovoked. She'd
even applied for some jobs. Aunt Sam said it was a bit premature, that
she'd only been out of the hospital for six weeks, but Mom said she
felt good on her new meds (finally). They balanced her out, unlike
the last ones, which only made her more uneven. I didn't know much
about mental sickness, but I'd assumed being diagnosed would be a
lot easier, a lot less time-consuming and confusing than it had been.
The idiots who passed for doctors in this town made matters worse.
Aunt Sam wanted to bring Mom to Toronto to see a specialist (and
eventually have us move there), but we both knew that was a long
shot—small town livin' was the only livin' Mom trusted.

I noticed that people on the road waved to us less, as though Dad's leaving somehow made us less worthy of the effort. Mom didn't care, as she'd grown a resilient skin. "Things are really put into perspective after you lose your marbles," she'd joke. Dad's leaving seemed to bother her about as much as the neighbour's changed attitudes, but that Isaac had become merely an honorary family member, that drove her nuts (oops, I had to remind myself not to use that kind of derogatory language anymore.) Let me rephrase: Isaac's prolonged absences drove her crazy. Wow, one more time: Isaac's absences thoroughly displeased her. But no matter how angry she got about it, she couldn't hide how much she enjoyed hearing him practise his guitar alone in his room. When he did make it to dinner, he looked as vacant as Dad's seat at the table, but she must have appreciated the semblance of normalcy—one empty seat was better than two.

I didn't look at either vacancy with disdain, and I didn't look at it with hope either. Isaac had become unbearable to be around unless he was stoned, so I was fine with him never re-entering his own consciousness. And Dad wouldn't live here anymore even if he did show up, so what was the difference? I thought about calling Dad's family in Ireland, to see if he was there. It was the only place in the world he had any family, and the only place I could imagine him being. I didn't want to hurt Mom, though; she was being proud, I just wanted to know. She said he'd want that, he'd want us to come looking for him, but we weren't going to. We weren't going to beg him to be a part of our family. Begging a man for anything didn't look good on a woman, she reminded me. She was back to reminding me of all sorts of things again, instead of me having to remind her of her own name (and the importance of personal hygiene). I had to bite my tongue last week when she asked me why it looked as if I hadn't brushed my hair since spring. She wasn't losing days or hours anymore, but she wasn't gaining back the days or hours she'd lost either. They were gone, they'd never come out of their hiding place, and she'd stopped seeking them. We all had.

Dr. Loverro told us it was pretty common to lose a bit of yourself when experiencing a "psychotic break." It meant exactly that; something in her mind had broken. She'd stopped retaining memories, identity, practicality, common sense—basically, she'd stopped retaining sanity. But then, like a broken bone, her brain started to heal. The cast stayed on longer than expected, but I knew it had been a bad break (worse than the clean fracture of my tibia). She had a lot more to heal from, and we weren't allowed to imply that Dad's leaving played any part in the that. Dr. Loverro suggested Aunt Sam and I remove anything from her room that could be "triggering"—things she'd fixated on before she broke. Sam removed the phone and the unplugged lamps from the nightstands, photos of Dad (discreetly), some books, and a weird stash of items she'd hidden in the wicker trunk (that for some reason smelled of vomit).

I only took her daybook, seemingly harmless with its sweet, floral-themed cover, though you can't always judge a book by its cover. We all wore the best versions of ourselves on the outside for everyone to see, bright and cheery, concealing the darkness that lined our pages. You had to look deep inside, between those lines to really know a person, and sometimes even then, you'd need to decode the message. Mom's daybook was filled with a mix of normalcy and absurdity, appointments and apparitions—it was *interesting* in the way people use that word for things that confuse rather than intrigue them. The gibberish she wrote about could have made sense to her at the time, but I wasn't going to risk it ever making sense to her again. When I showed it to Aunt Sam and she insisted on showing it to Dr. Loverro, it ultimately led to the booking of her little "vacation." Unfortunately, it wasn't in the tropics—it was in the psych ward. They'd decided that alongside the pages covered in cherry blossoms and chrysanthemums were encrypted plans of a disturbing nature. Plans that required a hospital stay. Plans that implied she'd wanted to kill herself. Not actual plans to do it, but plans to remind herself why *not* to do it. They said that if you might harm yourself or others, you couldn't stay at home. It didn't matter that she wasn't actually suicidal; to them one plus one equaled two in every situation.

She had ten extra hours put back into her daily schedule (from not sleeping), so I guess she had a lot of hours to think about weird things. I totally understood that—there are only so many butterflies and rainbows you can think about before you need to examine the more morbid aspects of life. Since Dad left, I'd be happy to find myself thinking about any of those things— butterflies, rainbows, death, even a dead rainbow-coloured butterfly, for all I cared—just as long as when I visited the halls of my mind, they weren't so painfully empty.

Mom's mind evidently never found itself empty—even when it appeared the most absent. In my opinion, she had an admirable system going, but of course, no one agreed with me. When her illness got the best of her and the halls of her mind filled up with dread, she'd write out scriptures over and over again until the thoughts or feelings went away. Meaningful stuff—stuff that told her suicide wasn't an option. She'd also write letters to her sicker self, reminding her of all the blessings she had to live for, all the reasons she had hope and strength. It was as though a small fraction of her sane self persisted, that she'd left a couple of lights on to guide her out of the shadows. To me, that kind of commitment to living was impressive, the opposite of what you'd expect would buy you a ticket to the Cuckoo's Nest. I was just glad it hadn't been a one-way flight; her brain had come back less broken than it was going in. I wasn't allowed to visit her there, so I called and requested all the pillows be removed from her bed and the beds of the other guests. The lady I spoke to sounded confused and after hanging up on me three times, asked me to stop calling. So much for the third time being a charm.

CHAPTER 37

July 2018

It's as though Isaac's plan to extend his number of properties has stirred something up inside of me. Sure, I'm a bit jealous that he's buying his second vacation home, and sure, I loathe myself for feeling that way, though jealousy and self-loathing are feelings I'm used to. Neither could cause a *stir* as it were. *Stirrr as it werrrre.* That makes me laugh, but I'm not exactly a tough crowd right now. I've done a shot of Canadian Club. Okay, okay—two (four) shots of Canadian Club.

I'm not sure if I'm trying to ward off sleep or bring it on. All I know is the idea of going to sleep is making me uncomfortable. It's normal for me to feel anxious (worried even) when it comes to sleep and how evasive it can be, but I'm not used to the idea of sleep making me feel uncomfortable.

Since Isaac called me from Coyoacán (where his other vacation home in Mexico is) to tell me he planned on buying a million-dollar cottage on Lake Scugog, I've been having some pretty gnarly nightmares. The type of vividly scary shit that's going to take years to unpack with my newest shrink. It's no secret there's still some trauma floating around in Lake Scugog. I heard it had to be dug out a second time because it sucked so badly at retaining water, its one job. By *heard*, I mean I read, because yeah, sometimes I check out the local newspaper online to see what's going on. No big deal. Even though I stopped resenting the lake for holding me back a grade, I still take pleasure in knowing it's a bit of a failure too.

I'm not a failure, Mom continues to remind me every single time we speak. When I called her last week, she'd just finished reading the *New York Times* bestselling novel that a client of mine wrote. My decision to become a literary agent is proving to be the first good decision I've made in probably a decade, and she's not letting me forget it. *Your father would be proud*, she said. I balked at the claim; it was bold, even for a bolder older woman. I mean an old and bold woman. No, I mean an older, bold woman. *As it werrrre.* Being older is only relevant because everyone knows that the more grey hair you have, the more shit you get away with, and Mom's curls have turned a distinguished salt and pepper. I was proud of myself for letting her say Dad would be proud of me and not spewing some hateful bullcrap right back at her. She knows my preference is (and always has been) to hate on him. Lately, it seems everyone got off the hate train, but it's just not my stop yet. I'm also not ready to . . .

I'm not entirely sure where I was going with that, but I just took another shot and it's clear I'm writing some kind of warped diary entry as a way to ward off sleep. Confirmed. If I have to walk through the halls of that house again and wake feeling as if I'm there and not here, I'm going to scream. In the years since we moved away from the Island, I've gotten used to it making the odd guest appearance in my dreams. My shrink says that's normal, since it's the house I've lived in the longest. The dreams are usually about innocuous activities, like sitting in the front window, eating at the kitchen table, or running around the basement with the lights turned off. One time I dreamed I was dusting my bookshelf in my bedroom, literally just doing some spring cleaning. Nothing major, and certainly nothing worth discussing ad nauseam in a therapy session. (My current shrink, Barb, is amazing and consequently charges $155 an hour, so I have to be chooooosy with my isshhhuuues.) But since Isaac shared his exciting (non-braggy) news about his impending purchase, my dreams have extended beyond the walls of the house and out into the forests and the trails behind it. I even dreamed about the tree house Isaac and I used to hang out in. I'd completely forgotten about it.

Sometimes, my old friend, Robyn, was there with me, or sometimes Chelsea was. At times it felt like a memory—as if I'd done it before, walking that path, picking up that grasshopper, throwing that rock, breathing that air. But people's memories don't just come back to them in their dreams. That isn't how it works. That's absurd . . . right?

List for Barb—Next Session:

+ *Do people's dreams come back as memories? Wait . . . does that make sense?*

+ *Is it okay to be jealous of your siblings?*

+ *Is your full name Barbie? By chance, is your husband's name Ken?*

I have to stick to the really important things with Barb's price tag—I keep notes between each session so I don't get off track.

I had to admit to Isaac, purchasing a cottage out there felt like an odd choice. With the sales from his solo album, he could buy a whole island. Why would he want a cottage on just a part of a muddy one? I mean, the water isn't even nice—it's half mud. In fact, all I can think about when I think about the Island is mud. It's just one pile of mud in the centre of a muddy lake made of mud. But as long as he hadn't gotten it into his muddled-up mind to buy our old house, then I was okay with it, I told him. Who knows if that house even still exists outside my dreams? It's likely been torn down and replaced with something nicer; I also read in the local paper that most of the waterfront properties have suffered that fate.

I remember that line about suffering fate from the John Frusciante tune "Omission," a song about omitting yourself for the sake of other people. See now, that's a chooooon. Not to imply that other tunes other people write are not tunes, but that's just a *tune*, ya know? I'll probably play it on repeat for the rest of the night—right until the morning, if it saves me from sleeping. The whole day today has gone by so quickly, I've barely had time to shake the heebie-jeebies from last night's dream. I could feel the dirt squishing between my toes and the rain falling on my face. The coals in the firepit radiated heat, and the pool water washed me clean. Everything felt so tangible and smelled so real. When I woke, eyes still closed, I had to glide my fingers over the scar on my thigh, then my palm, just to make sure I was back in my own body—that I was back in 2018. Even if I didn't want to be here, I didn't want to be there even more—not that night, doing whatever it was I was doing. Nothing appeared to be wrong, but it all felt wrong, really wrong. In the dream, I floated aimlessly in the pool while it rained, something I'm sure I've actually done before. But I had an overwhelming desire to hold my head underwater, to push my hands up under the ledge to keep my body from floating to the surface. No one was chasing me, but I still felt I was running and hiding from something. Whatever it was, it scared me enough to make drowning feel like a better alternative. I know it was only a choice dream-Ivy made, but I wouldn't be in therapy if I didn't believe my subconscious mind did things to fuck with my conscious mind (or in some cases—save it). Damn you, dream-Ivy. Ah, to hell with it—damn you too, awake-Ivy.

CHAPTER 38

Monday, June 19th, 2000—338 days since Dad left!

I survived.

I survived my first year of high school, and if that wasn't something to celebrate, I'm not sure what was. I managed a smooth 51 percent in math, not cause for celebration per se, but calculus wasn't my thing, and I wasn't going to force it. I had to believe that by the time I grew up, I wouldn't need to do math in my day-to-day life anyway. I already kept a calculator beside the register at Just Because, the craft store I worked at. Times, they were a-changin'.

We moved into town last December, about five months after Dad left. Mom and Dad had sunk so much money into that house, the mortgage was unmanageable. It was a long, depressing December, to say the least. It felt as if everyone was dreading the first Christmas without Dad, but much as I managed to finish my first year of high school, we managed the first big holiday without him. Not to mention we moved the contents of our entire house into a tiny apartment without his help. Getting by with just Mom turned out to be easier than we thought it would be. It also helped that Aunt Sam lived with us for almost six months after he left. I missed her being in the house with us, even if the apartment was too small. I missed walking in on her and Mom dancing in the family room while "It's Too Late" by Carole King blasted on the stereo. Aunt Sam said it was Mom's "get up and get over it" song. They seemed to regress to childhood together, dancing around, jumping on and off the couch, throwing pillows in the air like fools in the rain, but I loved it. If I didn't miss anything else, I missed that.

Well, that and the *old* Isaac. The Isaac who almost became my friend again. I knew it was hard on him, having a deadbeat dad. He said the hardest part was that Dad didn't even say goodbye. With the mess Dad had gotten himself into, Isaac would have respected his decision to leave, but he thought he could have at least said, "*Sayonara, kiddo.*" That's how Isaac expected he would have bid him, his *only* son, farewell—casual and partially in a foreign language. I would have preferred that to "You're a good kid, you know that?" Puzzle pieces had been permanently lost, but it was as if I had two of that one; it was burned so deeply into my brain some mornings, I had to check to see if it was written backwards onto my forehead, permanently, like a scar. You know, as if written from the inside out.

Normally, I'd feel inclined to write out some lyrics from the song "A Long December" by the crappy Counting Crows, but I'd gotten over that band. They'd moved to my Ex-Favourite Bands List. I tried to avoid thinking about them, even if I accidentally chose my words unwisely. That was just one way I made things easier for myself. I didn't talk with anyone about Dad leaving us, I didn't think about the details from last summer, I didn't listen to his music, I didn't tell his jokes, and since we'd moved, I didn't have to look at any of his stuff.

I liked living in town. I was closer to everything: the shops, the mall, my work, my school. The Island had been good when I was a little kid, but as an adult, I'd outgrown the country charm. I wanted practicality, not cow shit. Sure, I missed Robyn, Katie, Crystal, and Nick, I guess. We'd finally shared the same teachers and classes at the same non-Catholic school, but when I moved, I started running with a different crew of girls. A crew that knew nothing about the Island and everything that went along with it. A crew that saw me in my new and improved skin, my high school skin.

We got in trouble at school a few times for skipping class, smoking weed, boozing on school property, etc. But it was just regular stuff for us city girls. Robyn called us the Clueless Crew, and yeah, they were a bit vacuous, but I preferred them to the country bumpkins. I didn't care about doing all that immature stuff anymore—the farm frenzying or nicky nicky nine doors. In town, the parties I went to were house parties, not bush parties, the convenience store was actually convenient, not two hours away, and the Pretty Place was a beautifully maintained garden-park, not a stupid forest. I had a real job I could walk to, and oh yeah, I started to hang out with someone with a penis. A penis that liked me, I mean, *like, really liked* me. It was a nice change—all of it. How different my life was when it wasn't surrounded by a man-made pond. Isaac loved it too. Living in town meant he was closer to his gigs. And he was gigging a lot, taking full advantage of his dropout status. If he was home, he was writing music and practising. If he was out, he was at a gig or waiting tables to pay for a gig (or booze). I had to admire his commitment to his craft (and avoiding sobriety at all costs). I couldn't commit to anything anymore. I couldn't concentrate for more than fifteen minutes at a time, not even to write a journal entry. I used to love taking detailed notes about the boring details of my life, but I guess writing was just another thing I'd outgrown (same with all my bras).

When we moved, we had to take our big Viceroy home with the tower ceilings, three bedrooms, three bathrooms, two skylights, a wood-burning stove, a solarium, an acre of land, and a pool and compress its contents into a two-bedroom-plus-den apartment in town. It was a huge change, but I made a list of reasons why moving didn't suck:

Pros:

+ *No five-hundred-foot-long driveway to bring the garbage cans down/up*

+ *Only one bathtub to clean*

- *No mailbox to have to walk to*
- *No lawn to rake or mow*
- *No walkway to shovel*
- *No wood to stack against the shed we didn't have*
- *No pool that constantly turned green*

Cons:

- *No pets allowed*

I could have kept going with the pros. Overall, an apartment was easier for us. Simple and smaller, but easier. Isaac graciously accepted the den as his sleeping quarters, and Aunt Sam slept with me until she moved back to Toronto. The downsizing required a bit of a purge, but damn, did it feel good to dispose of our old life. Instead of the ceremonial end-of-fall leaf burning, we had a ceremonial purge fire where we burned anything we didn't want to take to our new apartment. I burned all sorts of things, most of my journals, my baby headboard, my paintings, and basically everything from the hall wall upstairs—we agreed there'd be no wall like that in the new place. It was satisfying to see so much of my childhood go up in smoke, figuratively and literally. That's what we Marshalls did, right? If we didn't know what to do with something, we either burned it or buried it. It felt like the most definitive way to do things, really. It was like a rite of passage into adulthood. I think I got my period the week after too (better late than never, as they say).

When I tried to burn the radio from the family room, Mom suggested I try to sell it like the trampoline. But I told her I wanted to give the trampoline to Nick since his parents would never buy him anything like that, and she was really touched by the "kind" gesture. Realistically, I was just too lazy to make up sale flyers. Robyn told me Nick sold it two weeks after we moved, likely for drug money. He'd gotten into some heavy shit when high school started. I'd seen him strung out in the halls, wandering aimlessly like an extra on the set of *Night of the Living Dead*. His eyes looked as dead as he did, staring at me as if he didn't recognize me anymore. I would have been embarrassed if my new friends had found out I'd associated with him in my past life, so I didn't make a fuss about it. Unfortunately, despite using an entire bottle of lighter fluid, I could only burn so much of my past into oblivion.

Mom. Is. Well. She's well. She's really well! I loved saying it because it took so many months to get her there. So many months, doctors, meds, and false diagnoses. But, almost a year later, I could confidently say she was finally, truly, beyond-a-shadow-of-a-doubt well. She was the best she'd ever been. She looked like herself again, having put on some "happy weight," as the doctor called it, which made me think I was the happiest I'd ever been too. She'd gotten a new job at the Freshair Heating Company in town, and she'd been seeing someone! Two someones, if you counted her therapist. It had only been a few weeks with the romantic someone, but Isaac and I thoroughly supported the decision to move on.

Even if Dad had come back, the damage was irreparable. His continued (unexplained) absence was as good as divorce papers. Though there were some legal matters attached to real divorce papers, I'd mostly kept myself out of the details. All I knew was that Aunt Sam called Dad's family in Ireland back in the fall, asked if he was there or if they wanted to investigate his whereabouts, and they said no. Sorry, they said, "No thanks, all good, no worries, he'll turn up!" They pretty much shared our sentiment, which was no sentiment at all. But I guess he had run away from Ireland too, all those years ago; this was nothing new.

Once Mom's diagnosis was confirmed and we finished some light renovations and put the house up for sale, it was as if we'd all made an unspoken pact. When that sale sign turned to a sold sign, that would be it—there would be no looking back. As fate would allow, moving was how Mom got her new job and met her new *someone*, too. That's how you know things are meant to be—when it all just falls into place like the checkers in a game of Connect 4. We were a family of three now, but we'd still win the game with just the three of us. Three was better than two; I didn't have to be good at calculus to know that much.

CHAPTER 39

September 2018

I couldn't get out of it, no matter how hard I tried. Isaac rarely came to Ontario, and when he did, he didn't stay long. This visit was booked entirely around the house viewing; we'd be in and out "in two shakes of a lamb's tail," he reassured me.

I was surprised we weren't being transported by helicopter, but he joked it was too ostentatious. The canary-yellow Corvette we drove in didn't win any awards for subtlety either, though it matched Isaac's distressed jeans, spiked hair, and tiny leather vest perfectly.

"Are you excited, Iv?" he asked, taking the bends on Island Road far too quickly. The potholes were smaller, but the curves were the kind that just wouldn't quit. Not even after twenty years (kind of like mine).

"Excited for what? For you to buy a cottage out here?"

"Well, yeah, and just to see the Island again. You never came back here after we moved, did you?"

I rolled my eyes as he turned the yellow death trap onto Pine Point so abruptly, it felt as if the road had snuck up on him. I may have never come back to the Island, but it didn't seem all that familiar to him either.

I scoured the farmlands, assessing the open space, looking to see what had changed since we moved away, but was in disbelief. Was I mistaken, and we were actually in a time-travelling DeLorean and not a Corvette? Why did everything look exactly as it did almost twenty years ago, with no new developments, no subdivisions? Had we stayed here, maybe I wouldn't have aged either. *That would be nice*, I thought, pulling down the visor mirror to inspect the wrinkles on my forehead. I couldn't possibly call them laugh lines; they were just stress lines to me, brought on by years of sunscreen neglect. Sun damage was one of the many things I'd been negligent about that I couldn't go back in time and change, and things I couldn't change also stressed me out—it was a vicious cycle.

"Ah! Look, there's Ghost Road!" he shrieked. "Mississauga Trail. I didn't even know it had a real name. Weird." He slowed down as if he'd decided to pull out of the race. I welcomed the rubbernecking—I wasn't in any rush to get where we were going.

"Let's drive down it and park," I said. I knew he'd mistake my stalling as nostalgic enthusiasm, but he'd offered the cottage to me on weekends, and I had to play his little game to reap the benefits.

The long dirt road looked the same as it always did, though it was even more boring and useless now that I was seeing it as an adult in daylight. There was still a forest on both sides of the road with the same kind of trees, the ones that don't lose their leaves during winter. They looked sparser and somehow shorter, or perhaps I'd just grown taller (and fuller too). The ditches were still lined with pussy willows and cattails, two unrelated plants with cat-related names. If nothing else came of the trip, I'd at least be pleased with that feline-ization (I had to). The only notable change was the sad attempt at spray-painted graffiti on an exposed rock at the foot of the road sign. Ghost Road, it boasted (or at least tried to) with wiggly neon-orange letters. The artist had a flair for the obvious, and if they hadn't written it with their non-dominant hand as a joke, I hoped for their sake they were drunk.

THE PRETTY PLACE

"Still attracting a high-class clientele," I quipped, pointing to the rock.

"Yup, I love it. It's like nothing's changed."

He smiled, looking out of the car through every available window space, desperately flipping his head from side to side as if he was hoping to prove himself wrong. It was disturbing to see that the Island had frozen in time while we continued to age not so gracefully. Isaac's dyed hair and ill-advised clothing choices weren't fooling anyone. Like me, he wore his neglect on his face too, only his lines were bottle shaped and needle scarred. It had been a rough few years for him after Dad left. We thought Isaac found solace in his music, though we realized later that it wasn't so much the music as it was the sordid bunch of drugged-up misfits. Of course, his craft flourished in that scene, but so did his affinity for cocaine. Cocaine led to heroin, which led to rehab, which ultimately led to a multi-platinum album. Rehab helped him understand how to access the pain he used for creativity without using intravenous drugs. It did, however, take a bit longer for him to learn how to coax it out without the help of a stiff drink (completely understandable). Although he appeared to have gotten dressed while drunk, the man next to me had been sober for at least two years. His choice of sobriety was definitely a noble one; I just couldn't hop on the bandwagon. Sure, addiction sucked, but was sobriety really the answer? Was that a stupid question? I think so. The distinct *lack* of pollution in the air messed with my brain functions.

"We'll go down Darley and back around. The cottage I want to see is closer to Pine Point, across from the water. It was the spot where Aunt Sam said she'd want to live if she had the money to buy something on the Island. Remember it?"

I did remember it—clearly. It still hurt to think about her alive, happy. It hurt to think about her in any capacity really, and buying the cottage she'd wanted was undoubtedly going to make that worse—for me, at least.

"Of course I know which one. Why would you do that, Isaac?"

245

"I thought you'd love that. Like I'm buying it in her honour, you know?"

I did love it—I also hated it. Hot tears welled up in my eyes as I thought about Aunt Sam, how she died, the way they found her. I'd admired that she left a note that was more of an unrequited love letter addressed to life than a list of her life's misfortunes. When I saw it, I tried not to take any pleasure in the fact that, in her P.S., she'd quoted a line from Kurt Cobain's suicide note—actually a lyric from one of Neil Young's best songs about how it is better to burn out—opposed to fading away.

She wrote it in big loopy letters at the very end, but you could tell it wasn't an afterthought—it was her love letter's finale. The rest of it looked as if it had been scribbled quickly, as though her hands weren't moving as fast as her brain was—or as fast as the sleeping pills. The part addressed to me made little sense, but the postscript said it all. It stood out, black and bold as if she'd traced it over and over again as many times as she'd contemplated her demise. There was an unsettling irony in the words then, and there still is now, considering Neil Young is still alive. He's out-living everyone—he'll probably outlive me too. I guess he decided burning out wasn't so bad after all. I had to stop myself from reading the note every single day (Why am I such a masochist?), looking for the *meaning of life* encoded in the words, wallowing in the tragedy that is suicide. The idea of spending weekends at this cottage (her cottage) was bringing me about as much joy as gargling glass shards.

We pulled up to number 332, almost bottoming out on the ditch hump at the end of the long paved driveway. A memory rushed to the vacant spot behind my eyes (the spot I liked to keep empty). I knew the driveway—I knew it well. I remembered Robyn and me panicking as we escaped down it to the road, too careless to pick a better getaway route before we'd knocked on the door. We were caught that night by a man and his baseball bat. He claimed we'd scared his wife and kid, but we'd never been so scared in our lives. The memory made me smile, even though the act was mischievous; it still felt innocent, and I couldn't remember the last time I'd felt that way.

"I remember it here," I said to Isaac as I gently closed the car door, careful not to slam it. I hadn't anticipated the incredulity in my voice. Was it so hard to believe I remembered the place I grew up in?

"Well, yeah, Ivy! Duh! It wasn't that long ago." He laughed. "And you kept about a thousand journals, so I'm thinking you have a detailed description of every inch of the Island, no?" He spoke as if he didn't remember the giant bonfire we had before we sold the house in 1999. Most of my journals had been burned in that fire, and my memories went up in a cloud of smoke with them. If they hadn't, I probably wouldn't have a perpetually lit vacancy sign at the front of my brain's hippocampus hotel.

The cottage yard was lined with towering pine trees. It was partially hidden and felt more rural than most of the neighbouring properties. The real estate agent showing the cottage was comfortable leaving us the combination to the lock box, so we could check it out on our own; Isaac's fame had some unexpected benefits. I checked the knob first to see if it was unlocked, to see if people's trust levels remained as unscathed as the surroundings, or if age had jaded the Island in invisible ways.

"No one's lived in it for a few months," Isaac said, punching the combination into the lock. "Good for me. It means I can lowball them on the offer."

He got his frugality from Mom. She's right to say there's a reason *the rich get richer and the poor get poorer*. I'm not 100 percent sure what the reason is, but I wish she'd tell me because I just keep getting poorer.

Inside, the cottage wasn't at all what you'd expect from the outside. It was unassumingly modern, open, and unique. It had the same vibe as our old house with cathedral ceilings and skylights, only it was a bit smaller and with more updated fixtures.

"It's beautiful, Isaac. How did Aunt Sam know?"

"She wasn't the type to judge a book by its cover. She was smarter than that."

I smiled. "She was."

"Right across the street, it has open access to the lake, and the backyard stretches out far—way back." He waved his hands back and forth over his head as if he was directing air traffic. "The realtor even said I could negotiate a piece of farmland into the deal if I wanted to. Wouldn't that be fun?"

"Fun? No."

Farming was a lot of work, not exactly a hobby. And I remembered precisely which piece of farmland sprawled up behind this part of the road. It would be near the rock pile we used to meet at, in the fields that were endlessly fallow. Barren. Empty. Just dirt. It made me uneasy thinking about it.

"Let's go check it out. Being back here makes me want to explore!"

I wasn't exactly wearing hiking boots, but Isaac's excitement was infectious. I'd never been able to say no to him, no matter how hard I tried. A classic second-born characteristic. Always eager to please, regardless of personal needs or wants—it's something I'm working on with Barb.

"Fine, but I'm not staying out there after dark," I replied, practising boundary setting with a spiritless compromise. It was early afternoon, and the sun was still hot and high in the sky; it was unlikely we'd find ourselves in an impromptu game of manhunt, but at least I'd dictated some terms.

He took off his vest and threw it on the deck, readying himself for our adventure. I'd had a major inner conflict about my outfit that morning, recognizing that Isaac's fame made me more self-conscious about my appearance. When my protracted deliberation put me at risk of being late, I grabbed the first thing I'd tried on, jean shorts and a V-neck. I was glad I'd decided against a sundress now that he'd gone and turned us into a modern-day Lewis and Clark.

"Let's go! We can even find a walking stick." He smiled a big toothy smile—the one part of him that still reminded me of his formative years. His eyes were a beautiful, new ice-blue, captivating, and the whites were whiter since he'd quit drinking. They reminded me too much of Dad's eyes still, and though his eyes never seemed as clear, the blue hue was identical.

Everything around us, every fallen pine cone and dying dandelion, every bit of soil and surviving anthill, every curled red leaf and enduring green one—everything had an alluring power about it, conjuring up mixed feelings from our childhood, a time that often felt fictitious. The little pieces of the world around me were creating a strange place in the middle of the past and the present, as if I, an adult, was walking around in a child's world. It made me think about that forlorn time in my life. I'd try to never forget, no matter how old I got. I remember the torture I felt when I realized my youth was fleeting and how contrary that was to the intense desperation I felt to grow up. I've always been conflicted, and not just about what clothes to wear—about everything. It was the first real hot-cold, love-hate relationship I ever experienced. I wanted to be a kid forever, but I wanted to be able to buy booze too. I was Peter Pan, but I didn't want to live in Neverland.

I walked beside Isaac, feeling just as conflicted. I wanted to please my brother, but I didn't like the feeling I had as we ventured deeper into the backwoods. It was eerie. I wanted to believe it looked different, that it had changed as I had, but at the same time, I wanted to believe it looked the same as it always had. Different but the same—the same but different.

It was like an episode of *Pop Up Video*; with every step I took away from the cottage and into the world behind it, intrusive memories popped up in my mind. Memories of things I had otherwise lost track of long, long ago. Without invitation, I recalled the kitschy, little pet names we had for our favourite landmarks. It wasn't a rock pile—it was Mount Everest! Tiny Trail was overgrown, but there were remnants of it still. We followed it toward Spooner Drive, almost tripping down Mount Rushmore, which wasn't a cliff at all—hardly even a dip in the ground. Either Robyn and I had been dramatic, or the earth had evened out over the years. When I dreamed about it, it looked the way it did twenty years ago, not the way it did now.

"You and Robyn had a place you went to around here, didn't you?"

"One, stop reading my mind—I was just thinking about her. And two, how did you know that?" I asked. I shared a lot with Isaac, but there were a handful of things I'd never told him about, and *the place we went to around here* was one of them.

"Did you actually think I wouldn't read your journal when you left it in the tree house? Come *onnn*," he said, mocking my ignorance playfully.

I shrugged while heat rushed to my pale cheeks. I couldn't remember all the embarrassing nuggets of self-deprecation I'd stowed away in that journal, but I knew I'd saved it for a special kind of extreme—the kind of self-loathing, parent-hating drama you'd only be foolish enough to write down if you thought for sure no one would ever read it.

"Don't worry, I mostly skimmed it. Ironically, all the written-out, angsty song lyrics didn't really do anything for me."

His attempt to make me feel better only made me feel worse. It had been two decades—I didn't think teenage shame was supposed to last that long. In fact, I *knew* it wasn't supposed to last that long. I let out a quiet, *I'm-not-ashamed* giggle and continued following the path, watching his self-assured feet in his self-assured boots as he led the expedition forward.

"Yeah, the Pretty Place or whatever," I said. "It's amazing how much is coming back to me, just being here. It's crazy!"

"Better tell Barb," he teased. It wasn't funny, but he remembered her name, and that made me smile. He supported my decision to be in therapy, but he wasn't a big believer in anything that didn't come completely validated with a side order of science. "Talk is cheap," he'd say (though he knew it wasn't—he often helped me cover the bill).

"Do you want to go see it? The way you wrote about it, it was like some kind of Fruitopia or something."

I couldn't tell if he was joking or if he'd fried the part of his brain that helped him distinguish fruit juice from literature.

"I think you mean utopia, but yeah, let's go."

CHAPTER 40

The Same Day

We couldn't find it—or it wasn't there—or at least the *pretty* wasn't. I was reluctant to enter the forest. My strides were slow and burdensome; it was like I was wading through quicksand. Without knowing where to go, I found myself being silently directed as if a map had been buried deep inside of me and my unconscious knew where to find the X that marked the spot. I'd taken the lead, bringing Isaac deep into the forest, where I (must have) thought the Pretty Place would be, but what we found was distinctly unremarkable. I knew I was looking for a place that had some significance to me—but it only made me feel significantly unwell. It was dank and gloomy because the trees had melded together at the top, starving the environment of the light needed for it to flourish. The density of the trees made the forest uncomfortably quiet, and I had to pop my ears to make sure I hadn't gone deaf. Everything about it was unsettling, from the empty quarry to the trashed old car; it was full of garbage and wild undergrowth. It wasn't a pretty place at all, but more like a place where pretty things went to die—it felt that way too. I hated it in there. I couldn't breathe, and there was no circulation. The air that did manage to get in smelled mouldy like a cheap basement apartment. Yes, that's exactly what it reminded me of: my first apartment in Toronto, the one that flooded each spring.

The Pretty Place seemed to be the one place on the Island that age had *not* been kind to. I ran out, pulling cobwebs off my face, hurtling toward what I hoped to be an exit. Everything outside it appeared to have met the years with notable poise and grace, but the heart of it all was diseased.

I stood outside the forest, catching my breath, focusing my energy on not throwing up. It had become more of a hellish dystopia than a utopia. But had it always been that way? Or had I been looking at it through different eyes—optimistic eyes, innocent eyes?

"Well, that was definitely it. I remember it from your description. The Beetle and stuff. Can't say I see the appeal," Isaac said, hunching over with his hands on his knees, winded from chasing after me.

"That's not what it looked like when I was a kid—I swear." I felt obligated to defend myself, forgetting I'd decided to place a statute of limitations on childhood shame. "Let's go see the old house!" I heard myself saying. I needed to get as far away from there as possible.

"I thought you'd never ask!" He was beaming with an enthusiasm I wasn't prepared for. He reached down to pull up his socks and tighten his laces; his rigid combat boots weren't prepared for more hiking either. They looked identical to the signature boots he'd worn in the nineties, though I imagined the price difference was more than nominal.

"Pitter-patter, let's get at 'er," I said, mimicking Dad's voice in my head. *Who am I morphing into out here?* I wondered. Out in the fresh air, surrounded by nature, where the birds were chirping and the beauty was free. Out where I missed the lurking smog and herds of people, the incessant car horns and the six-dollar coffees. Out where I missed the city. I missed being as far away from the Island as possible, and I missed feeling like myself.

"Ha, ha, ha. Okay, Henry. Which way is the fastest route from here, the *Ugly Place?*" Isaac said, quickly tying his second boot. His haste was part of his childhood shame story, the part where he'd hid his fear of being the group's *Slowpoke,* Dad's nickname for him. I knew it had always bothered him (but it beat the hell out of Fairy Flat Feet in my opinion).

I led the way back past Aunt Sam's cottage, past that poor kid's backyard, and turned on the trail between the fenced lots and the Dark Forest. As we came across the clearing, the silhouette of our old house came into view. At first it felt familiar, as if I were walking into one of my dreams, but as we got closer, we could see that only the bones of the house remained, and it was more like walking into a nightmare.

The backyard fence had fallen over, resting perilously on the birch trees, which didn't appear equipped to handle the weight. They looked as if they'd been diagnosed with a terminal illness that forced them to remain barely alive but always on the cusp of death. The back door of the shed was ajar, hanging precariously off the top hinge. The shed's vibrant green paint, which had once matched the deck, had peeled off both structures, now weathered beyond recognition. Inside, the shelves were empty, storing only rogue leaves and windblown garbage. The cinder blocks that used to enclose the firepit were holding down a black tarp on the pool, which evidently hadn't held anything other than rainwater in years.

The solarium windows in the kitchen were boarded up, making it look like a drab, colourless Rubik's cube. I wanted to see the front bay window, but I shuddered to think it might be boarded up too. I'd remembered it fondly (and vividly) ever since we left. Even when I could remember nothing else, the memory of the comfort I felt reading in that nook remained steadfast.

"What the hell happened here?" I glanced at Isaac to see if he shared the same disgust in our discovery, but his expression was indifferent.

"What? What did you expect? It was half rundown by the time we left."

"No, it wasn't. What are you talking about?"

In my mind, the house had been a palace when we left it. It sold quickly after Mom put it on the market—at least I thought it had. It was a travesty to see it left in such careless disarray, punished for a crime it didn't commit. Or maybe it was karma for the crime committed within it—being abandoned the way we were—deserted for the second time in its life.

"There was some work left to do inside. I think a foreign buyer got it and then sold it, and then the next guy probably gave up on the renovation. Who cares? It's a hunk of junk anyway."

His words punched me in the chest as if the insult was intended to pierce my lungs. It surprised me to feel anything for the house, let alone fondness. Last week I'd dreamed about drowning myself in the pool, but today, staring at its ruins, I felt it deserved something more, something better. It was ragged and hopeless like a homeless person—it was a house that had found itself homeless.

I stepped over the dilapidated fence toward the *hunk of junk*. I wasn't sure if I wanted to go inside or if I was even capable of it. More scenes of a past life flickered in my mind, fierce and uncontrollable. I was plagued by memories of toasted marshmallows and beach towels, barbecues and dog toys. There'd been a doghouse by the back door, a clothesline from the deck to the shed, and a metal two-seater swing by the evergreens. I could smell the chlorine, propane, and the sunscreen—scents I'd always had an affinity for, but I'd never understood why. Why hadn't these memories been available to me all the times I'd searched for joy but came back with nothing? Why had I buried even them?

Isaac meandered around the shed, opening and closing windows, inspecting the wood, lifting the tarp. He appeared to be looking for something, touching everything softly as if he cared for it, respected it. He wasn't treating it like a hunk of junk; perhaps he just needed to remember it that way.

"Didn't you bury a time capsule or something in the back by the fence?" he asked as he bravely ascended the decrepit deck stairs.

"I don't think so."

"Yes, you did. You were worse than Chelsea, burying stuff around the backyard. Henry hit something on the riding lawn mower once, and he lost it on you, remember? You hadn't buried it deep enough." He found the recollection especially hilarious, laughing hysterically until tears streamed down his face. I laughed along with him, finding humour only in his boisterous cackling—exactly like Dad's laugh— and I didn't want it to stop.

"I do remember we buried Chelsea's ashes over there." I pointed to the cluster of birch trees I knew protected her remains.

"Ewwww," he wailed, rushing toward me. "Where exactly? Do you remember? We should take them. They're ours!"

I wondered if Isaac treated each happening as potential song content. Digging up a dog's ashes was interesting, right? It would translate into some morbid song lyrics, but that would just add to his mystique.

"Yeah, I know where it is . . . generally." I went to the tree I'd carved a C in and walked three short paces south toward the lake. I tried to account for being bigger now, though my feet hadn't grown much since puberty. "Right here!" I shouted.

He handed me a stick he'd already grabbed for the excavation. Today we were home inspectors, explorers, historians, and archaeologists.

"Get diggin', sister!"

CHAPTER 41

The Same Day

Isaac was right—it was a time capsule, but I don't think that was my original intention. Had Dad not put a garbage bag around the cardboard box that held Chelsea's ashes, nothing would have survived. Mother Nature's a destructive bitch even under the surface. The contents of the box clanked together, sliding from one side of the bag to the other as Isaac slowly pulled it up from the earth.

"What else do you think is in there?" he asked, sitting down and resting the tattered bag on the ground beside me. He was proud of his retrieval but winded from an hour of laborious stick digging.

I shrugged. I sat down too, uneasy about what he'd retrieved and winded from an hour of (laborious) wondering. It felt as if I was fighting for oxygen with hundreds of people jammed onto a delayed subway train. My limbs were tingly and weighted like a cinder block resting on each arm, but I found myself tearing apart the weakened plastic, reaching inside without looking—fighting the desire to run to the pool and hold my head under the rancid rainwater.

"Damn, you're brave," he said, still trying to catch his breath. It was uncharacteristically brave of me, but I was compelled by something more powerful than courage—I was compelled by fear. The fear of finding out what could be inside but also the fear of never knowing. I dug around in the dark bag filled with moist chunks of cardboard and dirt, happy to feel it with my hands if not see it with my eyes. Chelsea's ashes were still enclosed in little sandwich bags. I remembered how they felt, gritty and squishy like fine grains of sand mixed with rocks from a rough shoreline. It was strange to think plastic could endure Mother Nature's wrath, but things made of the earth, like paper, broke down effortlessly, as if they longed to be a part of her again. I dug deeper, tracing what felt like a coin in the palm of my hand, smooth, round, and cold. I was disrupting a tomb and the remains were angry; some items moved away and others fell in on me (the same way the world did sometimes). Isaac ripped a bigger hole in the bag, and my hand emerged, gripping the tomb's most treasured possession.

It took less than a second for my eyes to tell my brain exactly what I held in my hand. And only a second more for my brain to tell my soul.

I fell back, resting on the broken fence, begging it to hold me up. My hands shook as I used my T-shirt to wipe the dirt and grime from the glass and silver. Though tarnished, its whimsical details were still as beautiful as the day I'd buried it. Suddenly, like a memory made yesterday, I could picture it sitting proudly atop Mom's vanity, coveted the way the earth had coveted it for the last twenty years. It had been so important to Mom and Aunt Sam, and though I hadn't seen it in decades, I knew it was important to me too. I remembered washing the blood from it in the sink, careful to clean every swirl, every crevice. It was meant to be mine when I grew older—a family heirloom with a tragic past.

I wiped the fog that clouded the mirror and saw the terrified reflection of a fourteen-year-old girl staring back at me. I too had a tragic past, and as I traced my index finger around the outline of her lips, I finally let myself remember it. I remembered it all.

"Oh shit, I recognize that!" Isaac shouted, grabbing it from my trembling hands. "What's wrong with you? You don't look *that* bad."

The holes in my mind I'd thought were empty hadn't been. They'd just been still—dormant but not hollow. Every memory I'd recalled with anger had only disguised a truth more painful than hate, a truth more powerful than the lie it protected.

He never left us.

For nearly twenty years I'd been blaming him for taking something from me: my youth, my normalcy, my family, my dad. When he was the one who'd given us everything. He was the one who'd sacrificed his life, his memory, to give us those things back. I'd been squandering the kindest gift anyone had ever given me: I'd been squandering my inheritance.

He never left us.

I'd left him. I'd left him to rest in the most sacred place I could think of, and when that thought had broken me, my brain made me believe it was the other way around. It had been so much easier to wonder about his whereabouts, to join in the search. It had been so much easier to place the blame on someone other than Mom, the one parent I had left. He never abandoned her. Us. But telling Mom and Isaac that now wouldn't give them what they needed. It wouldn't offer closure—it would only bury them alongside him. Alongside him in the Pretty Place.

***

I lay back and stared up at the cloudless sky. It was the same sky I looked up at in Toronto, but it was brighter, more vibrant now. The sun would set in a few hours, and Isaac would want to get back to the city. Before we did, I needed to breathe in as much country air as I could so there'd be some left in my lungs when I got home. Home. Where I'd finally be able to start a life without penance. A life without sadness looming in every nightfall, without shame in every shadow.

A life where, even though the light hurt to look at, it felt better than living in darkness.

"What's your deal, Ivy?" Isaac asked, resting the mirror on my stomach.

"Nothing, Issy. I'm just really glad we came back."

EPILOGUE

—

Found in Samantha Perruzza's apartment on January 3rd, 2014

Dear World:

Life itself is more fragile than any of the hardships people believe tarnish it, more precious than the special moments it's comprised of. The monotony of life is delicate, like the tissue-paper wings of the moth drawn to light, drawn to heat and fire. The world in which we live is and always will be the flame; some dance alongside it, others are the fuel on which it feeds. I could have been either. I could have taken what I wanted. I could have given it too, but I just didn't want to anymore, and for that, I'm sorry. Please don't mourn the loss of this life. I wanted to go where I'm going. I'm happy now.

For Ivy:

I told you I'd take it to the grave, and I did. I took it with me every-where I went, and here is no exception. There's no greater sacrifice than one life for another, so please don't let the sacrifice you made take away your life too. Blood runs thicker than water—remember that when you finally let the water wash you clean. I can be clean now too, Ivory.

P.S. I never wanted to fade away—my only choice was to burn out.

~Sam

ACKNOWLEDGEMENTS

Thank you, thank you, thank you!

Throughout this journey I've often likened writing a debut novel to the conception, growth, and birth of a first child. Though I have no actual experience with that, I have to imagine there are similarities—the sleeplessness, the obsessive consideration, the overwhelming excitement, and the sense of foreboding, even terror, that you tell yourself is "totally normal."

That being said, it truly does take a village! I was lucky enough to have mine filled with so many people who loved and supported me, fully aware I didn't know what I was doing, fully prepared to console me if I never figured it out.

I want to give special thanks to my parents: one who became a valued plot editor, the other my biggest fan. Both graciously allowed pieces of their truth to be woven into my story.

Thank you, Caroline Kaiser, for your patience and for editing my baby with as much meticulous attention to detail as if it were your own. There were times when the words on the pages began to look like a foreign language to me, and in those times, I trusted your eyes more than my own.

I want to thank my PR manager, Stephanie Leslie, for believing in me with the level of confidence only a PR manager (and sister) can have. Thank you for treating me like a published author before I'd even finished the book and for pulling me upright whenever you knew

I was going sideways. My deepest apologies regarding the Prologue. It was not my finest hour.

Thank you to my stylist and photographer, Courtney Caldwell. You were also a beta reader, consultant, and therapist, and you juggled all those titles while maintaining the most important role of all: friend.

Thank you to Charlette Brothers, Lesley Geddes, and all the other amazing beta readers who set time aside in their busy lives to read the various versions of my novel, even the ones that didn't come close to resembling the final product. Your eyes and your advice were invaluable and helped shape this book in so many tangible ways.

The list could go on and on, especially if I shared the names of everyone in my life who listened to me speak incessantly about the plot, the challenges, the submission process, and more recently, the road to self-publishing. You're all so dear to my heart, and your kindness will never be forgotten.

Last, but certainly not least, thanks go to my husband, the man who endured every bump in the road with me. And believe me, the road was bumpy. You helped me fight through every pang of self-doubt that halted my progress, every setback, and every rejection. You held me when reading someone else's book was enough to reduce me to tears, for fear I'd never have what that author had. Thank you for the way you believed in me, picking me up every time I was knocked down, reminding me why I was doing it, and remembering to celebrate even the smallest of wins along the way. This labour of love has been simultaneously the most taxing and most fulfilling experience of my entire life, and I know I wouldn't be writing this right now if not for you. I love you, Kyle.

Laura

CPSIA information can be obtained
at www.ICGtesting.com
Printed in the USA
BVHW032347200221
600568BV00003B/8